BRIGHTEN YOUR CORNER
Book & Mug Mysteries #3

Michelle L. Levigne

www.MtZionRidgePress.com

Mt Zion Ridge Press LLC
295 Gum Springs Rd, NW
Georgetown, TN 37366

https://www.mtzionridgepress.com

ISBN 13: 978-1-962862-19-6

Published in the United States of America
Publication Date: February 1, 2024

Copyright: © 2023 Michelle L. Levigne

Editor-In-Chief: Michelle Levigne
Executive Editor: Tamera Lynn Kraft

Cover art design by Tamera Lynn Kraft
Cover Art Copyright by Mt Zion Ridge Press LLC © 2024

All rights reserved. No portion of this book may be reproduced or transmitted in any form or by any electronic or mechanical means, including photocopying, recording or by any information retrieval and storage system without permission of the publisher.

Ebooks, audiobooks, and print books are *not* transferrable, either in whole or in part. As the purchaser or otherwise *lawful* recipient of this book, you have the right to enjoy the novel on your own computer or other device. Further distribution, copying, sharing, gifting or uploading is illegal and violates United States Copyright laws.
Pirating of books is illegal. Criminal Copyright Infringement, *including* infringement without monetary gain, may be investigated by the Federal Bureau of Investigation and is punishable by up to five years in federal prison and a fine of up to $250,000.

Names, characters and incidents depicted in this book are products of the author's imagination, or are used in a fictitious situation. Any resemblances to actual events, locations, organizations, incidents or persons – living or dead – are coincidental and beyond the intent of the author.

Chapter One

Wednesday, August 24

"Hey, Aunt Mel, it's David." The caller chuckled, a bit of static mixing with his tenor voice on the answering machine message.

Melba Tweed braced for his usual remark about needing to step into the twenty-first century and get a cell phone. She did have a cell phone, she just didn't bother giving the number to most of the members of the extended Tweed clan. Granted, David had reformed a great deal since his selfish youth, full of get-rich-quick schemes, and he was a dear, regularly checking in on her and Cilla, but she just didn't want to admit she had upgraded her technology. Simply because he wanted it so much. Maybe she was going back to her childhood. Cilla would say she had never left her childhood, and in many ways that was a good thing. She didn't understand what David did for a living. It was all electronic and all Internet, and while he claimed he was making people's lives more secure, she saw it as interference and invasion of privacy. Bad enough he had found her on Facebook. She wouldn't give him one more way to track her life. She had seen enough TV shows where overprotective sons and abusive husbands tracked women through their phones, and it always seemed to end badly, no matter how well-intentioned.

"Kind of glad you aren't home. I'd rather just give you the bad news in one lump. It's that cousin of Aunt Cill's. Charlotte what's-her-name. Westover, that's it. You really do need to pay more attention to social media, just to stay on top of things."

Melba snorted and sank down at her kitchen table, her gaze focused on the answering machine on the counter. Thanks to Eden Cole, she and Cilla both had figured out how to stop most people from following—i.e., harassing—them on social media. It worked if David didn't know just how active they were. Especially when it came to research and joining so many fascinating groups for senior citizens. Starting with their Silver-Age Entrepreneurs Forum. Right next to the landline and answering machine was her open notebook computer, where she was trying to figure out Wordpress, to design the website for Brighten Your Corner, the candle shop she and Cilla had been daydreaming about for years. They were finally taking the leap. Albeit, slowly.

"Anyway, I figured it was time to check what wacko stories she's telling lately."

"You're a dear boy, Davy, and we do appreciate it," she murmured. She almost didn't hear what he said next, as her mind skipped back to the most recent Charlotte "incident," two years ago. David had caught her announcing she was moving cross-country to move in with her favorite cousin, Cilla Tweed.

According to Charlotte, "the poor dear" was deteriorating, mentally and physically, and she would be giving up her footloose life to settle in and take care of her. Charlotte was so humbled and touched to have Cilla's utmost trust, starting with granting her power of attorney. Thanks to David's warning, Cilla hadn't been caught flatfooted when, less than ten hours later, the bank notified her that a collection agency was trying to put a lien on her family's home. Charlotte's debts, approaching one hundred thousand dollars, had been assigned to this agency, which intended to collect from the Tweed family estate, based on that power of attorney.

There was no power of attorney and no Tweed family estate. The bank contacted Cilla because the lien was placed on a home that had been sold more than thirty years ago. With the help of Eden Cole and Bill Worter of Worter, Worter & McIntosh, Cilla repudiated all the claims and proved the power-of-attorney falsified. David's social media and computer genius friends bombed every place where Charlotte posted, proclaiming her a liar and fraud, shaming her, and making her go into silent running mode. She left a string of furious phone calls on Cilla's cell phone, forcing her to cancel the number and get another one, unlisted. In return for two months of misery, they had enjoyed two years of blissful silence from Charlotte.

Melba supposed they were due for another attack, another scheme, to make Cilla responsible for Charlotte's debts.

"According to her, she's going into business with you two. She claims she's been dreaming for years of starting a custom-design candle business, and she's very generously — yeah, right, the only generosity she's familiar with is someone else paying her tab. Anyway, she says she's very generous to take you two on as partners, to handle the grunt work and the finances while she does the artistic design. She's calling it Wicked Delights, but she's got an apostrophe in place of the e. Supposed to be clever, I guess."

"She wouldn't ..." Melba whispered and gripped the edge of the table.

How in the world had Charlotte learned they were taking the big step? She and Cilla had deliberately avoided talking about Brighten Your Corner on any of the sites that Charlotte might frequent. They carefully searched the membership list of any groups where they had talked about their dreams for the shop. It was a given Charlotte wouldn't belong to any groups for entrepreneurs. While it sounded French, and she loved bringing out her fake French accent and boring people to death with details of her year spent in Paris, Charlotte probably didn't know how to spell entrepreneur, or what the word meant. Mostly because it implied doing honest, hard work, instead of tricking people into doing it for her.

"That woman would be a millionaire if she spent all that energy and scheming doing real work, instead of trying to trick everyone else into doing it for her," Melba murmured. She nearly didn't catch David promising he would get his friends to do some tracking and hunting and work on blocking Charlotte from going any further.

The message ended. Melba closed her eyes and rested her forehead on her clenched fists, took several deep breaths, then prayed, asking for strength and clear thinking. She considered what to do for a few minutes, before getting out of the chair and taking the first step: alerting Cilla. Charlotte was her cousin, after all, on her mother's side. Charlotte Westover wasn't a Tweed, but she certainly made every effort to profit from her tenuous Tweed family connection. Melba was bound and determined that would not happen this time, either. Especially since Charlotte had mocked their candle-making hobby when they were in high school and complained about Cilla's candles "cluttering" and "smelling up the place," whenever she came to visit.

Melba stepped to her open back door and looked out into the backyard she and Cilla had turned into a gardening paradise over their twenty years of sharing this duplex. Sure enough, her cousin was on her knees, adjusting that ceramic border they had bought at Menards this morning. She just couldn't wait for the cool of the evening to put it in place.

In the few moments it took to go down the back porch steps and walk to where Cilla was happily smoothing mulch back into place, Melba decided what to do next. Much as she appreciated David's warning, she wasn't going to ask him for help in dismantling the foundation Charlotte had started laying in social media. If he had his way, both sides of the duplex would be filled with all sorts of electronic gizmos. Everything would be wired to turn on lights and heat and appliances, and some disembodied voice would be responding to every chance remark she made when no one else was in the room. Melba just didn't trust computers. She had always cheered when Captain Kirk destroyed world-controlling computers on Star Trek. She wasn't about to let one control every aspect of her life.

David meant well, but when it came to computers and the Internet and all that rigamarole, Melba would turn to Eden Cole for help every time.

"Don't lecture me," Cilla said with a somewhat breathless chuckle.

She made one more gentle sweep over the mulch, sat back, pulled off her gardening gloves, and reached up to wipe sweaty hair out of her face. "This would just nag at me until …" She blinked several times as she looked up at Melba and her smile faded. "What happened? Did one of our suppliers call and change the prices? Don't tell me, Tracy says it's going to take even longer to get all of that junk out of the shop? The health department found out what's been causing those strange smells, and they've condemned the entire strip of shops?"

"Worse." Melba gestured for her to get up. "Hurricane Charlotte has struck again."

"Please don't tell me she's forgiven me and she's trying to move in again." Cilla ignored the hand Melba held out to her, shifted to her knees, and braced herself on the side of the wheelbarrow to get to her feet.

"Worse. She's trying to steal Brighten from underneath us."

"No." She shook her head hard enough to loosen the hairs that had been stuck to her forehead with sweat. "Not going to happen. Not in a million years." Her eyes narrowed. "She certainly wouldn't tell you what she's planning. How did you find out?"

"David did his usual social media check. He must have called while we were out running errands this morning. I didn't notice the message on my machine until I took a break from working on the website." Melba gestured at the back porch. "Get cleaned up. I'm going to call Eden and see if she has time to talk to us."

"Good idea."

~~~~~

Forty minutes later, the Tweed cousins settled down at the conference table of Finders, Inc., on the second floor of the building Eden shared with her cousins, Troy Hunter and Kai Shane. The three shared the office, but most of the floor was considered Eden's territory. In the time since Melba called, Eden had done a massive amount of work, judging by the piles of printouts waiting on the table and the two notebook computers sitting open, waiting for them to arrive.

"I'm a little worried that she has someone with some tech savvy helping her. Some of her earlier schemes were far too easy to track down and short circuit, but this time I ran into a few walls, some attempts to erase a lot of incriminating postings. From seeing her in action the last time …" Eden shook her head. "I seriously doubt she would take classes and gain some programming skills. Makes me wonder what she really wants this time, that she'd ask for help. The kind of help you pay for."

"What has she done?" Melba pressed her hand over her heart, where it seemed to try to drop and fluttered oddly for a few seconds.

"Let's check out the obvious stuff, first." Eden turned the notebook computer around, to show them Charlotte's social media postings. "The really concerning part is that she's going all out to establish documentation. As much documentation as you can get on social media. She forged a power of attorney last time, and got caught. If she learned her lesson, she's going to have a forged contract this time. Plus, a really good lawyer can use all this social media posting as evidence that at least at the beginning, you agreed with everything Charlotte was saying and doing. He can claim that you broke faith with her, that she was the innocent party in all this. But don't worry, I've been digging up gobs of postings where people argued with her and pointed out she was wrong. Whoever erased those postings was pretty good, but he's an amateur, compared to me. If this ever went to court, some of the battle would rely on how much electronic evidence the judge would allow. Just the arguments Charlotte got into with the dozens of people contradicting her is evidence enough for me that she's up to no good. Plus, I found proof that she's blocked you every possible place and every possible way you could have gotten a hint of what she's up to. But look at this first."

Eden moved the computer over to where both cousins could read the screen. Melba winced at the collage of shots of Charlotte in all her overblown glory that filled the banner at the top of her page. Charlotte dressed like she was on stage all the time, with makeup thick enough to need a trowel to scrape it off.

I'm so delighted to announce the imminent opening of Wick'd Delights. Of course, with my very active life, I can't be there full-time, much as I would love to do so. This is a dear, long-treasured dream of mine, and I am so very happy to be able to put much of the day-to-day operations in the hands of my favorite cousins, Cilla and Melba Tweed. They begged to be the money people in this venture, and how could I deny them? Such lovely dears, and so very much energy for their advanced years. I'm so pleased to give them something to focus their energies on. I trust them implicitly. Of course, all the designs will be by yours truly, but I have full confidence in them to handle the mundane details when I can't be there to be the face and voice of my lovely little candle shop.

"Advanced years?" Melba was glad she hadn't taken a sip of the coffee Kai brought up for them. She might have spewed it across the screen full of Charlotte's painted cheeks and smug grin.

Eden flipped to more social media sites, sometimes multiple pages belonging to Charlotte under different titles on the same sites. Each said much the same thing. She was the brains, the creative energy, and Melba and Cilla would provide the money and do all the work.

From there, Eden showed them screenshots and printouts of what seemed like hundreds of comments from people contradicting Charlotte's statements. Melba was encouraged by the number of people who reminded Charlotte how much she had mocked Cilla's candle making hobby and her insistence that candles were a waste of time and money. Eden had three pages of printouts showing the research Charlotte had done into the candle industry, showing how profitable it was and the prices people were willing to pay for designer candles. She even had a screenshot of an online discussion Charlotte had had with someone Melba and Cilla didn't know, where quite a lot of data changed Charlotte's mind about candles. Eden had already tracked Charlotte's searches, with the help of an as-yet-to-be-identified hacker, who found Melba and Cilla's online groups. She identified the fake profile Charlotte used to lurk on nearly every online group the cousins belonged to as they researched and prepared to set up Brighten Your Corner.

"We didn't post the address, did we?" Cilla said. "I can just see her sending all sorts of bills to the shop before we even open. If she knows where we'll be."

"It's not official yet. Something might come up at the last minute and Tracy won't be able to let us have that shop. Ernie is still threatening all sorts of lawsuits for evicting him," Melba said. "But I do have the address on the website I'm building. Is it possible someone could hack into my computer and get that information, even though the website hasn't launched yet?"

"It's possible," Eden said after a long moment of thought. "I have to head up to Sandusky for a couple days, but if you want to bring your computer in, Rufus can go through it and see if there are any spy bots or malware and set up some shields for you."

"Thank you, dear. That sounds wonderful." Cilla took a deep breath, let it out slowly, and her smile faded. "But we need to do more to protect ourselves, don't we? It's not like we don't have experience with Charlotte's schemes." A snort escaped her. "Starting with the time she tried to make my parents responsible for the bills for finishing school when she was thirteen."

"No, her parents were behind that scheme," Melba said. "Too bad Charlotte didn't learn from their humiliation every time one of their schemes faded."

As they went through the printouts and viewed different profiles and pages, Melba's dismay and disgust deepened. She felt a little sick, and more than a little frightened at how much Charlotte, or her accomplice, had been able to spy on them. On three different pages, she mocked their chosen name for the candle shop, to the amusement of her social media friends. One group got quite viciously nasty, when someone revealed that the title came from a Sunday school song. Charlotte spent a good four inches of posting venting her disgust for Cilla's devotion to anything religious and declared that anyone who took children to church should be charged and imprisoned for child abuse.

~~~~~

Eden adored the Tweeds. They were how she had always imagined favorite elderly aunts would be, from the moment she and Troy and Kai had moved to Cadburn. The two women had taken the trio under their wings and shared all their favorite places, gave good advice about who to turn to for help with renovating the Mug building and what community groups to join, and even who to avoid without speaking their own prejudices and bad experiences. That took far more tact than Eden thought she would ever possess.

She had enjoyed listening to them and offering bits of advice as they researched their business idea and slowly built up their knowledge. Eden was glad to inform them that registering for their business name put a date stamp on their idea, and provided further proof that they had no intention of going into business with Charlotte. Therefore, protecting them from the claims of anyone who would try to make them responsible for her actions and debts. She advised them to talk with their small business advisor at their bank, which was a local rather than national chain, to put flags on the account if anyone tried to annex it or obtain information about their financial activities.

Fortunately, common sense was still a good defense. The moment someone realized how much work the Tweeds had done to set up their own business, and asked why they would duplicate all that effort to go into business with Charlotte, the falsehoods would disintegrate. She could forge all the signatures and documents she wanted, but none of that would hold up against the testimony of Bill Worter and other local business experts, and the piles of documentation the Tweeds had generated already.

Eden had helped them dismantle Charlotte's schemes before, so she knew the woman's past nasty tricks. This time was different. Someone was likely using Charlotte as a shield for illegal activities. She couldn't imagine anyone giving her all that technological help for free. Accessing her financial records was relatively simple, and proved she hadn't paid with money for that assistance. Eden was determined to ensure that when Charlotte fell, she wouldn't drag Melba and Cilla down with her.

This new scheme roused Eden's ire like it hadn't been since the early days, when social workers and other authorities tried to separate her from Troy and Kai. And worse, kept trying to take away their Venetian glass hearts. Someone was always insisting that the trio had "obviously" been given stolen goods, or they wanted to set up a nest egg for the children by selling the hearts. And of course, pocketing a good share of the profits. Or flat out wanting to confiscate the hearts in the guise of "enabling" the children to "pay their own way" as they grew up. Those people were the visible enemies. Then there were the ones who played with the records, erasing or falsifying them, creating false trails, setting up roadblocks and lies that Eden still ran into now, twenty-plus years after she and her cousins had been dumped into the system. Someone wanted them lost, and they were good at fuddling trails and destroying evidence. But Eden was better, and this was personal.

Charlotte came by her scheming, greedy ways naturally. Her parents were users, liars, and thieves. Apparently, Cilla's mother was one of the few decent, honest people in her generation. Charlotte's parents constantly took off across the world on another scheme and dumped her on Cilla's family for months at a time. Charlotte learned early to tell everyone a different story, and then turn people against each other, so they couldn't compare stories until it was too late for her victims to get out of the mess she created. That left them to clean up the mess, take the blame, and pay the bills.

Fortunately, Cilla had Melba and other relatives, and now Eden, Troy, and Kai to watch out for her. Charlotte hadn't been able to hurt her for more than ten years. She couldn't seem to learn her lesson and kept trying. Eden wished Cilla would wise up just a little more, and entirely block the obnoxious woman from her life, but she knew that would never happen. That just wasn't Cilla. She had a backbone, and she wouldn't put up with garbage from anyone, and she certainly could rip off snarky responses when necessary, but she was also forgiving and willing to give someone another chance. Even troublemakers like Charlotte. Eden suspected that if Cilla ever changed, that would be a sign of the world coming to an end.

So, she was determined to help fend off this newest scheme. Gut instinct told her that if Charlotte was bringing in big guns to help her, there was far more at stake than just stealing Cilla's dream and creating a cash cow Charlotte could milk for years to come.

Chapter Two

In the hour of free time Eden had between the Tweeds leaving her office and when she had to leave to head up to Sandusky, she found more of the hacker's fingerprints in the work done to scrub Charlotte's Internet trail. It was a sloppy job. He was either complacent, or he was setting up Charlotte to take the fall, but bottom line, he was sloppy. He didn't follow up on the scrubbing and erasing work he did, to look for bits and pieces and stray threads that were glaring alarms, alerting anyone who looked that someone had been erased. He either didn't care, or he didn't know to check all the layers of security and redundancies, and all the archival programs that essentially took snapshots of website content. The adage was true: when something appeared on the Internet, it was forever. Either he didn't have the chops to get into those sites, or he didn't know about them.

Many of Eden's contacts were zealous when it came to defending web content from those who would scrub and destroy records, essentially trying to rewrite reality. All she had to do was give them some identifying markers for the hacker, and they would be on the hunt, eager to exact some justice.

~~~~~

"What in the world ..." Cilla sat forward, resting her hands on the dashboard, as Melba navigated the corner onto their street, preparing to pull into the driveway of their duplex.

"What? Who's—is that Heinrich?" Melba tapped the brake, but Heinrich and the young man he stomped after, up the driveway, stepped onto the sidewalk before she pulled in. Not that she would ever willingly hit Heinrich, or even tap him with the bumper, but she thought some honest fear might be good for the old curmudgeon. She swore he had been impossible to live with ever since Cilla turned him down in eleventh grade and went to the prom with Eddie McGillicutty.

"Is that David?"

Melba didn't turn her head to look. She pulled into her usual parking spot in front of the garage, put the car into park, and turned off the ignition first. By the time she got the door open, Cilla was sliding out of the passenger seat. David walked down the driveway to meet them, alone. Heinrich wasn't visible, out in front of the house, but Melba thought she heard his stomping, slapping footsteps and his grumbling voice as he headed back to his house three driveways down the street.

"Gee, I come over here enough times, you'd think the neighborhood watchdog would recognize me by now," David greeted them, and grinned.

"He's just being a good neighbor," Cilla said. "You were walking around the house, weren't you? Checking the doors and windows, like you always do?"

"Well, yeah. Gotta look out for you, y'know?" He shrugged. "I'd feel a lot better about you both if you'd let me install that home security system my company designed. Especially with all the weird stuff that's been going on in town lately. Who'd ever have thought sleepy little Cadburn would have murders?"

"We appreciate your concern, but we're fine." She patted his hand. "Now, I'll just bet you're here to follow up on that message you left before. Not to worry. We got our investigator friend working on the problem. She says we're well protected against Charlotte's schemes, thanks to all the preparation we've been doing for our business."

"Investigator?" David blinked a few times. His mouth moved like he was going to say something else, but didn't.

"Yes, you remember our friend Eden, from when Charlotte tried to move in with Cilla?" Melba said.

"Oh, yeah, right. I remember. You threw me off track. I'm talking about security for your house, keep someone from breaking in, or at least send for the cops if something happens, and you talk about that lunatic." He chuckled, but the sound didn't entirely convince Melba.

"Never to worry." Cilla gestured at the back door. "Ted keeps an eye on things, and if he thinks the situation is dire enough we need a burglar alarm, he'll help us with it. Not that we don't appreciate your help, but he is a police officer, he lives here, and he knows how things are done."

"Yeah, yeah," he said with a grin that didn't quite reach his eyes. "I'm big city and you're little township, with nothing in common."

"I wouldn't put it that way." She chuckled. "Now, would you like to join us for dinner? I've got a lovely batch of chicken and potato wedges I put in the slow cooker this morning, and we've got the last of the corn on the cob from Dalrymple's. Their corn is always so good."

"Thanks, but ..." David shrugged. "Got a business meeting on this side of town. Just thought I'd check on you before I headed over there. You didn't get back to me, so I figured maybe you were out of the house all day, or out of town or ..." Another shrug. "Glad you're okay and on top of things."

He turned like he would head down the winding path of paving stones through the middle of the garden, and out the back of the yard, then stopped after two steps and headed up the driveway to the street.

"Give our greetings to your folks," Melba called. "How are they doing, by the way?"

"Fine, fine. You know how it is with them. Always running around." David walked backward a dozen steps as they made their farewells. He turned left at the end of the driveway and in a few steps vanished behind the house next door.

"Huh, that doesn't make sense."

"What doesn't?" Cilla was already on the back porch and fumbling with her key. "How about dinner outside tonight? It's cooled down enough."

"Fine." Melba couldn't recall seeing any cars parked on the street between Overview and their house, so where was David going? A sigh escaped her as she turned and headed down the path through the flowerbeds. She stopped halfway there, so she was partially hidden by the line of skinny evergreens that stood as a threadbare sort of barrier between their back yard and the parking lot of the apartment building behind them. Sure enough, she saw David jogging down the sidewalk and turning left into the parking lot to a car parked next to the driveway.

He had come up through the back of the house, like he had done dozens of times before when he came over for picnics or brought his parents for a family get-together, whenever relatives dropped in from out of town. That explained why Heinrich went after him, coming through the trees like that. The old curmudgeon certainly wouldn't have believed David when he claimed he was there on a legitimate visit, if he didn't come to the front door "like an honest man with nothing to hide," as he often finished so many of his complaints nowadays. But why didn't David want them to know where he had parked?

By the time she got back to the house, Cilla was all excited about a text from the clerk at Megan's Hobby House. The silicon molds they had been waiting on had arrived. Melba let her questions about David slide to the back of her mind, and most of their dinner conversation focused on color and scent combinations to compliment the candles to come out of those molds.

Thursday, September 8

Melba watched Cilla read through the lease agreement. Again. She took a sideways glance at Tracy Adams and fought down the urge to apologize, *again*, to the young woman who would be their landlord in another minute or two. If she didn't get frustrated with Cilla and change her mind and tug the paperwork out of her hands. Melba knew Cilla was being logical and cautious, and Tracy didn't mind them checking over the contract yet again. She had said so and even laughed when Cilla apologized and asked for one more look-through before signing.

She had had a nightmare three nights ago, where Charlotte had bombed through the door, waving documents, declaring that she had already signed the lease on the shop. And worse, the previous tenant, Ernie Benders, was the fourth partner in their business.

"I wish I had a few more clients who were as careful about details as you two," the young woman had assured them. "If you're sure of the details before we get started, then we'll have fewer chances of problems later on."

Around them, Morning Folks Café's traffic dwindled visibly as the breakfast rush cleared away. Melba considered opening their candle shop an hour early to take advantage of the people leaving the café, then shook her head. Five days a week, anybody leaving the café would be on their way to work and wouldn't have time to linger and certainly not step into the shop and sniff candles and examine all the unique designs she and Cilla intended to feature. The most they could manage would be window shopping.

Measure the display windows, Melba noted on the tablet in front of her. *Shelves? Stair step display? Check the angle of the sun during the day, and heat in the window.*

They certainly couldn't take the chance of their stock fading or even melting.

Creekside Shops were charming and old-fashioned with their deep-set display windows, wooden floors, and fancy crown molding. The traffic on Creekview Street wasn't as steady as on Center, but that was a good thing. Chances were better of people actually seeing what was in the display windows and stopping to investigate.

"Okay." Cilla took a deep breath and put down the last page of the leasing agreement. "I think we're ready."

"I'm glad to welcome you to the Creekside Family." Tracy picked up the pen with deep green ink that matched the letterhead for Creekside Shops, and the paint on the trim around the shop windows.

Fifteen minutes later, after leaving a generous tip, because after all, they had taken up a table at the café far longer than a normal breakfast hour, the three of them stepped out the door and walked two doors down, to the shop that was now officially the future home of Brighten Your Corner.

Tracy held her breath as she unlocked the front door, pushed it open, and leaned in. She sniffed cautiously. Winced. Turned back and handed Melba the keys. Three sets of five keys. For the front door, the back door, the utility box that served all the shops on that side of Creekview, and two for the gates on the concrete deck that ran behind the stores and extended out over the rocky drop down to Cadburn Creek. One set of keys for Melba, one for Cilla, and one set of spares, to be safely hidden somewhere at home, and hopefully not forgotten.

"These look new," Melba said, turning the ring of keys over in her hands. They made a nice, solid jangle.

"They are." Tracy stepped into the shop and spread her arms, welcoming them in. "Sorry about the smell. It's actually better than it was. I don't know what that man was doing in the back room ..."

"We never did understand what he did here." Cilla pulled out the tape measure from her tote bag and headed for the left-hand display window.

"I'm pretty sure he didn't understand, either." Tracy shook her head. "He definitely wasn't dealing in collectibles, which is what he stated as his business when he signed the lease. I could have evicted him just on that detail alone. There were more deliveries to this place, at all hours, in all weather, than the entire street combined. A couple people complained about yelling screaming arguments, and the smells that seeped into the shops on either side weren't ..." She shrugged. "They just weren't natural."

"He wasn't cooking meth or anything like that, was he?" Melba asked. Cilla muttered, "Meth" and sighed. Melba wrinkled up her nose at her, and they both chuckled.

"I almost wish he was." Tracy shook her head. "He still owes me five months' rent, and replacing the glass on the front door, twice, and the lock on the back door three times. I could legally charge him for replacing the locks on this shop and the back deck gates and copying keys for everyone."

"It's a crying shame," Cilla said. "Ernie used to be such a nice guy, back in high school. What happened to him?"

"Besides going anti-establishment and running off to some commune and then advocating burning down the White House every time a new president got into office, no matter which party?" Melba shook her head. "Haven't the foggiest."

"He claims I broke his heart," Cilla said, punctuated by the snap of the measuring tape as it retracted back into its case. She snickered as she wrote down the measurements of the display window.

"Grandpa should have broken his head." Melba chuckled. "Our grandparents had that big old house the Gallery took over. We used to have sleepovers, all the cousins, maybe once a month. Ernie decided he would play Romeo and tossed rocks at the dormer windows to get Cilla's attention. The problem is, he used really big rocks and broke Grandpa and Granny's bedroom window. The big buffoon actually refused to pay to replace the window, because he claimed Granny insulted his family, getting her landscaping rocks from someone else. Can you believe that?"

"Ernie's father and uncles had a landscaping business," Cilla explained.

"Well, that's a chunk of Cadburn history I never heard," Tracy said, punctuated with a chuckle. "So Miss Cilla, you're a heartbreaker, are you?"

"There's gotta be a heart to break," she muttered, and stepped over to the built-in counter that divided the front room in half, lengthwise. She extended the measuring tape down the long side and paused to run her fingers over the dings and gouges and dents and what certainly looked to Melba like burn marks in the wood.

"Some common sense would have been nice, too," Melba added. "Remember the time he showed up to take you on a date, and he wouldn't take no for an answer because he had paid Boyd for the right to take you out? He wanted exclusive access to you for the entire week."

"Wait," Tracy said. "Who's Boyd?"

"Our money-grubbing cousin."

"Makes those stereotyped ambulance-chasing lawyers on TV look like Boy Scouts," Cilla added. Then she giggled. "Remember the time he tried to convince Aunt Myrna to join some pyramid scheme, and when she didn't give in fast enough, he stole the old glass piggy bank where she put her egg money? She went chasing after him with her rolling pin and he fell going down the steps and ..." Her laughter faded into a sigh and she shook her head. "Oh, my, listen to me. Gossiping."

"It's not gossip if you'd take Ginny's advice and put all those family memories into a book and sell it as humor," Melba said.

"And get sued by three-quarters of the family for embarrassing them."

"They did it to themselves!" She snickered. "We really should. Even if it's just as a joke. Let's talk to Charli Hall, since she knows writing. Or Saundra Bailey. What do you say?"

"It might be fun," Cilla admitted and chuckled.

"What are you doing in my shop?" a rusty tenor voice bellowed. It cracked and squeaked on the last word and shattered into coughing. Ernie Benders staggered into the shop, arms spread to brace himself in the doorframe. He gasped and heaved, eyes watering, glaring at the three women in turn.

Tracy jammed her fists into her hips and stomped forward, putting herself between Ernie and the Tweed cousins.

"This isn't your shop. It isn't," she insisted, when he opened his mouth to argue.

Yep, same old Ernie, Melba thought. She recognized that sizzling fury in his eyes, and the spark of what she had long ago suspected was insanity. Maybe chemically induced. According to the gossip and the complaints from the owners of other shops in this strip, Ernie had been manufacturing something highly toxic in his back room. He had probably poisoned himself. She wouldn't be surprised if the FBI someday linked him to a string of homemade bombs placed around post offices and other government buildings.

"Everything was handled properly and legally, and I gave you twice as much time as was spelled out in the lease that you signed," Tracy continued, waving a finger in Ernie's face. He choked and swallowed and rubbed his watery eyes. "You were served multiple notices, and the judge listened to you argue and you were warned multiple times about all the violations to the lease agreement. I should have evicted you four months sooner. I had every legal right to do so."

"A man's business is his castle," Ernie snarled, and broke down coughing.

"What business?" Tracy spread her arms, gesturing for him to look around.

"What the—where's all my stuff?" He staggered around her, reaching for one of the empty built-in shelves, then turned and yanked on a door under the counter. "You can't do that! You cleaned me out!"

"I did not. Although I would have been completely within my rights to confiscate everything you left behind, to pay the back rent you owe me."

"Filthy lying—" Ernie staggered backward, as if propelled by the force of the filth spilling out of his mouth.

"That is enough!" Cilla snapped, and swung hard, slapping Ernie so he staggered sideways. "You have no right to use such language around this lovely young lady whom you cheated and stole from and abused her property and lied to and—and—and a couple dozen other nasty, selfish things that are just typical for you, Ernie Benders! You're the same selfish oaf you were in high school. When are you going to grow up?"

Ernie shook his head. His eyes seemed unfocused for several moments. Melba didn't doubt his ears were ringing and he couldn't see straight. She fought not to cheer. That slap was many years overdue. She had always told Cilla she had been too nice all the times she turned down Ernie and tried to gently discourage his interest in her.

What was it about Cilla that attracted the worst sort of boys, when they were growing up? None of them could take no for an answer, and that was the only answer she ever gave them. Too bad the one time she did say no to Heinrich, over the Prom, he never came back. He would have been good for Cilla, and under her influence he never would have become a paranoid curmudgeon.

"Ci—Cilla?" Ernie finally mumbled. She nodded, lips pressed tightly together, probably holding back another volley of rebuke, if Melba knew her cousin. "What are you doing here?"

"This is my new shop. Mine and Melba's. And you will not be welcome here if you can't control your filthy mouth or learn some manners."

"Control my—" He staggered back another step, and broken laughter spilled out of him until he fetched up against the wall next to the door. "Oh, that's rich. No, really, what are you doing here?" He straightened and peered around, and for a moment he looked confused, even surprised. Melba wondered just how hard Cilla had hit him. Maybe they should join that Autumn Fellowship baseball league like Pastor Roy kept urging them. "I'm kind of embarrassed for you to see my place like ..." He shook his head, and his gaze seemed to sharpen and focus. "What did you do with my stuff, you sorry—" He flinched when Cilla raised her hand.

"I. Didn't. Take. Your. Stuff," Tracy enunciated with care. "And don't go making up another of your stories about people stealing from you. I've got you on a security video two weeks ago, breaking the lock on the deck gate and breaking the window on the back door and coming in here and taking everything, with the help of three shady-looking characters in a brown pickup. Even got the license plate."

"That's what's wrong with this country," Ernie snarled, building up volume and momentum again. "Locking a man out of his own shop. Making him break in to get his own stuff."

"I gave you a full month to clear out your stuff." Now she sounded more tired than angry. "Everything is documented. Every legal notice. Every certified letter. Every run-in with the server or the police who were involved. Every broken window and lock. Every complaint of stink. Every violation of the lease agreement. Every unpaid bill. You don't have a legal leg to stand on."

"Yeah, with a crooked judge in your back pocket," he sneered.

Chapter Three

"Get out." Tracy pointed at the door. "As the landlord, I don't want you stepping into any business in the Creekside Shops. I'll swear out a restraining order if I have to, and I'll bet you every shop owner will support me. Starting with these nice ladies."

"Nice ladies?" Ernie raked his eyes up and down Melba and then Cilla. For a moment, Melba could have sworn there was more confusion in his eyes, as if he didn't recognize them.

Maybe some of those rumors and speculations about what Ernie was doing in his back room, the source of the disgusting chemical smells, had some basis in fact. Maybe he had done damage to his brain?

"You can't throw me out of my shop." He stomped and swung around, as if he was about to punch, but he slammed his arm against the doorframe. Ernie let out a howl and punched at the frame again, earning a shriek. He clutched his fist to his chest, hopping up and down, hunched over.

"Maybe we should call for ..." Cilla gave Melba a wide-eyed look. "EMTs? The hospital?"

"The loony bin," Melba said under her breath. She started digging in her purse.

"What's going on in here?" Officer Ted Shrieve called, as he hurtled past the display window and flung himself through the doorway.

He nearly ran into Ernie, but the writhing, sobbing, cursing old man hopped out of his way in time. Ted looked around, his frown deepening to concern as soon as his gaze met Melba's.

"Are you two all right? What'd this whack-job do to you?" he demanded.

"Same old, same old, Ted," Tracy said on a sigh. She seemed to wilt a little. "Can you take care of him? He started beating up on the wall and the wall beat back."

"Did not!" Ernie shrieked and twisted aside out of Ted's reach. He staggered toward the door. "This is still my place! The law is on my side. I've got rights. You can't have it." His gaze fastened on the keys Melba held tight clutched in her fist. "Those are mine!"

He lunged at her. Melba turned to the right, out of his way. He caught hold of her jacket sleeve, twisting her. She spun, flailing to catch her balance, and slapped him across the face with two sets of keys. Ernie shrieked and clamped his hands over his nose. The sound cut off with an audible snap. He darted for the door, and this time didn't miss. In seconds, he had staggered down the street, out of the line of sight through the display window.

"Wow," Ted whispered.

"There is something definitely wrong with that man's brain," Cilla pronounced. "Always has been."

"Yeah." He sighed. "I guess I should go after him, make sure he doesn't start foaming at the mouth or falling down in a fit. You sure you're all right?"

"I'll check in at the station and file another report," Tracy said. He nodded his thanks, rolled his eyes, and headed out the door after Ernie.

"If you ladies want to change your minds," she continued, "I wouldn't blame you at all. He's going to keep insisting this place is still his, even after it's been redecorated and renamed."

"Not on your life," Cilla said.

"Ditto," Melba said. "I suggest our first purchase with our nice new business credit card is a security system."

"Definitely. With cameras that feed straight to Eden's office at Finders."

The two cousins nodded, gazes locked. Then the idiocy of the whole situation struck them, and they laughed. Tracy gave them a confused look for a few seconds, then she joined in.

Wednesday, September 14

The gossip suited the rainy, gusty weather. A body had been found under the floorboards of Windows on the River. Conrad Price was missing, and as the day progressed, the gossip changed to say that Conrad was the body. By the time Book & Mug was about to close for the night, the rumors multiplied. Conrad had two identical brothers who tried to steal the Fontaine family business and might even have killed Raymond Fontaine, the young man found dead in Cadburn Creek the week before.

Melba wished she and Cilla hadn't come to Book & Mug and made it their center of operations while they worked on plans and ran errands for Brighten Your Corner. Far too many people came into the coffee shop during the day, not just to get out of the rain, but to try to catch Eden or either of her cousins, to see what they knew, to verify the gossip. And of course, everyone had to add their own personal speculation to the chatter, which just expanded things to the edges of believability. The worst part was that Melba remembered how Becca Sheridan and Conrad had been starting to build a nice relationship that promised to turn into something permanent. If even a tenth of the speculations were true, then Melba feared Becca's life might have been endangered. Where was Becca right now, and how did she feel? The Four Corners dancing club had discovered the body, and Becca was their leader, so she would have been right there when it happened.

Cilla finally had the common sense to insist they leave. They had picked out the color of paint, ordered it from Lumberville, and had samples of the different borders they wanted to put up in the shop, and the stain for the woodwork that needed approval from Tracy. What else was there to do? Besides, they were going to miss *Jeopardy* and *Wheel of Fortune* if they lingered any longer. And who really needed to hear all those ridiculous stories, just twisting things so they bore no resemblance to the truth?

Saturday, September 24

"We're probably going to regret this," Melba whispered, as she and Cilla pulled into the parking deck behind the strip of shops early that morning. Early for shoppers, but not for eager, soon-to-be shop owners. That deck made her nervous, but not enough to use the municipal lot on the east end of Creekside and walk two blocks to their shop.

Their shop. Entirely legal now, signed and sealed, and about to have the last outward vestige of Ernie Benders' noxious presence removed. The interior of the shop had been steam cleaned last week and the last of his illegal renovations had been reversed. Not that Tracy had any hope of getting him to pay the fines that he had agreed to when he signed the lease. If he wouldn't abide by the agreement in other areas, such as making no changes to the shop's paint and furnishings without permission, why would anyone expect him to pay the fines for violating the agreement?

The judge who had to look over Ernie's latest legal action to stop the Tweeds from moving into "his" shop commented, off the record of course, that if Ernie ignored everything he had agreed to in the lease, then Tracy and the Tweeds had every right to ignore his complaints. He advised them not to ignore his threats but stay on the alert for trouble. He had even heard several threats Ernie had made that they hadn't heard yet.

But none of that mattered this morning. The sign for Benders Outpost was coming down at long last.

"Just what does 'Outpost' mean, anyway?" Cilla said, once they had come around the side of the building. She glanced back over her shoulder at the deck, clearly marked as "tenant parking only," and shuddered. "Do you feel safe parking there? I just have this vision of the whole concrete and iron monstrosity collapsing into the creek." She managed a grin. "Like those shelves Rupert put up for Granny when we were fourteen, remember?"

"Oh, how I wish I could forget." Melba grinned and turned to look down past Morning Folks to their shop, where the Monroe Brothers van had parked on the street. Their little crane was already rising up to the sign. "Uncle Vincent kept telling him he had to find the studs before he drilled and put up those railing thingies that the shelf brackets slid into, and Rupert just said he knew what he was doing, he aced shop class, didn't he, and went on. And then the crash when he had all the shelves in place and it all fell down, and the holes in the drywall!"

Cilla cast one more glance at the end of the building, as if she could see through it to the parking lot. "I know that deck thing passed inspections, and Jorgenson Construction is a good company, but just the word 'cantilevered' sounds unreliable to me. I guess I don't trust something that's just too convenient. Does that make any sense?"

"Unfortunately, yes." Melba patted her cousin's arm. "If it's any comfort, I think we've earned some grace and greasing of the wheels, after all the fuss Ernie put up last week. The nerve of him, trying to file a restraining order to stop us from moving in. And suing Tracy for defamation. How can you call it defamation when everything people are saying about him is true?"

"Trying to sue," she retorted as they linked arms and headed down the sidewalk, to get a better view of the removing of the old sign and the raising of the temporary sign. Just a sturdy vinyl sheet, proclaiming this the future home of Brighten Your Corner candles. "He has to go a couple towns over to find a lawyer greedy enough to take on his case."

"I heard he's threatening to sue the Worters for refusing to take him as a client. He actually had the gall to insist that lawyers were public servants and they were obligated to assist everyone who came to them for justice."

Cilla snorted loudly and rolled her eyes. A few heartbeats later, they both muffled giggles.

"Stop that! Stop that right this minute!"

Melba had to look, because that cracking screech didn't sound like Ernie, even at his worst. Yet it was. His voice bounced off the storefronts. He trembled visibly as he stomped down the street from where he had parked in front of Goody Two Scoops. Right in front of the handicapped parking sign, straddling both blue-outlined spaces.

Where was a police officer when they really needed one? Preferably with a tow truck to haul away the offender and his offensive car? She swore all those nasty, threatening, self-righteous bumper stickers covering Ernie's car, proclaiming support for all sorts of extremist political groups and militias were all that held the rusty, dirty contraption together.

"You can't do that! This is my shop." He stomped up to the van and pounded with both fists on the side. Then he threw himself at it, as if he could topple the van with just the force of his skinny frame. "You're not allowed to park here."

"Permit." Jake hooked his thumb at the piece of paper taped to the inside of the windshield.

Ernie threw himself at the driver's side door and tugged up on the handle, and howled pain when it didn't open. Jake turned to glance at the Tweed cousins and winked.

Clearly the van was locked. And clearly, Jake had experience with people giving him grief in the course of his work and knew to prevent them from reaching in and tearing up the permit. Jake and Joe knew what they were doing.

"This is my place." Ernie stomped, several times with each foot.

Melba recalled the story of Rumplestiltskin in that moment, and how he stomped so hard in frustration he sank down into the ground and vanished and was never heard from again.

"Oh, if only," she whispered.

"I paid my back rent. You can't take down my sign. This is my place."

"We really need to get out of here," Cilla whispered.

"You think?" Melba whispered back. She knew better than to move, however. Not while Ernie was snarling and digging in his pants pockets. She had seen several of those Jurassic Park movies, and Ernie reminded her so clearly of those nasty hunting lizard creatures, she firmly believed if they stood still, he wouldn't be able to see them.

Wrong.

"You two! It's all your fault," Ernie snarled, spitting with every word, even with only one sibilant among them. He stomped up the sidewalk toward them, hands outstretched, waving a piece of paper. "This is my place. Here's my receipt! I paid that lying, greedy—" He spilled more vulgarity, clearly aimed at Tracy.

"You shut your nasty mouth!" Cilla cried and swung with her purse.

Her Saturday morning shopping purse, with her notebook and a coffee can full of change to take to the CoinStar machine.

Ernie went stumbling backward, eyes wide enough Melba thought they would pop out of his skull. He hit the bracing strut for the crane with enough force to make it clang, toppled sideways, and went to his knees on the sidewalk. His eyes rolled around for a few seconds. Melba didn't want to get close enough to be sure, but she thought they rolled in opposite directions.

"Yeah, we're gonna need some medical help here, along with that cop," Jake said.

Melba looked up to see him holding a smartphone facing outward.

She had the awful feeling he had recorded that. Hopefully, he had recorded enough to prove that Ernie was the aggressor, and Cilla had clobbered him in self-defense. She muffled a giggle, as she thought of the reaction on the Internet if that video ever got released to the public. Maybe they should talk to Rufus, who was so good with computers and the Internet. Or maybe Becca Sheridan. She handled that sort of thing for some of her clients, didn't she?

"You ladies probably want to get out before the circus lands," Joe said, and gestured with a jerk of his chin back the way they had come.

"Yeah, we're pretty much done here," Jake added, and lowered the phone. Meaning the camera was off.

"Thank you, boys. I'm going to design a candle and name it after you. What kind of scent would you like?" Melba said, as she and Cilla backed up a few steps.

"Anything with coffee suits me," Joe said with a grin.

Jake tipped two fingers off his eyebrow in salute and bent to offer a hand to Ernie. The curmudgeon had recovered enough to bat it away. Melba turned herself and Cilla around and they scampered the last twenty feet to the end of the building and the parking deck. They were in her car, pausing at the end of the driveway to check the traffic on the street when the EMT truck pulled up behind the Monroes' van. Melba focused on getting around the truck. From the corner of her eye, she saw Cilla slide down in the passenger seat so the top of her head barely cleared the door. They were both giggling by the time they reached the bridge at Apple and turned right.

~~~~~

Allen Kenward had the bad luck to be involved in writing up the incident report, and he called the Tweeds two hours later to get their story. He informed them then that Jake Monroe had been on the lookout for Ernie to show up and had turned on his phone's camera the moment the man's car appeared. All evidence clearly put Ernie in the wrong. He was already shouting that the entire video had been fabricated, that he had been lured there with the intention of attacking him, and a man disguised as Cilla Tweed had assaulted him with brass knuckles.

Ernie's proof that he had paid the five months back rent was nothing but a PayPal email receipt, reporting the email address where he had sent the money. Ernie insisted that he had gotten an email from Tracy the night before, promising he could move back that afternoon if he paid his rent right away. It wasn't Tracy's email. Allen had asked Eden, in her role as an occasional consultant for the police department, to do some digging to identify who had sent it.

Whoever had received that money, their email address was different from Tracy's by five transposed letters. Ernie had screamed and spat when

Allen told him he needed to get online and reverse that transfer of money before the person on the other end accepted it. Then the money would be gone for good.

"It's too easy to mess things up, going all electronic like that," Melba said, as she and Cilla discussed the situation with Rufus that afternoon, at Book & Mug. After hearing about the mess Ernie had gotten himself into, they agreed they needed to get advice from an expert for handling online payments. Rufus was the nearest computer expert, and gladly wheeled over to join them at their table when they called to him.

"Should we keep things as simple as possible?" Cilla said. "Taking payments, I mean. We were talking about setting up a website and taking orders through the Internet, but we aren't sure if we should get into the whole fuss of shipping and all that. Even after all the talking and planning we've been doing for months, you'd think we'd have every contingency covered, but ..." She sighed. "What do you think?"

"I'm not the one to ask when it comes to running a business." He hooked his thumb toward the front door. Becca Sheridan was just coming in. "She's the one to ask. Get her in on the ground floor."

"She's next on our list of people to talk to. But you will handle our website and security, won't you?" Melba hurried to add.

"For you ladies, anything." Rufus winked and backed his wheelchair away from the table. He popped a wheelie and turned to the left, aiming toward the bookstore side of the coffee shop, where his sister Devona's head was just visible above the shelves.

They gave Becca time to settle in and get her drink, and chuckled a little to realize that they were so busy cornering Rufus for advice, they hadn't ordered anything. They picked up their usual iced chais and sauntered over to Becca's booth. Melba thought she looked good, more rested, finally recovering from all the stress of the last few weeks. She considered Becca one of the good ones in Cadburn Township, who deserved far better than what had happened to her.

Becca's face lit up when the cousins finally talked long enough that she understood they wanted her help setting up their business. Another knot of tension and doubt eased out of Melba's neck and stomach. Becca loved the name for their shop, and eagerly agreed to help them. She pulled out one of her notebooks and the three started brainstorming. And laughing a little about the whole mess with Ernie Benders. Becca had heard about what a troublesome tenant he had been for Tracy.

"I don't think the old fusspot sourpuss is anywhere close to giving up," Melba admitted. "This is going to go on for weeks. I wouldn't put it past him to throw a brick through our window or try to do something to melt all our candles, or even badmouth us in the newspaper."

"That costs money," Cilla said, and wrinkled up her nose. "Ernie has been a tightwad since kindergarten. All he can get for free in the newspaper is a letter to the editor. The only thing that's kept him out of a lot of trouble over the years has been having to pay for the supplies to do all the things he threatens to do to people. He'll give up just as soon as he realizes how much it'll cost him." She nodded for punctuation. "Now, we need to find lovely old, eclectic sort of furniture to use for display racks. No boring old shelving. Where do you recommend we go?"

"Well, maybe you should decide how much of the shop will be used for display, and how much room you need for making your candles," Becca said, as she drew several lines down the notebook page, dividing it into columns. "That'll give you an idea of how much room you have, before you buy furniture."

"I had an idea," Melba said. "What do you think? Do the production out front where people can see. We have two huge display windows. Do our designing in front of one window, where people walking by can see it. Then show them the finished product in the other window."

"I like that," Cilla said slowly, her gaze going distant.

Melba chuckled, practically hearing the gears of thought whirring in her cousin's head. This was the fun part, the dreaming and imagining and figuring out how they could make it happen.

Chapter Four

Sunday, September 25

"Oh, no," Cilla whispered, as the cousins paused on the steps of Cadburn Bible Chapel that morning.

"No, what?" Melba looked up, expecting the gray threat of clouds to have thickened while they were inside at worship. No, the sky had improved. She lowered her gaze to the people spreading across the small parking lot and heading down the street to the municipal parking lot just around the corner.

Then that falling elevator feeling hit her stomach.

"What is she doing here?" she whispered.

"More important question is how we can—" Cilla let out a whimper. "Too late."

"Darlings!" Charlotte Westover spread her arms wide, making her dozens of glittery bracelets jangle. "How are my favorite cousins in the whole wide world?"

Melba knew she was being nasty, and only ten minutes after a sermon on showing mercy to the merciless and irritating, but she said a prayer of thanks that she was not indeed any relation to Charlotte. She was Cilla's cousin on her mother's side, while Cilla and Melba were cousins on their fathers' sides.

Charlotte was in what Cilla's older brother Calvin had called her Carmen Miranda mode. All she lacked was a mountain of fruit stacked on her head. She fluttered with multicolored scarves and some sort of gossamer overshirt and a butterfly hem on her enormous skirt and if Melba wasn't mistaken, had three different colors of eyeshadow.

"Charlotte, what brings you to town?" Cilla said as she descended the front steps of the chapel.

And what will it take to get you to leave? Melba thought, and then apologized to God. Maybe she needed to apologize to Pastor Roy, too. She had the awful feeling God had a lesson for her to learn. Today's sermon certainly could apply to this situation.

She knew things had been too quiet on the Charlotte front. Eden had reported that after she "set the dogs loose," Charlotte had vanished from social media. Not that either Cilla or Melba had any way to know, since Charlotte had blocked them. Not that they had looked for signs of her anywhere online. None of their mutual acquaintances had reported Charlotte in victim mode and wailing about how everyone was so unkind. On second thought, that should have been a warning in and of itself.

Melba fought down a brief stab of resentment. The only person in the world who could be counted on to be kind to Charlotte when she least deserved it was Cilla. If Charlotte wasn't here for revenge, which implied she had figured out that they were to blame for her downfall, then she was here to hide from her latest disaster and try again to guilt-trip Cilla into helping her put her life back together.

After her failure two years ago to essentially hand Cilla's childhood home over to her creditors, why hadn't Charlotte learned her most painful lesson yet and just stayed away permanently?

"Well first on my list is finding a place with some air conditioning. How can you stand living here? It shouldn't be so unutterably hot in September!" Charlotte giggled and jiggled and hurried to smother Cilla in an embrace that made the smaller woman rock back on her heels for a moment. The dispersing members of the congregation shuffled outward, creating an open area around them, as if pushed by a small shock wave. "I've just been waiting for hours."

"You could have come inside," Cilla said, when she could finally step back and regain her breath.

Melba wondered how Charlotte had even figured out what church they were attending now. The church they had grown up attending had merged with the Chapel eight years ago. Charlotte had loathed their former church and always played sick on Sundays to avoid going, when she stayed with Cilla's family. Not that her act ever fooled anyone.

"Oh, don't be ridiculous." Charlotte giggled. "Darling, I was so embarrassed. I knocked on your door, and there were strangers living in your parents' house."

"Aunt Candace and Uncle Royce have been gone more than ten years," Melba said.

"What does that have to do with it?" Her lip curled up and she turned slightly, putting her back to Melba, edging closer to Cilla.

Some things never changed. Already, she was maneuvering to cut out Melba.

"Then I remembered that you sold the house. How could you do that? I loved that house. I insist that you buy it back."

"It was much too big for me," Cilla said. She met Melba's gaze and rolled her eyes, just for a few seconds, while Charlotte dug in her purse for a handkerchief to blot at her sweaty face.

"Oh, but you need room to entertain. Darling, you can make every bedroom a different theme and open a B&B. They're all the rage now. Besides, I need a place to stay when I come to visit and catch up. Surely you won't make me sleep in the street?" Charlotte chuckled, sounding like Elmer Fudd. Another warning sign that she was up to something and faking her emotions.

"The house was much too big for me."

"But didn't you realize I was looking forward to having a vacation house in my declining years? I adore this part of Ohio."

Could have fooled me. Melba wished she had made a recording of some of Charlotte's complaints whenever her parents had parked her in Cadburn for months at a time. According to her, the entire state was boring and smelled bad, and the weather never suited whatever mood she happened to be in.

"Vacation house?" Cilla's voice lost the weary, polite tones she always used with Charlotte and took on a sharp edge. "You're not making my home your vacation house."

"Oh, but darling, it would be my home, too. I mean, it's been in our family for generations!" Again, with the Elmer Fudd chuckle.

"No, it wasn't. My father bought the house before he married my mother. It's Tweed property, and as you let us know whenever you didn't want to abide by Granny Tweed's rules, you aren't a Tweed."

"Oh, I can't believe how cruel you are!" Charlotte dabbed at her eyes and looked around, probably seeking sympathy from onlookers.

"What do you want, Charlotte?" Cilla said with a sigh. "You never show up unless you want something."

"Cilla ..." Her shoulders slumped and she rubbed at one eye with her knuckle, instead of dramatically dabbing with a lacy handkerchief.

That was new. Melba and Cilla exchanged glances. Charlotte had learned her mannerisms from old black-and-white movies full of dramatic, fainting, scheming heroines. That had become her handbook for dealing with life in general.

"You're absolutely right." The false brightness dropped out of her voice, which lowered about half an octave. "I'm just ... I'm putting my life back together. I thought I'd go somewhere that ... well, one of the few places where people treated me decently even when I was a brat who needed my 'tude slapped out of me, as Grandad ... as your grandfather used to say." She shrugged. "Would you let me stay a few days to catch my breath?"

"How many is a few?" Melba asked, before Cilla could. Someone had to protect her cousin from her soft spot. It had hardened over the years when it came to Charlotte, but unfortunately, not hard enough yet.

"A week?"

Charlotte didn't give her the stink eye for, as she put it, intruding into a private conversation. Maybe she had finally gotten knocked back on her padded, self-important behind hard enough to learn a long overdue lesson?

"Well, that sounds ... reasonable," Cilla said. "I just have to warn you that Melba and I have a lot of community activities and commitments. You'll have to entertain yourself while I'm busy."

And please, please, please make it clear to her she has to stay out of my half of the duplex, Melba silently begged. *I really need to grow up. Lord, were You whispering in Pastor Roy's ear this morning? I certainly needed today's sermon to prepare me for Hurricane Charlotte.*

She missed the next couple of sentences Charlotte and Cilla exchanged, until Cilla asked, "Did you drive here, or did you take an Uber?"

Charlotte muttered something about refusing to get in a car with strangers, of course she rented a car. Typical.

~~~~~

They agreed that Cilla would feed Charlotte and keep her on her side of the duplex. Melba would watch the Guardians game and check out the websites for all the secondhand furniture stores Becca had recommended they visit. How Cilla was going to visit the stores with Melba without Charlotte finding out about Brighten Your Corner and trying to take over, Melba had no idea. She would need to spend a good chunk of time praying and planning for contingencies. And repenting of her attitude toward Charlotte. Cilla was definitely the kinder, more patient member of the team.

"Here." Cilla stepped through the kitchen door Melba had left open. She had the plastic milk crate of all the paperwork she had been handling for the business, including designs for the candles they had been creating over the last month. "Out of sight, hopefully out of mind." She set the crate down on Melba's kitchen table. On top of everything was a cross-stitched heart-shaped pillow. She flushed a little when she caught Melba's crooked grin. "You know she'll start looking for it the second she walks through the door. Why she keeps trying to take it, after all these years—"

"She knows it irritates you." Melba snatched the pillow out of the crate. "I'd better hide it somewhere good and deep, because sure as shooting, she'll weasel her way in here to look for it, once she figures out it isn't at your place."

"And whining the whole time about how it's such a precious memento of Granny." Cilla headed for the door. "She says that just to rile you. I can't figure out why she wants it when she made fun of us for making all the heart pillows for the craft sale." She shook her head, grinning wryly. "And I won't give her the satisfaction of asking."

"She's not going to leave after just a week, is she?" Melba already knew the answer to that. Charlotte always contradicted herself, not just everyone around her.

"I don't know. She has to be in trouble with someone. I'll wait until she calms down and stops playing queen of the world. She really isn't so flamboyant when it's just the two of us. Whatever she's hiding from this time, I'll figure out a way to help so she leaves us alone." Cilla gestured down to the basement. "You need to lock your basement door. Not that she'll lower herself to use the laundry room, but you never know when the bug will bite her to try to redecorate your place again."

Melba nodded. That was the smart tactic to take. Eventually, Charlotte would brace herself to climb down the stairs to the basement on Cilla's side and back up on Melba's side, just to prove that she could go anywhere she wanted. Melba despised playing games by Charlotte's rules, but the alternative was to leave the woman free to invade the moment Melba left the house and help herself to whatever she wanted. *Well, I'm a guest, and you need to be hospitable, make me feel welcome*, she had said numerous times over the years, when forced to give back something she took without permission. Starting with money, house keys, expensive cooking ingredients, and mementos of Granny Tweed.

Cilla hurried back to her side of the duplex. Just in time. Melba heard the heavy sound of a luxury car's engine pulling into the driveway. She hurried to close and lock her door and pull the blind down over the window. She tucked the pillow back into the crate and hauled it to her spare bedroom, which served as her office.

How many times over the years had Charlotte gone after that pillow? The first time was while the family had gathered to clean out Granny's house after the funeral. Amid the fuss of finding out the labyrinth chest and several small pieces of valuable furniture had simply vanished, Charlotte managed to sneak into the house and start digging through rooms. If she hadn't snarled at Ginny's six-year-old, making the little girl go running for her mother in tears, they never would have caught Charlotte stuffing the pillow into her enormous purse.

The irony was, if Charlotte had just asked, they would have let her have the pillow. And a dozen other things. The house was overflowing with Granny's crafts. But Charlotte had trespassed and then got nasty when she was caught. The family council convened right then and there and agreed: Charlotte had to leave immediately. No one was to let her into the house. If she wanted something that belonged to Granny, then she could come back for the auction and the yard sale next week. Cilla's mother made sure the none of the heart pillows went into a yard sale box, specifically because Charlotte wanted one.

Melba scolded herself for griping about old arguments and petty feuds. She tried to pray, first for strength and cleverness for Cilla, then for forgiveness for herself, as she dug through her leftovers for an easy lunch. Her spirits were in much better shape by the time she combined several dabs of vegetables, pasta and potato salads, and a leftover Italian sausage into a satisfying meal. Then she stretched out in her recliner and leaned back and turned on the TV. The timing was perfect. It was a home game and the opposing team had gone through their half of the first inning in rapid-fire order without scoring. The home team was up.

Monday, September 26

Melba woke up that morning to find several emails from Cilla, discussing the paint they had ordered from Lumberville, then suggesting several changes, including paint swatches for accent colors. She had gotten out of bed more than an hour early that morning, just to give her time to get a head start on her share of the list of chores for the week before her houseguest woke. Not that Charlotte would wake before 10am, but common sense said to never trust her to stick to a routine.

Still, that woman's presence did complicate the simple, easy routine the cousins had established after years of sharing the duplex. For one thing, Melba would have to keep her doors locked. Maybe it wasn't safe, and Ted lectured them every few months, but they left their doors open whenever they were home, just to make it easier to step out the front or back door and pop in through the matching door, with an idea or a question or to share some fresh cooking they had done.

Melba spent a pleasant half hour on the phone with Tammy, Mo's grand-niece at Lumberville, discussing color schemes and ordering the accent paint. While she was on the phone, she scheduled the Richardson twins, grand-nephews on the other side of Mo's family tree, who had a stripping and refinishing business, to come in and refresh the hardwood floors. Melba opened up her notebook with the list of chores and checked off two more items. She sighed, wondering if they had given themselves too tight of a schedule, and they wouldn't get all of this done before the grand opening, during the fall street festival.

A banging on the front door startled her, shortly after ten. She listened for Cilla's quick tapping footsteps, but nothing came. Sighing, she got up to go to the front door. As far as she could recall, she wasn't expecting any deliveries. The motion of the door opening stirred the envelope taped to the woodwork of the frame between the two front doors. The envelope had nothing on it other than *TWEEDS*, in all-cap letters. No return address. Sighing, she glanced up and down the street, to see if she could catch a glimpse of who had taped it there. No one in sight. She flipped the envelope open and slipped out the bundle of several folded pages.

"What in the world ..." Melba paused with her hand on the door to push it closed and stared at the seal for the Cuyahoga County Municipal Court. Underneath was the word "INJUNCTION," and underneath that, "LEGAL ORDER," in all-caps. She was growing tired of all-caps. Someone had told her using all-caps online was equivalent to shouting. Now she could understand why.

She read through the orders for "the Tweed women," rather than giving their names, to cease and desist all activities to start their new business. The business wasn't named, either. It looked rather official, but it just felt wrong. Melba couldn't be sure, because she had never had any reason to look at anything like this before. She read through the two pages a second time. Shouldn't there be more details, more pages, more legal language? She finished closing the door and headed back into the kitchen, where she had left her phone. First, she texted Cilla, asking her to stop over. Then she called Lisa Pascal, executive assistant to Bill Worter of Worter, Worter & McIntosh. A Worter had been lawyer for the Tweed family for generations. Cilla came in through the front door while Melba was waiting for Lisa to finish taking care of another call and pick up the phone again. She explained in whispers about the arrival of the document and handed it to her cousin to read. Lisa picked up the phone just seconds later. Melba put her on speaker so Cilla could join the conversation.

"I don't suppose you can scan it and send it over here?" Lisa asked, once Melba explained what she had found.

"How about we just take photos of each page and send those over?" Cilla suggested.

"That works for me."

Cilla whipped out her smartphone and got to work.

"Without even seeing it, I can tell you the documents are fakes. Legal documents like that are delivered by couriers, and depending on the severity, you have to sign for them. Benders put it together to scare you."

"He did a pretty good job," Melba said. She shuddered, her mind filling with all sorts of implications at this newest attempt by Ernie Benders to stop them setting up their candle shop.

"So we can ignore this?" Cilla asked, tapping away on her cell phone. There was a whooshing sound, meaning an email had been sent.

"Well, ignore the orders, but not the threats. I can't break confidentiality to give you any details, but this is going a few steps beyond the nasty tricks he pulled to keep Tracy from evicting him. I wouldn't put it past him to hire someone to dress up in a police uniform and threaten you face-to-face. Okay, your email just got here. I'll take this to Bill. You might want to get one of those doorbell cameras installed, or even talk to Eden about security cameras like she used for Rufus and Becca's duplex. Just to gather evidence."

"Thanks. Starting up a new business is turning out to be more expensive than we anticipated."

"You didn't hear this from me," Lisa said with a chuckle, "but if you help us pull this nasty little rat's teeth, once and for all, I wouldn't be surprised if any legal help you end up needing turns out to be pro bono."

"Well, that's something," Cilla said, once they had thanked Lisa and hung up the phone.

"The important thing is that Lisa told us, completely official and on the record, that we have every right to keep working on the shop."

"I have to wonder ..." Cilla rubbed her eyes, looking like a weary five-year-old needing a nap. She sighed and headed for the door. Charlotte would come looking for her if she didn't return soon.

"Wonder what?"

"What kind of man Ernie would be if I had dated him."

"Somehow, I doubt the influence of a good woman would have done anything to change him. You would have suffered, and I refuse to sacrifice you on the off chance you might have done him some good."

"Or been dragged down to his level?" Cilla paused in the door, one foot on the front porch, one inside the house. "I wasn't a very strong Christian back then, just attending, learning the Bible stories but not letting them sink in. I cared more about what Granny and Grandpa wanted from us and thought of us, than I did about obeying God."

"We were all self-centered to one degree or another back then. That's what teenagers do. Babies think the world revolves around them, and teens haven't progressed very far past that stage. Some never progress past that stage," she added, dropping her voice to an ominous tone.

That got a chuckle from Cilla, who ended on a sigh and pulled the door closed before she stepped over to her own front door.

Chapter Five

Lisa Pascal came into Book & Mug shortly after eleven. Kai was surprised when she didn't step up to the counter and order something. Before he could call out to her, Eden came downstairs with Rufus. They gathered at a four-seater table near the door and only chatted for ten minutes before Lisa waved and hurried out.

"Problem?" Kai asked, when Eden stepped behind the front counter to pick up one of the bottles of cold brew he kept waiting for her.

"The Tweeds are getting some hassle about their new shop. Lisa asked us if we could set up a system like we had for Rufus and Devona's place." She unscrewed the lid on the bottle and reached for the box with the packets of stevia, to refill the dispenser bowls in the self-service station.

"Who'd be hassling them over their shop? What kind of trouble could a candle store cause anybody?"

"Former tenant. That Benders troll over at Creekside." She grimaced and tore open three packets.

"Ouch. Don't suppose it'll lighten up the atmosphere on the other side of the creek now that he's gone?"

"If only." She finished replacing the cap, saluted him with the bottle, and hurried away.

"You heard?" Rufus paused at the end of the counter, where he could look over the drawbridge.

"Yeah. What's the guy been doing to them?"

Rufus shrugged. "Wouldn't be surprised at anything, from the stories I've been hearing about him."

"You guys need any help with the installation, let me know."

Rufus thanked him with a nod and turned his wheelchair to head for the little brass cage elevator.

"What kind of trouble is that scumbuzzard Ernie causing now?" Heinrich shuffled up to the counter and thumped an armload of books down. A pale green receipt stuck out from under the cover of the third book down, meaning he had already paid for them on the bookstore side of the shop. Kai was relieved, because he just wasn't in the mood to deal tactfully with Heinrich and remind him to pay for the books.

"He got evicted—"

"About time. That Tracy's a sweet kid. Deserves better than to have to deal with him. The things I've seen, working late. Shady types coming in and out of the back door of his shop when an honest man would be gone for the night." Heinrich's scowl turned thoughtful. "I've got a great view right across the creek from the side window of my shop. Guy like Ernie just ruins the whole street. Wouldn't be surprised if the whole building blew up one of these days, y'know?"

"Well, it won't, because he's gone." Kai silently urged Heinrich to gather up his books and go back to his den. He had a business to run, after all.

"Yeah, you said. Good for Tracy. Giving her grief over evicting him like he deserves?"

"And the Tweeds. They're taking over the space."

"He's going after Cilla?" For a moment, Heinrich seemed to go pale, then an angry flush washed upward from his collar. "Not on my watch." He thumped the counter once more, making a few mugs jump, then scooped up his books and stalked to the door, muttering under his breath.

Kai watched him go, exhaling slowly, trying not to let the idea coalescing in his brain solidify. There was no way Heinrich … and Cilla … just no way.

Still, if Heinrich took it into his head to keep an eye on things across the creek like he had watched events in the Windows building, that might be a good thing. He had complained often enough people ignored him, but his comments had been clues to help trap Conrad's murdering brothers.

Kai mulled the situation over in his head for the next few hours as he performed late morning chores and handled the lunch rush. Who could be so nasty and self-centered to cause trouble for two elderly ladies as sweet and fun and kind as the Tweed cousins? He hoped whatever evidence Rufus and Eden's equipment caught, it would be enough to hang the guy.

~~~~

Melba tapped on Cilla's back door four times and headed down the back porch steps to the garage to get her car. She got in but didn't start the engine. While she waited for Cilla to come out, for their first errand of the day, she looked through the printout of addresses and descriptions of the secondhand furniture stores Becca had recommended to them, to find interesting display pieces for their shop.

"Lord, You're going to have to help me today. It's already started on a sour note, but if she comes with us, You know she's going to try to force her tastes and choices on us and insist that we want her help, no matter how many times we tell her no, we don't. Please, a couple of miracles would be nice. Starting with laryngitis?"

Cilla's back door creaked open. Melba flinched. Thank goodness they had never gotten around to asking Curtis to take care of that creak. At least she had a warning. The last thing she needed was Charlotte hearing her praying and asking God to intervene. That would lead to Charlotte whining that everyone was being mean to her, they didn't understand that she was only trying to help.

"How many times does someone have to be told not to do something before they realize that excuse doesn't cut it?"

Melba snorted, remembering a friend whose handicapped brother had an aide come every morning to take care of a few tasks he couldn't handle. Every other week, her friend had to leave a note for the aide, telling him to stop rearranging the house for his convenience. He constantly moved food and dishes and personal items out of the reach of the wheelchair-bound man. Every time she left a note, the oblivious twit left a scribbled note saying, "I only wanted to help. God bless." God finally blessed them by his agency firing him after far too many complaints.

"Punch it," Cilla muttered as she slid into the passenger seat. She slammed the door for punctuation.

"Where's ..." Melba shifted into drive and barely refrained from stomping on the gas.

"I hurt her feelings," Cilla said, once they were two blocks away down Overlook, heading south into Strongsville.

"How?" She managed to keep her voice down, in fear she might erupt in a cheer.

"First of all, remind me never to go out to dinner with Charlotte unless we go somewhere ten miles outside Cadburn." She sighed. "Carly Pembroke stopped by our table last night and gushed on and on about how delighted she was to learn we're opening the shop."

"Oh ... no..." Melba would have closed her eyes and banged her head against the steering wheel, but she was driving.

"I warded off trouble for a little while, because she didn't mention candles, just offered her services with decorating and color schemes. Her brother now sells store furniture, so we absolutely have to go to him for everything. As if." Cilla snorted for punctuation.

Melba grinned. Carly's brother had a new sales job every three or four months. He always managed to close down his affiliation with the company in time to let him say, "Sorry, you have to go to the parent company for all warranties and services."

"On the positive side, Charlotte got into an argument with her, declaring that she was our design and interior decoration consultant. Carly has hurt feelings now and will leave us alone for a few months, and Charlotte sulked for the entire evening. I wasn't going to tell her flat out that no, we hadn't hired Carly. Then this morning, she decided that we had taken her up on her generous offer to *let us* run *her* candle store and went on and on about her requirements for the shop."

"So why isn't she coming with us?" Melba wasn't sure if she really wanted to know. Charlotte in a snit, left alone in Cilla's side of the duplex, could lead to all sorts of horrific discoveries when they returned from their shopping trip. Staring with ransacking or rearranging the whole house. It was a good thing Cilla had moved all the shop records and research to Melba's place yesterday.

"Well, she didn't listen when I played dumb and asked when she made the offer. I even said we had never discussed a candle shop with her, so how could we accept?"

"She's conveniently forgotten she blocked us." Melba grinned. She considered making notes about all of Charlotte's ridiculousness, her idiotic schemes and tantrums, and hand the document to Charli Hall. Charlotte would be a mock-worthy villain for one of her stories someday.

"She ignored me, like she always does, and then went on and on about all the fun we had in junior high, designing candles for the craft fairs, and all the awards we won in art competitions."

"Uh, no, that was you and me."

"I know that. Well, I finally got fed up and reminded her of how many times she mocked us for our old-fashioned, stupid hobby that wouldn't make a useful career." Cilla snorted. "Useful. What would she know about that word? Starting with how to spell it."

"So I take it she got her itty bitty feelings hurt that you kept contradicting her?"

"And then some. She insisted that Jeffrey and Tyrone were the ones who made fun of us, and she always defended our delightful little hobby."

"Delightful little ..." Melba groaned her exasperation.

"Exactly. I kept telling her no, we never agreed to go into business with her. And she had the gall to correct me, we weren't going into business together, we were working for her. I asked her for paperwork, some proof of the agreement and she had the gall to say that family doesn't need any such foolery. I was getting this close—" Cilla measured a tiny distance between forefinger and thumb, "—to telling her all the legal work we've done to protect us from her schemes."

"You should have. She'd be packing in a huff right this moment."

"I know." Cilla sighed and deflated in her seat.

"What happened?"

"She was working herself up to lecture me. I could see it in her face. Then she got a phone call and the moment she looked at the screen, she just went white. And there was this terror in her eyes ... I know she deserves all the trouble she's brought on herself, and I am sick and tired of how she tries to force us to bail her out, but ... I felt sorry for her."

"You're a better person than she is, that's all there is to it." She snorted. "And a better Christian than me."

"Not so sure about that. A part of me kind of ... well, I kind of enjoyed knowing she was getting her comeuppance once again."

"You're only human. And Charlotte does deserve what punishment she gets."

"You are far too reasonable and calm and philosophical this morning." Cilla reached over and lightly tapped her arm.

"Maybe. I think it's time to ask Eden to do some more digging and find out what new trouble she's hiding from."

"What would we do without her? And the boys? We really need to get them to come to church more often."

"We need to kick Kai's butt and get him in gear and solidify things with that lovely Saundra before someone else wakes up and starts pursuing her." Melba tapped the steering wheel for emphasis.

"Agreed!"

Laughing, they turned down Royalton Road, heading for their first stop.

~~~~~

After three hours, they had found two pieces of furniture, both along the lines of what was once called a breakfront, to display their products. Both pieces of furniture were what the store owners called "distressed," but Melba considered them abused. The grain was dry and had opened up, and in some places splintered, stained in others, and would require quite a lot of work and time to refinish them. She was willing to risk someone else snatching up the furniture before they came back to buy it, rather than putting down a deposit at the store owners' urging.

On the way to Vintage House, the fourth store on the list, they discussed in more detail the idea of setting up production out in the shop itself, so customers could see what went into making their candles. They were refining their plans for candle crafting classes as they turned onto the street.

The old Victorian-style house stood guard at the street, soft gray with lavender trim. A dignified sign in the same color scheme directed them between two luxurious box hedges that had to be six feet tall, to the parking area in back. Bushes and climbing ivy softened the lines of the warehouse that sat low to the ground. The smell of turpentine and paint drifted on the warm afternoon air.

Melba was pleasantly surprised to step through the double-wide open doors into the shadowy interior and find the floor tiled, not cement. A few steps in, she realized the dark green tiles weren't placed haphazardly among the speckled beige. They marked aisles through the warehouse and delineated "rooms" with groupings of furniture set up for inspection.

The people running this place knew furniture, keeping the styles and periods together. This was the kind of furniture store several of the women in their book club had been looking for. They had been complaining about the bizarre taste dictating modern furniture styling, how much quality, solid furniture cost, and how hard it was to find the really good, tasteful furniture they remembered from childhood.

Melba split her attention between making note of the groupings of furniture and a mental list of the specific women who would like each grouping. Cilla pointed out a table here, a lamp there, a desk over to the side. Nothing they saw so far really suited what they had in mind to use for displays in the shop.

A muted pastel rainbow caught her attention. It was almost hidden behind a long row of mismatched freestanding bookshelves, arranged like dominoes ready to be tipped over. She gestured vaguely for Cilla to follow and stepped across the aisle for a closer look.

Dozens of faded, cobwebby childhood memories swirled through her mind as she studied the cabinet. It stood maybe six feet tall, maybe four wide, nearly three deep. The front was evenly divided into squares, six inches on a side. Small knobs that looked like miniature thread spools sat in the middle of each square.

"No maybe about it," she murmured, and rested her hand on one of the knobs.

The paint looked airbrushed, in fanciful swirls of dusty rose and blue, deep lavender, and soft avocado. She imagined an up-and-coming artist, maybe at the local vo-ed school, having fun sprucing up the old, blocky, utilitarian-looking cabinet. Something caught in her throat as she tipped her head back to study the carved top, really the only decorative part of it. The upward curve in the middle had been broken off. Someone had made a little effort to smooth it down. Only the bottom two-thirds of the broken spiral of a maze remained, carved into the wood. Her hand trembled as she reached up to touch it. The painter had been faithful to delineate the design with colors, so it stood out, as if it were the most important part.

"It's lovely, but it really isn't our style," Cilla murmured from behind her. "We agreed on red oak, remember? To go with the paint for the trim." A chuckle. "Not nouveau psychedelic."

"It's a labyrinth chest."

"I know that." She sighed. "I remember Granny's."

"Excuse me?" A woman who looked like the typical New York editor, according to Charli Hall, stepped out of the aisle to their right. She was skinny and pale and wore all black, and even had a pen tucked behind one ear, partially tangled in her dusty-looking red hair. "What's a labyrinth chest?"

"It's like a puzzle box. There are hidden compartments in the center of the chest. Depending on which drawers you have open, and even the order in which you pull them out, that dictates what compartments you can find."

"We used to have such fun, hiding things in Granny's chest, when we were children." Cilla chuckled. "And got in major trouble when we couldn't remember what compartment we hid some things in, or how we got it open in the first place."

"Why would someone make something like that?" the woman asked. She grinned, her tone and expression indicating she was intrigued.

"You know, I don't really know," Melba admitted. "We just knew it was a fun puzzle to play with when we were little. Granny got it from her mother, as an engagement present," she explained to the woman, who certainly seemed interested.

"I've never heard of a labyrinth chest," the woman said. She stepped up and reached out a hand to run a finger over the beveled edges of the drawers, then traced the swirls and swoops of the paint.

"There was this furniture designer, back in the late 1800s. Algernon Duchene. They called him Dizzy Duchene, because every piece of furniture he made had that spiral labyrinth carved into it somewhere." She reached up to touch the spiral, remembering the time she had spent following the labyrinth with her gaze, trying to find the way out. "There's a little bit of a scandal associated with the chest, according to family history. Supposedly, Duchene was a suitor for our great-grandmother, and the chest was a courting gift. Supposedly, her father sent him packing after he gave it to her. A gift of furniture was basically saying he wanted to set up housekeeping. Not over that grumpy old man's dead body." Melba sighed into a chuckle. "The scandal got worse, because legend says Duchene carved the labyrinth into every piece he designed because he was pining for his lost love."

"Your great-grandmother?" The woman's eyes sparkled.

"Hardly. Legend also says he had to pack up his business several times, run out of town by angry fathers and brothers. Dizzy Duchene wouldn't take no for an answer, until a shotgun backed it up."

"Uh huh." She gave the chest a speculative look. "That's a lot of drawers to play with, to find the hidden compartments."

"Not really. Here, look." Melba held her breath and tugged on the second knob from the right and three down from the top.

Three squares straight down opened in one piece. It revealed an opening with tall, thin slats of wood, perfect for holding folders. She left it open and tugged on another knob. This only opened a drawer as big as one square. It stuck when Melba pulled on it.

"That needs to be fixed before we buy it," Cilla said. "What use is a drawer you can't open to put something in it?"

Melba stared at her, a smile growing on her face. It wasn't like they had agreed to buy the chest. They hadn't even seen the price tag yet. And yet, this would be just the thing for their shop, all the odd drawers pulled out at different depths, holding candles. It would certainly draw attention. Although no, the current color scheme wasn't exactly a good match for how they intended to paint the shop.

She nodded to Cilla, who nodded back, and Melba laughed, with a funny catch in her chest. The labyrinth chest from their childhood had been stolen during the long months of confusion and sadly waiting for Granny to die.

She did want this one, if only for the memories.

~~~~~

The memories came back in the quiet of the drive home. Melba smiled, seeing images from happy visits lasting weeks at a time at Granny Tweed's house. Despite being an only child, she never felt like one, because there was always a gaggle of cousins at the house or nearby. Laughing and genially arguing, singing and cooking, and often just sitting and rocking on the massive wraparound front porch. The memories spilled out in words, when Becca came by to check on how their first foray went and give them some designs for business cards and letterhead.

"We used to store our treasures in the secret compartments and behind panels. Oh, the fights we used to have, when we'd come visit and find someone had moved our things out, to put their own books and toys away. Franklin insisted there was a master key that made all the secret panels open, and compartments that would only open for the key. He claimed he found the key, and where to insert it, but he would never tell us. At first, it was just because he was so much older and so scornful of us. Then ..." She sighed, the warmth and laughter fading out of her memories. "He followed the family tradition on his father's side of the family and went into the Navy. They gave him special training, special missions. A precursor of the SEALs, I suppose." Another sigh. "One day, he didn't come home from a mission. The kind where no one will share the details. So the secret vanished with him."

"Shades of *National Treasure*?" Becca murmured.

Chapter Six

That evening as she tried to decide what to make for dinner, Melba's phone chattered at her, signaling a text from Cilla. It had to be something big, because neither of them liked to text.

Problem. Look outside. I'll run interference.

She hurried to the front of the house. A delivery truck from Vintage House sat on the street and two young men in T-shirts from the House of Blues were studying the steps that broke the sidewalk into three sections. Probably trying to decide how to get the labyrinth chest from the street to the house.

It wasn't supposed to come here. It was supposed to go to the shop. In two more hours, once the traffic on Creekview had slowed for the evening, so they wouldn't block anyone. And Ernie was less likely to be out, spying and trying to stop them from accessing the shop. Melba feared they would show up to open the shop for the delivery and find the door plastered with more fake court orders denying them access.

None of that mattered right now. The delivery was at the wrong address. She glared at the gray, churning sky as she snatched up a sweater and headed for the front door.

"Stop!" she called, as the taller young man fiddled with the door at the back of the truck. Probably preparing to lift the gate. "You're not supposed to deliver that here."

"Nobody at the other address," the shorter one said.

"That's because we aren't expecting you until eight." She jumped down the first set of steps and wondered for the umpteenth time what idiot thought it would be clever to put steps in the long path between the duplex and the city sidewalk. It made shoveling snow inconvenient. What would have been so hard about just making a long, gently sloping path?

"Yeah, but we got the other deliveries done earlier," the taller one said, and slammed the sliding door upward.

"Aren't you supposed to call ahead before you attempt a delivery?"

"Well, yeah, but ..." He looked at his partner. "There was nobody at the address when we got there."

"We would have been there if you had called ahead, like your boss said you would do." Melba gestured at the back end of the truck. "Close that up. I don't want the cabinet falling out on the way over to our shop, and I certainly don't want to risk any rain getting inside on the way over."

"But there's nobody there," the shorter one said, with that tone of voice that clearly meant he thought she was an idiot.

"I will be when you get there. I'm going to get my keys right now and follow you right over. And even if you don't remember me, I remember you, Tanner Wilcox." Melba muffled a chuckle when the taller one straightened up and his mouth dropped open. "Don't make me tell your mother how you cut corners and don't follow procedures to save time. That was your problem eight years ago. And look how much time you've just wasted, trying to save time."

"Yes, Miss Tweed," he mumbled, and jumped up into the back of the truck, reaching for the strap to close the gate.

She darted back into the house, pulled the front door closed, made sure it was locked, and hurried through to the kitchen. She snatched up her purse and was out the door before the truck's engine had even started up again. No rapping on the wall to signal Cilla this time, and no waiting for her cousin to accompany her and deal with this problem. She had to get out of there and get that truck out of there before Charlotte realized something was happening. They didn't need her to stick her nose into their business.

Although ... Melba knew she was being nasty, but she found great amusement from the idea of Charlotte rushing to lay claim to the shop and running into Ernie. Maybe she would finally get frightened away for good by the crazy old nasty.

On the other hand, she might find him to be a man after her own heart, team up with him, and never leave Cadburn Township. No, better that Cilla keep her distracted.

Melba grumbled as she pulled out of the driveway and followed the delivery truck down Overlook. By all rights, Cilla should be with her, overseeing the delivery of the first piece of furniture for their shop.

She mentally went over the list of things to do as she drove, but it was hard to keep her mind on that when the truck seemed to deliberately hit every bump and pothole in the road. When had Overlook gotten so many potholes? Would the township fix them before winter? Was it useless to do that? The snowplows would just dig them out again. Why did that truck have to bounce around like that? She imagined that lovely old labyrinth chest toppling over and bouncing against the sides of the truck, just on the short drive to Creekview. It wasn't Granny's labyrinth chest, but it was close enough to bring back dozens of lovely memories, and for that alone she cherished it.

Although ... not enough to put up with that airbrushing in colors the craftsman had never intended. Or maybe she should leave the chest as it was? She could work around those colors, to set off the candles she would display on it.

Melba hadn't made up her mind about refinishing the labyrinth chest by the time she pulled into the driveway to the parking deck. She parked, shook her head to clear it, and hurried down the street to open the front door of the shop. The parking deck was too narrow for the truck, otherwise she would have had them bring the chest in through the back door.

A pyramid of paint cans nearly blocked the door. She flipped on the light switch, stepped into the shop, and let out a sigh of delight. A note taped to the top can was from Tracy. She had let Lumberville in to deliver the paint, as the order had come in a day early.

A pile of drop cloths and brushes and the pieces of scaffolding sat against the wall, ready for the painting team to get to work. Mo and his grandchildren at Lumberville were wonders. She would never work with a franchise again for services. People in Cadburn Township took care of their own.

Tanner and his red-shirted partner took extra-long getting the chest out of the back of the truck. Probably because now he did remember Melba as a substitute teacher when one of the math teachers at the high school was on maternity leave. They slid the chest onto a wheeled cart, thickly padded with carpeting, rolled it down the ramp right onto the sidewalk, then bumped up the single deep stone step into the shop. Melba opened the door into the back room and directed them to set the chest right in the middle. She would worry about maneuvering it onto a drop cloth to protect the floor when they got to work stripping and refinishing. If they did. She needed to talk with Cilla about whether to restore the chest or leave it as it was. Now that she looked at it again, she rather liked the colors, the swoops and swirls. And the drop cloth might not be necessary. The floor was in such bad shape from whatever Ernie had spilled on it over the years, it was scheduled for stripping and refinishing too. Once the floor in the front of the shop had been refinished they would set the chest and any other furniture they obtained into place, then refinish the back room floor. Tracy, as landlord, was paying for all that, but she gave the cousins total freedom to pick their colors and finishes.

Melba watched the delivery truck pull away from the curb. Less than half an hour from the time they parked until they were gone. Not bad. They weren't as helpless as she had feared.

She stepped back into the shop and leaned against the far wall, to look straight through the door into the back room. Framed in the splotchy and battered trim of the doorway, the chest didn't look that bad. That shade of pale yellow really was lovely.

Tuesday, September 27

"Oh ... my," Cilla whispered, and stopped short in the doorway at the back of the shop. She turned around to face Melba, her lip quivering.

"What?" Melba gently moved her aside and stepped into the back room. Her foot skidded on a slick patch on the floor at the same moment the smell of fresh paint assaulted her nose.

The painters weren't supposed to start working until Thursday. There shouldn't have been paint in the back room. And certainly not on the floor.

Buckets were overturned, spilling puddles of sage green and warm sand. Footprints tracked through the puddles, creating a trail out into the front room and back, multiple times. Melba swallowed hard a few times, took a deep breath, nearly choking on the paint smell, and tiptoed through the mess, careful not to step in any of the paint. She paused in the doorway. The footprints were even worse out here, with big blotches of paint on the wall, nearly up to the height of the counters. How had the vandals managed that? Taken their boots off? Or were they incredibly limber?

"Check the front door," Cilla said. She stayed in the back room and just leaned her head through the doorway. "The back door was locked. They must have gotten through the front door."

"That would be kind of stupid," Melba said as she tiptoed her way through the footprints and puddles. She frowned at the puddle of sky blue that filled the left display window and dripped down the wall. She hadn't ordered sky blue. Did that mean the vandals had brought their own paint?

"I can see nasty, but how is it stupid to come through the front door?" her cousin said.

"Valerie mentioned she was having trouble with the new security system she had installed last week." Melba's mouth stretched in a flat, grimly satisfied smile as she recalled the conversation with their neighbor across the street. Valerie Carter was setting up a boutique promotion and publicity firm and had stopped by yesterday afternoon to introduce herself when the delivery truck left.

"What about her security system?"

"The computer controls insist on pointing two of her five cameras across the street, to catch traffic. If we're lucky, and the vandals are unlucky ... Valerie's cameras caught them coming in."

Cilla caught her breath, then she laughed as she pulled out her phone. "I'm calling Ted."

Melba nodded as she reached for the doorknob. Then she thought better of it and tugged down the sleeve of her light sweater to cover her fingers. If there were fingerprints, she didn't want to cover them with hers. She also didn't want to wipe them out with her sweater, either.

The doorknob didn't stick like it did when it had to be unlocked. It turned easily and she pulled it open a few inches.

"Well, now we know how," Cilla said a few moments later, as she lowered the hand holding her phone. "Now we need to figure out when and who."

"We know who."

"Let's just hope Valerie's cameras give us proof. We both know what Ernie's like when he's accused. Even if he's guilty, he'll shriek that he's being persecuted, and stereotyped, and profiled, and all those ridiculous trigger words, and ..." She sighed and gestured for Melba to look across the street.

Valerie was walking to her front door to open up and continue getting her business up and running. Melba hoped she had far more success and fewer obstacles than they did. Taking a deep breath, she hurried out the door and called, to catch Valerie before she went inside.

~~~~~

The investigation revealed Valerie's cameras weren't equipped with night vision mode, but a streetlight spilled almost straight down at the door for Brighten Your Corner. All three cameras caught Ernie, accompanied by a man that Chief Sunderson identified as a locksmith under a court order not to practice his trade. He had been implicated too many times in assisting burglars, troublemakers, and men like Ernie who took the law in their own hands. By 9:30am, Chief Sunderson sent Ted Shrieve out to confront the locksmith, while Allen Kenward went to confront Ernie. Because Ted was a relative of the Tweeds, any contact with Ernie would give grounds for a harassment lawsuit.

Ernie, of course, denied being anywhere near Creekview or the shop. When shown clips of the security video, he shrieked that it was a setup, the pictures of him were fake. He made the mistake of waving his arms around. Allen noted that he was wearing the same shirt that appeared in the video. When he raised his arms, the movement revealed splotches of warm sand paint. He had blue paint under his fingernails that matched the shade of blue spattered around the shop.

Allen called the station and within twenty minutes got verbal permission from Judge Evans, followed by an email with a search warrant. He found Ernie's boots, sitting at the top of a trash can, coated in all the colors of paint spattered around the shop. Plus, he found a nearly empty can of blue paint, still with a receipt from Schurger's Hardware, in Medina.

Ernie shrieked that he was framed, someone had used computers to create images of him to frame him, while Allen handcuffed him and led him to his patrol car. He insisted later that Allen had denied him his rights and refused to Miranda him, but the dash cam proved those claims false.

Ernie then claimed that the reciting of the Miranda rights had been edited in later.

Interestingly, the troublemaker lawyer whom everyone agreed was trying to make a name for himself, who usually arrived before Ernie was finished being processed at the police station, never showed up to defend him. Ernie used up his guaranteed phone call and got in a fight with Bernadette, the officer who processed him, when she tried to take all his personal effects and he refused to surrender his phone. She was smaller than him, but demonstrably stronger and more agile. Ernie yelled and argued until he went hoarse. He had to stay overnight. Chief Sunderson allowed him a phone call in the morning and another in the afternoon. Finally, one of Ernie's troublemaking, hyper-critical friends showed up on the third day of incarceration with bail and to take him home.

While there had been enough paint on hand to fill the first order for Brighten Your Corner, now Lumberville had to wait for a new shipment. The painting crew had another job they needed to start before the new order of paint came in. The schedule for renovations and decorating the shop had to be redone.

Now was the perfect time to examine the labyrinth chest up close, while no one was in the shop. How it had escaped being doused in paint, they couldn't imagine. Unless Ernie was so intent on vandalizing the front room, he ran out of paint by the time he got to the back room.

To Melba's relief, Cilla was free for the afternoon. Charlotte had a mysterious appointment she tried to play coy about, leaving little hints that she wanted the cousins to beg her to reveal the secret. Melba ignored her and prayed Cilla would hold strong. She nearly laughed aloud when Charlotte gave up in a huff and left for her mysterious appointment.

"I'm just sick, thinking of all the years trying to change her by being nice. It just encouraged her. We should have just kept hurting her feelings so she would give us the silent treatment," Cilla exclaimed, as they watched Charlotte's rental car head down the street. "Let's hope she stays away a long time, trying to make me worry."

"You are a nasty old biddy, Cilla Tweed." Melba chuckled. "I'm proud of you."

The amusement had faded by the time they deemed it safe to get in her car and head to the shop. Part of that was anticipating the paint smell, and the reminder that Ernie wasn't giving up. Once he recovered from this setback, they could expect his nasty tactics to escalate. She needed to get her mind off that depressing subject, and talked about the chest as she drove, how similar it might be to their grandmother's chest. Cilla got on her phone and looked up labyrinth chests and Duchene by the time they parked behind the shops.

There were other references that came up first before anything directly referencing Duchene and the short period of time in furniture making when labyrinth chests were in vogue. Cilla read aloud from an article that called them puzzle boxes and treasure chests combined. Decades after family heirlooms had been forgotten, or considered lost for all time, someone opened the secret compartments and brought old treasures to light.

By that time, they had opened the back door. The thought of a piece of furniture being used as a treasure chest got Melba thinking. About treasures that went missing when she and her cousins forgot how to get into the hidden compartments of the labyrinth chest between one visit and the next. She got down on her knees in front of the chest and tugged the bottom row of squares open. Just like with Granny's chest, they were all connected together, making a single drawer. It stuck, stopping after only five inches. That left enough room to get her hand in and thump the bottom of the drawer. She caught her breath when the panel visibly shifted under her touch. A false bottom, just like in Granny Tweed's labyrinth chest.

She stepped over to her purse, sitting by the back door, which they had left open for ventilation, and retrieved her metal nail file. She caught the tip of her tongue between her teeth and slid the nail file down the side of the drawer, gently prying up on the false bottom. Just like she had done as a teenager.

"Melba, listen to this. 'The secret compartments and false drawer bottoms varied from piece to piece, to suit the needs of the individuals who commissioned them. While Duchene went out of fashion before his death, his work is now increasing in desirability. A labyrinth chest damaged in the Ohio River flood in 1937 sold at auction for $5,000.'"

"Wonder what this would go for, despite the new paint job," Melba murmured as she lifted the thin drawer bottom. It creaked and splinters came off. She needed more room to maneuver.

Another yank on the drawer knobs. One came off, but the drawer opened ten inches with a horrendous screeching noise. She pried up the false bottom. A sheet of paper and a cloud of dust swirled up from the air movement. Two teardrop-shaped objects lay hidden in the dust and splinters from the shredding false drawer bottom.

"A pristine labyrinth chest sold at a Sotheby's auction in 2016 for $35,500." Cilla slowly lowered her smartphone. "Holy guacamole."

"You said it," Melba whispered, brushing curdles of dust off the gold clip-on earrings, with the initials F.A.T. picked out in what looked like diamond chips. She wiped off the dust and stared at the earrings, silent for so long, Cilla put down her phone and leaned over to look at them.

"That can't possibly be ... but what if ... Aunt Felicity?" she whispered.

Their aunt had hated her initials, and had joked every once in a while, when she was irritated with Uncle Titus, that she should have thought twice before marrying him, changing her name from Felicity Abigail Newsome to Felicity Abigail Tweed. She had been infuriated with Uncle Titus at the last family get-together before Granny Tweed died, and had taken the earrings off, saying she should have lost them years ago. The only times she wore them were when she had been running late or left the house without them and had to depend on him to get her earrings. He always chose the initial earrings because she refused to wear them.

Melba tried to remember the circumstances of that get-together. The labyrinth chest had been a topic of conversation. Granny Tweed had asked several of the great-grandsons to move it out to her workroom, on the sun porch, where she spent most of her time. She didn't say what she wanted to do with the chest. She was so feeble and delicate by this time, and so sad after the loss of Grandpa Tweed, no one had questioned her or even hesitated to fulfill her every wish. Melba remembered now that Uncle Titus had tried to discretely ask around about the earrings for more than a month after the get-together. She remembered Aunt Felicity had never worn them again. If Titus and Felicity fought over the lost earrings, no one knew. It made perfect sense now that she had hidden the earrings in the labyrinth chest and proclaimed them lost.

"Do you think?" Cilla said after they had both looked over the earrings. The odds of finding earrings with these specific initials in a labyrinth chest with that broken piece on the top, just like Granny's labyrinth chest were ... well, Melba couldn't calculate odds to begin with.

"We need to find out how the chest got from Granny's to the store where we found it," Melba said.

Chapter Seven

Wednesday, September 28

Charlotte's fancy champagne-colored rental car was gone from the driveway, so Melba didn't hesitate to rap their "come over, this is a good one" signal for Cilla on the shared kitchen wall. She chuckled as she spread what she had found on the kitchen counter, and for once didn't suffer that flare of resentment at how Charlotte had put a cramp into their daily routine. Melba didn't realize how much she enjoyed the freedom to leave the doors open for either of them to visit the other, until that freedom was restricted by the need to keep Charlotte from intruding. Especially since the woman seemed constitutionally unable to accept the fact that yes, she was intruding.

Charlotte had worked herself into a tizzy, ransacking every closet, refusing to admit she was looking for something, and then refusing to clean up the mess she made. Common sense said she was searching for the heart-shaped embroidered pillow. Melba found great satisfaction in knowing it was safely hidden away on her side of the duplex. It was childish, of course, but then again, so was Charlotte.

"Here I go again, Lord. Help me stop doing this," she muttered, and slammed one of the photo albums closed for punctuation. She grinned again as she looked at the stack of photo albums and photo boxes she had gone through. The time of enforced silence between her and Cilla had been well spent. Then she thought a prayer of apology for abandoning her cousin. Well, it was Cilla's idea that Melba just step back and leave her to deal with Charlotte, but it still felt like abandoning her.

Cilla let herself in the front door. Melba fought down a moment of panic at the thought of Charlotte finding out Cilla had that key. Either Cilla held onto the key, or she had to leave her door open for her cousin to come in and out. Not much of a choice.

"Good news?" Cilla called out.

"Proof." Melba held up an earring, then gestured at the series of six photographs laid out on the counter, and the two photo albums with the pages marked by sticky notes, so she could return the photos to their proper places.

Cilla chuckled as she leaned over the counter and studied the photographs, taken from several different family gathering occasions.

Granted, Aunt Felicity's earrings had never been the focus of the photos, but with the help of a magnifying sheet that Melba needed for some of her cookbooks, getting details of the earring visible in each photo was easy enough. Melba set the earring down on the magnifying sheet, next to the image, and they compared the details. They did it twice with each photo.

"It's amazing," Cilla whispered. "To think that we found the labyrinth chest again."

"No, it's frustrating." Melba tried to laugh. "We shouldn't have had to find it. That chest never should have left the family. Much less gone to someone who would paint it up like that. I mean, yes, it's a work of art, but ... well, for one thing, the chest is too big for just one person to have taken it. At least two people, maybe more, were involved in getting it out of the house. And how did they manage it when the house was full of people coming and going, in those weeks when Granny was dying? People lied, when they said they didn't know. I can't imagine we'd have any success backtracking the route that chest took between there and here, but I would certainly love to try. Just to settle those arguments. Some of our relatives haven't talked to each other in decades."

"Things were such a mess when Granny died. So much arguing. And then even after we discovered the furniture was gone, people kept trying to take things without asking, and everybody was on edge and ... I'm surprised all that fighting didn't make it into the papers."

"If there's one thing the Tweeds do right, it's keeping our family business our family business." Melba sank down into the nearest kitchen chair, her elation draining away. Maybe finding the photos to prove this was Aunt Felicity's loathed earring, meaning they had found Granny Tweed's labyrinth chest, hadn't been a good idea after all. All the memories being dredged up from behind the hazy wall of years just reinforced why she hadn't looked at the family photos in such a long time. The hurting memories threatened to overwhelm all the good ones.

"So, who do we contact about returning the earrings?" Cilla asked after several minutes of quiet, looking over the photos again.

"My first thought was Francis, as the only daughter, but since she's gone, and she had only sons ..." Melba shrugged.

"Andrew is the oldest son, with two daughters. We haven't heard anything from him or about him in ... how long?"

They put the photos back in the albums and Cilla helped Melba haul the albums up to the bedroom that was library and office. As they worked and then settled back at the kitchen table with a notebook, they discussed what they knew about their many Tweed relatives and their descendants and who would know where and how to contact whom.

Melba got up to find her address book. She had put it away probably two years ago when she got her cell phone and decided to store everything electronically. The front screen door squeaked open. She froze. Cilla's mouth dropped open, and she got that guilty look on her face that might have been comical in any other situation.

"I'm sorry," she whispered. "I left the door open. It's such a nice warm day ..."

"Yoohoo!" Charlotte yodeled, her voice dripping with Southern molasses. She only got that tone when she felt utterly triumphant and vindicated.

Melba put the list of names away while Cilla got up and headed for the front door. Too late. Charlotte bombed her way into the kitchen, beaming with delight, and looking around. Melba braced for another immediate lecture on how her kitchen needed redecorating and Charlotte, of course, was the only one who knew the proper way to do it.

"What's that?" Charlotte pounced, reaching for the earring that had been left sitting all by itself on the counter. Before Cilla could do anything more than say, "No," she swooped it up and held it close to her face, studying it. "Oh my goodness gracious! Do you know what you have here?"

"Yes, in fact, we do." Melba moved over, holding her hand out. "It's none of your business, Charlotte."

"How can you say that? I remember dear Aunt Felicity, how heartbroken she was when one of you naughty little children stole her earrings."

"Uncle Titus was the only one who was upset. Felicity laughed louder than anyone," Cilla said. "She hated those earrings. And we weren't children. We were in high school."

"Still naughty, though." Charlotte bubbled that Elmer Fudd laughter that had made Melba want to slap both hands over her mouth, even at the risk of getting bitten. Charlotte had been a biter all the way through elementary school and junior high. "Where did you find it? What are you doing with it after all these years? Oh, I can't wait to tell dear cousin Francis we found her mummy's earrings after all this time!"

"Francis is our cousin, not yours," Melba snapped. "Stop re-writing the past, Charlotte. It's a very ugly habit."

Charlotte's glare might have set Melba on fire just a short time ago, heavy on a sense of guilt. And hadn't she been praying God would help her have a kinder heart toward the woman? But sometimes enough was enough. What was wrong with her, to blithely change every detail of solid, established, accepted family history?

"You're planning on keeping it, aren't you?"

"Don't be ridiculous." Cilla snatched the earring from Charlotte's hand. "We just finished verifying it really is Aunt Felicity's earring, and we were just sitting down to decide who to notify."

"Well that's just ridiculous. Francis is her only daughter, so she gets it. I'll get my phone and call her right now, if you two don't have the good sense and the courtesy to do the right thing."

"Oh, really?" Melba leaned back against the counter. "And just how are you going to call her? The last I knew, they didn't have phone service to Heaven."

Charlotte stopped short, her mouth open. A flush crept up her neck, and two bright splotches on her cheeks appeared from under her usual heavy coating of makeup. "Oh, you are just awful. How dare you shock me with such horrid news? Francis was one of my dearest cousins—"

"Not your cousin. And not dear enough to keep in contact. She died five years ago."

Charlotte's mouth worked several seconds and her eyes lost focus as she visibly struggled for a retort, a denial. Melba mentally slapped herself for finding some glee at her difficulty in coming up with a new lie and justification.

"Why didn't you notify me?" she finally whimpered.

"Because Francis is our cousin, not yours," Cilla said, her tone weary rather than frustrated. "Because the last time you talked with her, you had a horrid screaming fight with her in front of half the family and told her — well, I won't repeat what you told her, but you reminded her that you weren't a Tweed, so she had no right to criticize how you lived your life."

"I never!" She backed up, reaching out behind herself.

Melba silently urged her to find the doorway out of the kitchen, rather than a chair to sit down. If Charlotte sat down, they would never get her out until she had gone through her usual litany of histrionics.

"Yes, you did."

"How can you say that?" Charlotte stamped her feet, three times each. Another of her calculated mannerisms that she had never gotten the trick of. "I was proud to call all of you my family."

Could have fooled me, Melba silently retorted. She knew better than to give Charlotte more fuel and bring on the next martyrish explosion.

"I adored Granny Tweed. Those summers spent in her home are some of my fondest childhood memories! I looked forward to my annual visits. I adored my room—"

"You stayed in my house, not Granny Tweed's," Cilla said. How she managed to keep her voice soft and even, Melba had no idea. She adored her cousin for that restraint and self-control. "You didn't have a room of your own at Granny Tweed's. When you stayed over, all us girls shared the dormitory room in the attic."

"Oh, you're so cruel! Destroying my most treasured memories!" Charlotte fluttered her lashes. Melba had the horrified suspicion she was trying to drum up tears.

"You really need to stop trying to rewrite the past, Charlotte."

"Oh, how can you be so cruel?" She heaved a deep, trembling breath, and pressed the back of her hand over her eyes.

Melba tried to remember in which melodramatic movie she had seen that gestured used. Definitely black-and-white. Maybe silent? Her conscience prickled, and she remembered her prayer, so easily discarded, asking God to help her be kinder. The best she could do right now was keep her mouth closed and let Cilla deal with her. After all, Charlotte was her cousin, not Melba's.

"You keep saying that. If the truth is cruel, so be it," Cilla said. "And another truth. I told you to stay out of Melba's side of the house. Why is it so hard for you to remember?"

"Oh! Oh! Oh!" Charlotte fluttered her lashes more, looking back and forth between the two of them. Then letting out a wail, she managed to half-fall, half-bolt from the chair and fled, back through the living room and out the front door. The floor seemed to tremble a little under her stomping footsteps.

"How long until it's safe to go back to your own house?" Melba whispered. Not that Charlotte could hear her.

"It's not my safety I'm worried about, it's anything breakable Charlotte might accidentally run into while she plays tormented martyr." Cilla took a deep breath, held it a few seconds, then let it out slowly. "Keep working on that list and figure out who to contact. I'll deal with the hurricane before she redecorates my place the hard way." With a crooked smile, she hurried out after Charlotte.

~~~~~

Emails were the easiest way of making contact, and getting the whole story out, while avoiding interruptions and attempts to reignite family arguments that should have died years ago. Melba was a little dismayed at how many of her cousins and their children and their parents she had lost touch with over the years. Exchanging Christmas and birthday cards wasn't the same as sharing family news and showing concern. Keeping updated on weddings and graduations and births and deaths didn't qualify as staying in touch. They had been so close when they were younger. The months between visits hadn't mattered, because they had been able to catch up in a matter of hours during those blissful, adventurous months of summer and holiday get-togethers. When everyone of their generation had started getting married, getting jobs, heading off to college, and raising families of their own, they had drifted apart. Selling Granny Tweed's house hadn't shattered the family, in the final analysis. It had been the mercy stroke to a lingering death.

With that thought in mind, Melba decided that relating how she and Cilla had found Aunt Felicity's earrings might be a good way to start the email. Fun family memories. The joy of solving a puzzle. Not until she had sent the third email out did it occur to her that some of the cousins getting that email might not like being reminded of those last few months of arguments.

"Well, what's done is done," she whispered, and decided that changing the contents of the emails now or not contacting some people at all might lead to trouble. She had no idea who was in contact with whom, and who would compare their emails before responding to her, and who would whip up more hurt feelings if they were treated differently.

All the time she was digging up addresses and phone numbers and emails, the quiet from Cilla's side of the duplex worried her. She hadn't heard Charlotte wail or shriek one of her infamous lectures, and she hadn't heard slamming doors or the roar of that obnoxious luxury car racing away. Cilla was playing peacemaker once again, as she had been forced to do so many times when Charlotte had herself exiled from Granny Tweed's house for her rudeness.

Charlotte was over eighty years old, and she had yet to learn that hospitality and good guest manners were a two-way street. She had just as much an obligation as her unwilling hosts to be polite and considerate.

Melba shook her head, silently prayed for help in being kinder, then asked for what felt like the hundredth time just this week if God was trying to teach her a lesson or make changes in her character. Could He save the reformation for next week? Then she got back to work.

~~~~~

By dinnertime, the responses began trickling in. Most of her phone calls had been to simply leave messages, and that suited Melba just fine. Some responses were angry at this reminder of how family relationships had splintered in the wake of Granny Tweed's funeral. Several speculated on what kind of ripples would result from the discovery. Some even hoped this might bring about some healing, or at least closure relating to the questions and accusations. Most wanted Melba to investigate and backtrack the path the chest had taken since it vanished from Granny Tweed's house. Several cautioned that the truth would just make things worse. Several commented on stories they had heard over the years, about a final treasure hunt Granny Tweed had been putting together for them, as a last gift once she was gone. Was it possible that information had been hidden in the labyrinth chest? Could Melba get all the compartments open and find more answers for the family?

Many responses were positive. Someone had talked to someone else, and they were considering getting together a family reunion, which hadn't been done in years. They would brainstorm and reminisce, bring family photos, eight-millimeter family films, journals, anything they might have to jog memories.

Most of the irritated responders limited themselves to texts or emails. Why did she contact them about something so trivial or painful or embarrassing? Despite them being in the minority, Melba wished she hadn't contacted anyone. She remembered the anticipation of the treasure hunt, Granny's last gift to her family, the disappointments, the arguments and accusations that followed, when the treasure hunt never materialized. Granny's treasure hunts, when all the grandchildren had sleepovers, were some of her favorite memories.

One thing was settled, by an email that pinged on her phone just before she turned off the nightstand lamp to go to sleep. Andrew's oldest daughter, Alicia, didn't care about the earrings. She remembered the teasing arguments between her grandparents about the earrings, but more important, she had fond memories of the stories her father told her about the labyrinth chest. Could Melba document the whole process of opening all the hidden compartments and what she found in the chest? Her sons would be fascinated. If she could manage a visit next summer, would the chest still be there? Maybe they could arrange a family reunion? Maybe get a private tour of the old family home?

Once she turned off the light, Melba's mind swirled with ideas and possibilities. She smiled into the darkness, grateful for the positive note to send her to sleep.

Still, there were so many unanswered questions, emails and phone calls still waiting for responses. Would this discovery help their family, or reawaken old hurts?

Thursday, September 29

The Dragnet theme music droned, muffled, from Cilla's purse just as they were heading out the door of the sixth used furniture store in their hunt for display pieces. Melba shook her head, wondering what prompted Cilla to program that music into her phone. Her cousin chuckled and pulled it out of the front pocket of her purse. She waved it in front of Melba as they crossed the parking lot to her car. The screen said "Ted."

"You didn't." Melba chuckled at the ringtone assigned to Ted Shrieve. Then her amusement died, as she wondered what would prompt their police officer cousin to call them in the middle of the day.

They got into the car while Cilla answered the phone. Most of her responses were, "Oh, my," and "He didn't," and "Well, that really is rather nice of him," and "Yes, that makes sense." Melba waited, not even starting the engine, until Cilla thanked Ted, asked him for the third time if they should go home, then said goodbye.

"What happened?"

"Someone was skulking around in our backyard and Heinrich came racing over, waving—" Cilla broke off with a chuckle. "Waving a paintball gun, of all things. I don't even want to know what that grump was doing with a paintball gun. But anyway, he scared the intruder off, and then he took it on himself to walk around the house, until Lois across the street saw the gun, but didn't recognize Heinrich, and she called the police. Heinrich didn't want to leave until he was sure we were all right, so Ted called us. Heinrich knew your car was gone, but he was worried about me, that maybe I was hurt, since he had …" She sighed and rubbed at her temples. "Well, he heard Charlotte shrieking the other day, and he thought maybe someone had attacked me. Then when he saw someone sneaking around the back yard, trying windows, he thought the worst."

"The man still has that silly high school crush on you," Melba offered, when she couldn't find words to deal with the chill that settled in her belly at the image of Cilla injured and unconscious in her own home. Yes, it was nice of Heinrich to be worried, and yet at the same time, she didn't really like the idea of knowing the man kept that close a watch on their house.

"It's only silly because he never did anything about it. How strong were his feelings, if he gave up the first time I said no to a date?"

"It was the prom. That kind of a wound leaves a deep scar."

"I suppose you're right." Cilla sighed. They were both quiet, thinking, until she sniffed and reached to tap the steering wheel. "Are we going to sit here all day?"

"I don't really feel like doing any more shopping, do you?" Melba turned the key in the ignition.

"No." Cilla chuckled as Melba put the car into reverse and backed out of the parking space.

"What?"

"What if Charlotte sneaked back after we left, and was trying to get into your place to look for the pillow? And Heinrich scared her off with the paintball gun?"

"If so, we both owe him a big kiss, at the very least."

That got Cilla giggling, and they were both still smiling when they pulled into the driveway, half an hour later.

Chapter Eight

David called that evening while Melba was throwing together a quick, solitary meal before going to the Guzzlers meeting, the group who met at Book & Mug to brainstorm new drinks for the coffee shop. She still wasn't sure if Cilla could come. That would all depend on whether Charlotte had come back to the house. Cilla didn't want to leave her alone, to dig and pry and confiscate any items she considered "treasured mementos."

He had been out of town for a few days and hadn't checked his personal emails until after dinner. He was excited about the discovery and recovery of the labyrinth chest, and wanted to know if he could stop by to look at it.

"Dad talked about it all the time, and I can remember digging through Great-granny's back room and playing with the drawers. What are the chances of you finding it, after all these years?"

"I have no idea how to calculate the odds." Melba bit back a remark that David's father would know. Boyd was the gambler, the schemer, in the family. He and Charlotte were so much alike when they were younger, they were constantly clashing. At least Boyd had learned his lesson.

"How much do you think a piece of furniture like that is worth?"

"Oh, I doubt anyone would pay anything for it. Someone refinished it. I mean, it's beautiful, and we're considering leaving the paint job as it is, to go with our shop as a display piece, but the color scheme is nowhere near the original. It's been altered too much for a collector to want it."

"Gee, that's too bad. It'd be a great nest egg for you two. So ... is it okay if I swing by, take a crack at decoding some of those combinations for the drawers, for old time's sake?"

"Sorry, Davy, but it's not here. We have it in the back room of our shop. If we do refinish it, we just don't have the room here at my place. And Cilla's cousin Charlotte is here. The last thing we need is her figuring out we're going ahead with the shop."

"You got a store already? When did that happen?" He chuckled. "Hey, need some help offending the old bat so she leaves town fast?"

"You're still a troublemaker." Melba chuckled. "No, let Cilla and the Lord deal with Charlotte, and you keep your nose and your conscience clean." She stopped herself before adding, "For a change."

They chatted for another ten minutes or so, basically filling him in on the progress of setting up Brighten Your Corner. He made his usual offer to set up a security system, for the shop as well as the house. Melba tried to be vague in her answer, not promising him anything, but not hurting his feelings by saying no. If they did go with any kind of security system for the shop, they would use the system and service Tracy recommended, to tie into the one she used for Creekside Shops. Or maybe they would ask Eden to set up what had been so useful in protecting Devona, Rufus, and Becca's duplex, and helped capture Conrad Price's murderer.

She chuckled when she hung up. David was so eager to see the labyrinth chest, but he couldn't get away during the day, and he had all sorts of meetings in the evening for the next week or two. Maybe by the time he came to see it, they would have the interior of Brighten Your Corner painted and the floors refinished and they could start setting up for the grand opening.

~~~~~

Kai stepped out of the back room of Book & Mug that evening and grinned at that increasing sense of everything being right where it belonged. On the other side of the glass block wall, Saundra and the Tweed cousins were pulling tables together to prepare for the Guzzlers meeting. They looked like they were having a serious conversation. At least, until Saundra blinked a couple times and shook her head, and then Cilla chuckled. All right, that looked interesting. He wondered if they would tell him when he joined them or make him wait until the rest of the Guzzlers showed up.

"I hope you did your homework," he greeted them, as he stepped behind the counter. All three jumped and turned in nearly perfect unison to look at him, wide-eyed and startled. Definitely a serious conversation. "Homework?" he prompted, when none of the three responded.

"What homework?" Saundra gave the table she had been leaning on one last nudge to line it up with the four others that would probably be enough to hold all the Guzzlers attending tonight.

"Some new flavor for fall," Cilla said. She shook her head and sighed heavily. "While I enjoy pumpkin as much as anyone else, I agree, we need to find something new. Long before Halloween, I'm sick to death of the word, pumpkin, forget about the flavor."

"Cinnamon and nutmeg, without pumpkin?" Saundra suggested. She moved down the length of the table, heading for the opening in the glass block wall. The Tweed cousins followed her.

"That's been tried." Kai ducked down and retrieved the pitchers he had prepared earlier in the day and put in the under-counter refrigerator.

"I always loved caramel apples," Melba said.

"Oh, I know," Saundra said. "Candy apple, with red hots, bits of red hots swirled through cider flavored latte."

"An oldie but a goodie." She followed Saundra up to the counter. "If I remember correctly, Kai had that on the fall menu ... three years ago?"

"Time to bring it back out." He nodded and slid a tray onto the counter and started filling it with the squat, pebble-bottomed glasses he liked to use for the samples and testing for the Guzzlers meetings. "I actually forgot about that one."

"Does that mean it wasn't very popular?" Saundra asked.

"I liked it," Cilla said, joining them.

"So what had you three looking so serious? Good things, or Ernie problems?" He turned back to the counter with another handful of glasses.

"Don't get me started on that ridiculous man," Melba said with a groan.

"Or all the whackadoodles coming out of the woodwork," Cilla added. "We were at the shop this morning, to let the cleaners in to clean up all that paint, when this disgusting creature banged the back door open and stomped in and dropped an old crate on the floor. Then he looked around and cussed us out for being there where we had no business. The nerve of him!"

"How disgusting?" Saundra asked, and grinned.

The Tweeds blinked in unison, then chuckled.

"Just filthy. Grimy clothes, like he'd been working under an old car. And the smell." Melba shuddered, but her eyes sparkled with humor.

"Turns out the big idiot had a delivery for Ernie. The language, when we finally made him understand that Ernie had been evicted!" Cilla added. "He was muttering all sorts of threats of what he'd do to Ernie for not telling him he didn't need whatever disgusting things he had brought for him to sell."

"No, not sell," Melba said, her humor fading. "Handle. He said 'handle,' and I think something about distribution. Wouldn't be surprised, from his language, and his smell, if it wasn't something illegal."

"Wouldn't be surprised if that chemical smell was gunpowder or explosives of some kind." Cilla shuddered again. A tiny snort escaped her. "Serve the nasty old poop right if he blew up his house, or someone did it to him. The things I've heard about the people who went into his shop ..."

"Be careful you don't get blamed for it," Saundra said. "It's amazing the gossip that preschooler mothers share, when they're bringing their children in for story time. Someone is claiming that Ernie had to go to the hospital when you beat him down in the street, Cilla, and he has broken ribs and a broken nose."

"I hit him once in the face with my purse!" Cilla cried.

"From the talk around town, you're up for a medal. It's amazing the number of people who wanted, and I quote, 'a piece taken out of him, to give back all the crap he's been tossing around.' I don't even recognize you, when I hear some of the stories about how you jumped on him and gave him a few karate chops and threatened to break his neck if he stepped foot in your shop ever again."

"I never!" She flushed bright pink.

"Nobody who stops and thinks for a few minutes will believe any of that," Kai hurried to say, when Melba got those crinkles of worry around her eyes and Cilla's high color started to cool. "It's just Ernie's bad reputation working against him. I heard Valerie's security cameras caught a lot of that, along with the break-in and vandalism."

They chatted a few minutes more about the situation as they set up for the Guzzlers meeting. The four agreed, before anyone else showed up, the best way to handle the gossip was to ignore it, or just laugh and try to make a joke if people persisted in talking about the conflict. Kai stepped away for a few moments to text Eden and ask her to investigate the rumors going around about Ernie and the Tweeds. She would have ideas for how to protect the cousins, if the wild stories grew to the point Ernie tried to sue. It was his standard reaction to whatever irritated him. He usually lost. His last lawsuit was against a judge who threw out his claims as frivolous.

Fourteen total Guzzlers showed up that night, and Kai pretended to be greatly disappointed when no one came up with a new flavor to be associated with fall. He laughed, though, when four other people brought up the red hots and cider drink and suggested it reappear on the menu.

Eden came downstairs to join them just after the conversation had shifted to whether Kai needed to have a booth out in the street during the fall street festival or set up a table on the sidewalk outside the doors. She had caught some social media posts about Ernie's shop and threats against Melba and Cilla for "scheming" to evict him. Supposedly a growing number of Ernie's loyal customers were infuriated at the "injustice." She thought they should be warned and added that she had already passed the information on to Chief Sunderson and Tracy to take precautions.

"I've started some searches into Ernie's loyal customers who only seem to show up every four or five months," Eden added. "Seems kind of funny that despite being so loyal, he never griped to them about being evicted, and they didn't know he's been gone a month now."

"Should we delay opening the shop?" Cilla murmured. "It's bad enough we've had to replace all the paint."

"Ernie will pay for that. Eventually. As long as he doesn't realize that the fines he's been charged include money to go to Tracy for the paint," Melba added.

"Yes, but still, we had to go to the effort of replacing. I'm just afraid that we'll have to keep replacing things, if Ernie's friends are as nasty as he is and keep coming in and damaging things."

Kai steered the conversation to their shop, what they had been doing, the small steps of progress, their plans for the grand opening during the fall street festival.

"The other day," Cilla said, "we bought a labyrinth chest at a lovely secondhand furniture store Becca found for us. To use as a display piece in the shop. It's all painted up, all sorts of swirls of color. I'm still undecided if we should refinish it or leave it as it is because it's so eye-catching. A labyrinth chest has all sorts of hidden compartments, false drawer backs and bottoms and such, and to open them, you have to arrange the drawers different ways. Fully open, half-open, whatever. Anyway ... we started digging around and to our utter shock, we found our Aunt Felicity's gold earrings that she hid in our grandmother's labyrinth chest years ago."

"It's your grandmother's chest, then." Kai grinned. "Good news or bad news, finding an old family heirloom?"

"Don't get me started on all the reactions from our relatives," Melba said with a sigh. "I made the mistake of notifying our cousins that we found the chest and earrings. I never stopped to consider how many Tweeds there are now, with our cousins' children having children. The memories are wonderful, but the accusations and rumors and arguments ... I have to wonder if the good memories are worth it. And at least five more people have mentioned that last treasure hunt Granny was making for us, that just vanished. Or else she never got around to it. All the speculation of what was at the end of the hunt." She sighed.

"It does sound like a fun puzzle," Saundra said. "I've never heard of labyrinth chests. Are they something I can research for you?"

"I hope so. The maker, Duchene, had a reputation for specializing in them," Cilla said, nodding slowly. "Supposedly, the chests were all the rage for a short time. They were sort of like safes and puzzle boxes, combined. You'd hide family treasures in them. I can't see the sense in it, myself."

"Considering how we'd often get a hidden compartment to pop open without knowing how we did it, and then made the mistake of closing it after we put something inside, and couldn't get it open again?" Melba grinned at what seemed to be a fond memory.

"It seems to me, something like that would be documented," Eden said slowly. "There would have to be a standard for construction. Maybe even diagrams for the inner core of such a thing." She turned to Saundra. "Race you to find the answer?"

"Could be fun." Saundra nodded.

Friday, September 30

Mid-morning, Ted Shrieve stopped into Book & Mug and swung by the counter to ask Kai if he could go up to Eden's office.

"She's at a client meeting in Columbus. Should be back by 4:30," Kai said. "Have her call you?"

He took a step back and looked around the coffee shop in the mid-morning lull. His frown deepened, then he stepped up to the counter and leaned on it.

"I was just going to ask her to keep an eye and ear out, but all three of you are close to Melba and Cilla, right?"

Kai nodded slowly, with a dropping, chilled sensation as he realized this wasn't Ted Shrieve, police officer, but Ted Shrieve, concerned relative. Or maybe police officer *and* relative, which was an even more serious combination.

"I'm heading over to the house to let the ladies know, but ... there was an attempted break-in last night. You didn't hear any of the ruckus, did you?"

"That was ..." Kai shook his head. "We thought those re-enactors were running around down in the creek, shooting off blanks or cap guns or whatever."

"Re-enactors?"

"There's a group who dress up in Civil War costumes and are really intense, if you ask me, about historical accuracy with their clothes and props and even the language. They re-enact battles and do encampments, and there was some talk a week or so ago about using the creek to stand in for one of the battles down in a river valley in ... now I can't remember, but it was down south." Kai reached for the pot with Ted's usual dark roast decaf to fill a cup for him. "Not re-enactors?"

"Someone was trying to break in, back of the shops. Looks like they were targeting the ladies' place."

"They shot at one of the shop owners?"

"This was way past midnight, so nobody was there." Ted scratched at the back of his neck, frowning in thought. "Funny thing is, we're starting to think there were two guys, or maybe two groups. One was trying to break in, and the other caught them at it, and one or the other started shooting." He snorted. "Got a call from Heinrich, of all people, before any of the alarms went off in the shops. He's got his security cameras sweeping the creek. Probably afraid someone's going to climb up and break into his shop. Whatever was going on, they broke the window of the door, but it doesn't look like anybody got inside. I'm about ready to ask the ladies if they'll consider setting up shop somewhere else."

"That might be a good idea," Kai said. He handed over the cup and held up a hand to stop him when Ted reached for his wallet.

"Thanks. But you know Melba and Cilla. They won't admit it, but they're hacked off enough with Ernie already, they're going to stick to their guns." He snorted. "Almost feel sorry for him. When they're finished with him, he won't know what hit him."

Kai thought about what Ted had said. On a break, he contacted Tracy to find out if any other shops were coming open soon and checked some of the other landlords in the downtown area of Cadburn. There were no other locations. Melba and Cilla had been lucky that Ernie's former shop had come open when it did. He left a note for Eden, in case he was too busy to talk to her when she came home that afternoon and talked over the situation with Troy on his lunch break. They agreed to keep an eye on the ladies. Maybe they could make arrangements with the owners of one of the shops in the Windows building, to set up cameras focused on the shops on the other side of the creek.

Sunday, October 2

Eden Cole dithered until the last minute before making up her mind whether to go to the memorial service for Conrad Price that Sunday afternoon. The little bursts of "no way" that hit her at unexpected moments made no sense whatsoever. Conrad had been a friend and client. Sarah Fontaine had depended on her to find out what was wrong, what had brought about the great change in her grandson.

She needed to be there, yet at the same time, perhaps for the first time in her life, she cringed away from facing public opinion and questions. In this case, a whole church full of people who had been listening to the rumors and asking questions and speculating, ever since Conrad's body had been found. She knew quite a few people would turn to her for answers and clarification, and that was the strongest reason to stay away as well as show up. If she wasn't there, Eden knew people would be badgering Sarah and Becca, who had been dating Conrad at one time, for those answers and explanations and clarification. Many of them in the nicest way possible, without meaning to be intrusive. Many of them out of genuine concern. And that somehow would make the interrogation worse. Kai and his loyal staff had been gathering up all the overheard comments and questions from Book & Mug, and her voicemail was full of people asking even more pointed questions. What made her itch was the growing number of comments that tried to paint her as one of the heroes of the story.

If she could get Nick West and his federal contacts to show up and deflect some of the heat, she would do that. However, that meant owing him a favor. There was just something about Saundra's smart-mouth, wise-cracking knight in dented armor that bothered her. Starting with that look in his eyes that seemed to declare he knew secrets that included her, and he was going to make her pay to reveal them. Or worse, he knew her secrets, and he was either going to reveal them at the most inconvenient time, or he was going to use them against her, as well as Kai and Troy.

Kai and Saundra were getting closer, warmer, and Eden refused to do anything that might encourage Nick to hang around Cadburn Township and threaten that relationship. Yes, he had given Kai a big brother warning talk, but could she really trust him when he said he thought of himself as Saundra's big brother and he wanted her to be happy, and if Kai did that, then he gave his blessing? Nick was even deeper into the whole espionage and secrets game than her mentor, Royce. That made him even less trustworthy in all the small things, even if he was the one to be depended on in the big things, life-threatening things.

Chapter Nine

Everything added together resulted in Eden feeling like a coward, with a growing headache, by the time she dragged herself into her bathroom to put on some rarely used makeup. When she stepped out into the office, heading for the stairs, she found Kai and Troy waiting for her, both in dark suits. Not unusual for Troy, who dressed up for all those financial meetings he handled, whether in person or over video calls. She always enjoyed seeing him in a combination of suit coat, dress shirt and tie, with the grungiest sweatpants or wildly colored shorts, and barefoot. Kai, however, looked unexpectedly somber and stylish in a navy suit with dark purple pinstripes that she didn't even know he owned.

She had to blink away a few tears, because she hadn't expected them to accompany her. Eden wished they were a more huggy-kissy family, because she wanted to hug both her cousins right that moment. Of course, then she might cry a little, and that wouldn't do. She had to be strong for Sarah and her daughter, Julia, and her husband Rick, Conrad's parents. Then she felt a little guilty, feeling so selfish. Of course they weren't coming to support her. They both thought the world of Sarah. Conrad, until he had been replaced by his identical brothers, had been on friendly terms with them both, if not actually friends.

"Thanks," she said. "Miss Sarah will appreciate it."

Kai just shrugged. Troy patted her shoulder as they headed for the stairs.

They arrived at Cadburn Bible Chapel a good twenty minutes before the doors were supposed to open for people to gather for the memorial service. Saundra was watching for them at the front door, which surprised Eden a little. She knew Saundra attended the church, but she hadn't been in town long enough to become close friends to Sarah or Becca. Most of the people who attended the Chapel were caring people, and Saundra certainly fit in. Maybe she had joined the funeral committee?

Then Eden figured it out. Saundra often rode with the Tweed cousins or drove them to church, and the Tweeds were part of the funeral committee.

"How is everyone doing?" she asked, once they were inside.

Saundra shrugged and glanced toward the open doors leading into the sanctuary. "From what I've overheard, they've got some of the stages of grief out of order. I think Mrs. Fontaine is going to ask you to do some more digging into the adoption, just to assure her daughter that there was no way they could have known Conrad was one of triplets." A tiny chuckle escaped her when Kai and Troy exchanged confused frowns. "She's been working herself into tears, wondering if they overlooked that detail, and if they had known, would they have offered to take all three boys, and if all three would be alive right now and ..." Another shrug. "You wouldn't happen to know off the top of your head, would you?"

"Actually ..." Eden thought a moment, then pulled out her phone to get into her OneDrive files. By the time she had walked to the front of the sanctuary, where Sarah, Julia, and Rick were sitting with Pastor Roy and Patty, she had the information she hoped would help lessen some of the family's guilty wonderings, if not their sorrow.

"Conrad's documentation never stated he was one of triplets. There was no way for you to know. By the time you showed up, Nathan and Steven had both been sent out into the system for fostering. Someone messed up big time with the paperwork." In the back of her head, Eden heard the comments her cousins would make if they heard that statement. She was grateful they both had elected to stay back in the narthex. The three of them had more than ample evidence of how the system could be manipulated, to hide records and change documentation without anyone realizing it. She knew firsthand how digitizing records just made it easier to twist the proverbial paper trail and hide facts. Without Nick's help, she might still be digging, and Sarah and her family might still have dozens of questions of just how two men had showed up in Cadburn to steal Conrad's life and identity out from under him.

"There, you see?" Sarah said, tightening her arm around her daughter's shoulders. She gave Eden a grateful, somewhat teary smile. "There was nothing you could have done because you didn't know."

"I know, but just the thought ..." Julia took a deep breath and held it for a few seconds, visibly bracing herself. Rick held her hand, eyes glistening with sorrow, and probably feeling guilty over the relief clear on his face from Eden's information.

"Take it from me," Eden offered. "Even if you had known, it would have been very hard retrieving the other two brothers from the system, once they got sucked down. Whoever messed up their paperwork violated several rules and practices for dealing with siblings. Steven had to use his military connections to find Conrad. He and Nathan would never have found each other or even suspected their past if they hadn't ended up going to the same schools as children. That separation never should have happened."

"Still, it would have been fun, and hectic as all get out, having three Conrads running around," Rick offered. He let out a gusting sigh. "Thanks. It's comforting to have some answers."

"You two did a good job with Conrad," Sarah said. "He was a good man, respected, admired, involved in the community. He made us all proud. You saved him from ending up like his brothers."

Julia's mouth twisted, and something hurting and hot flared in her eyes, just for a moment. Eden could guess what she was thinking: What good had all that done Conrad? He was dead because he was a good man and got in the way of his brothers' schemes. Maybe he even figured out what they were doing and tried to stop them.

"Excuse me." Becca stood at the back of the sanctuary. "We're ready to open the doors. People are starting to arrive. Do you need more time?"

"We need you here," Julia said, and held out a hand to beckon for her. "You're not going to work this whole time, are you?" Her voice broke for a moment. "If things had been different ..." She looked around the sanctuary, full of flowers, surrounding a display of dozens of photos of Conrad, on a sailboat, involved in sports, receiving awards, at his high school and college graduation, and other activities and events. "Today might have been ... sweetheart, we would have been so happy to have you as our daughter." She sniffled.

Eden decided this was a wise time to make her escape. She passed Becca on her way up the aisle to join Sarah, Julia and Rick. Becca's eyes were glistening.

Diane Musgrove stepped up and shut the doors into the sanctuary once Eden left. She shook her head and heaved a sigh. "This is a hard one. I used to think that the deaths of children were hard to handle. I've been griping at God a lot longer with this one than I did when Shelby Tanner drowned last summer."

"They always hurt, just in different ways," Cilla Tweed said.

She and a number of older ladies had come from the hallway that led to the church's small gymnasium, what they called the fellowship hall. Eden shivered a little, deciding she had come to the Chapel for twice as many funerals as weddings since she and her cousins had settled in Cadburn.

"Eden, good, I've been thinking about calling you," Cilla continued, joining the three cousins by the far wall, to keep out of traffic. The doors had been propped open and people were visible in the parking lot and coming up the sidewalk from both directions. "Have you found out anything about Duchene or just labyrinth chests in general?"

"Actually, yes. Labyrinth chests did have a few standards, but every designer had their own quirks. Unfortunately, so far it looks like there were no set patterns that were the same from one design to another. Duchene had an interesting quirk, though. He always put a compartment or two in his chests that couldn't open unless you had the master key. You could play with drawers and combinations of opening and closing all you wanted, but without the key, those special compartments would never open. The key also made all the other compartments open. It really was clever, and it made his designs stand out from all the others, in terms of security."

"Well, that's some help, but that just adds another item to the list. Where did Granny's key go, and who took it?" Cilla shook her head. "Honestly, I wish we hadn't asked if anyone remembered anything. There's a family feud brewing over who took the chest and lied about it." She looked around, as the first arrivals came up the steps to the front door of the church. "Tweeds may grumble, but at least we're not nasty fighters. If we could find that key and make sure all the compartments are empty, that would calm things down. Too many people are talking about the treasure hunt Granny was supposed to make for us, but ... I don't want to use up any more of your time, but if you could find out if it was a general key, like a skeleton key, and where to find the keyhole, that would be a big help."

"Don't worry, I'm glad to do it. This is a fun kind of hunt. It's a break from what I usually deal with."

"You're a dear." Cilla patted her shoulder, then scurried away with the other ladies of the funeral committee.

Eden made notes on her cell phone, brainstorming who to contact first for that very specialized information. Then Charli Hall arrived in a large knot of people, all talking quietly, with more of those dreaded questions and speculations about Conrad and his brothers. She wore that Venetian glass heart locket for the first time since coming into the Book & Mug with Saundra back in August. It hung out in the open, clearly visible against a dark gray, high-neck short-sleeve knit dress. Nothing for it to slide into hiding behind or inside. Eden knew she stared, but this was her first good look at that heart. Frustratingly, neither Kai nor Troy were standing with her when she saw Charli come in, so she couldn't nudge either of them and gesture for them to look, to verify what she saw.

From the front, it certainly looked like a duplicate of the Venetian glass hearts she and Kai and Troy had been protecting since they were children dumped into the foster care system. Without touching it, feeling for the seam that turned the heart into a locket, feeling the tiny hole to insert a pin to trip the latch and open the heart, or seeing the strip of colored glass on the back, she couldn't be sure. Over the years, she had tracked down a handful of glass hearts that had looked similar, in photographs and in antique store displays, but when she got her hands on them, they always turned out to be disappointing copies. The color wasn't right, they weren't lockets, and other little details were missing. She had spent hundreds of hours trying to track down the makers of those copies, to find out where they got their inspiration, if they had actually copied a heart like hers, to try to find the owners of those original hearts. All broken or cold trails and disappointment so far.

Was she setting herself up for disappointment, placing so much hope on Charli Hall and her heart necklace?

Before she could move down the hall to intercept Charli and strike up a casual conversation and get a closer look, Charli waved to someone and changed direction and hurried out of sight. Eden sighed and went to look for her cousins. With three of them on the alert, they at least had a decent chance of getting a closer look.

"Eden?" Julia caught up with her just moments after she, Kai, and Troy had their meeting and roughed out a plan of attack. "We're going to need your help with damage control. When the rest of the Fontaine clan shows up, could you help us sort of … corral them? We need to have a short conference, bring everybody up to speed. And most important, keep Ray's mother away from Devona."

"She's not blaming Devona for his death, is she?" Eden shuddered, trying to imagine the grief the woman had to be going through, losing her son and husband.

Her pain had to be awful, to the point of blaming Devona, when all the young woman had done was break up with Ray before their romance truly got started. Yes, his mother could claim Devona had broken his heart, but he had stayed in Cadburn to try to heal the family rift. He had made a nuisance of himself until Steven threw him off the bridge. Devona couldn't be blamed for his decision.

Eden had seen enough in her investigative work to know that grief had very little to do with common sense at times.

"No, it's worse than that," Julia said. "Mother had a talk with her before the family left Columbus this morning, and she realized nobody knows the truth about the family rift. Apparently, none of my idiot brothers told anyone why they cut off our parents when I was still in high school."

Julia looked around and gestured for Eden to follow her into a room across the hall from the side doorway of the sanctuary. A wooden plaque on the wall designated it the prayer chapel. Eden's first thought was that people were more likely to fall asleep, with the low lighting and dark wine-colored wall hangings and matching, thick carpeting making it a very restful, quiet place.

"Mother said I could tell you, so you can understand. The important thing is that we protect Devona and Rufus. There's no telling how my brothers brought up their sons, if they're as self-righteous as they were in college. Just because they were raised going to church is no guarantee they'll act like Christ. Look at how my brothers …" She closed her eyes, rubbed her forehead, and let out a ragged little chuckle. "And look at me, for that matter. No, essentially the family split was that my brothers couldn't forgive our father for having an affair and having a daughter, Laura. Devona and Rufus's mother. They couldn't forgive me and Caroline, and especially our mother, for forgiving him, when he was truly repentant. And they especially couldn't forgive Laura. How was any of that mess her fault? Our parents took her in when her mother died, made her a part of the family, and my brothers cut off all contact. Devona and Rufus didn't know the whole ugly story until Ray showed up and they ...." She shrugged. "It was like love at first sight, from what Mother says, and she couldn't let that go on. Well, Madeline said several times just this morning how much she had looked forward to getting to know Devona, how much Ray loved her, how she hoped Devona would be part of the family."

"That's the last thing that poor girl needs to hear," Eden murmured.

"So we need to have a family conference before the service, and if we can't manage that, if they get here too late, then we have to keep Madeline and Devona apart until afterward."

"I'm on it. And Kai and Troy will help. We all consider Devona and Rufus part of our family, too."

"Thank you." Julia surprised her with a brief hug, then hurried away, dabbing at her eyes.

Eden stayed in the chapel a few moments longer, catching her breath. Just when she thought the surprises were over, this had to pop up. She ached for Devona, especially as she remembered how happy she had been in the first few days of her relationship with Ray, and then the sudden change, most likely after Sarah had told her that they were cousins and couldn't be sweethearts. She remembered the times Ray had come into the Mug to find Devona and try to reason with her. For some reason, Devona had never told him. Or if she had, he hadn't told his mother. Eden wondered if knowing that bit of painful truth could have avoided some problems. At the very least, Ray might have left Cadburn to have a fight with his father over the secret, and neither man would have been available for Steven to murder.

Speculating on what might have happened or what should have been done wouldn't help anyone. She shook off her speculations and headed out to find Kai and Troy and give them new marching orders. The family search and the mystery of the Venetian glass heart lockets had once again taken a back seat. Protecting Devona was top priority this afternoon.

The Fontaines all arrived together. They were easy enough to spot, with all the men looking like younger versions of Albert. Eden did a quick tally of numbers. All of them had come, and it looked like several of Sarah's grandsons had brought dates. She wasn't sure about the etiquette of bringing a date to a funeral. Maybe they were fiancées, or at least serious enough to believe it was the right thing to do? There were so many elements of family dynamics that Eden had never experienced. She tried to imagine Kai or Troy bringing a date to her funeral and necessitated muffling her laughter into coughing. At the very least, she hoped that by the time she was ready to be buried, Kai and Saundra would be married and have a few children, and hopefully grandchildren.

And that was a more sobering thought than she expected. Eden straightened her shoulders and headed through the front doors of the church to intercept the Fontaine contingent in the parking lot. She looked back and signaled Kai. He nodded and went back into the church. As agreed, he was heading to notifying Sarah, Julia, and Rick, while Eden guided the Fontaines to the side entrance, and Pastor Roy's study.

Mission accomplished.

~~~~~

Eden discovered she had relaxed too soon, although there could be some argument that just before the final hymn of the memorial service could not be considered "too soon." She caught movement from the corner of her right eye and turned to see Elli Parsons, in uniform, creeping up the outside aisle to the pew where Chief Sunderson sat with the remaining trustees and representatives from the Chamber of Commerce. Fortunately, the police chief sat two seats from the end of the pew, so Elli only had to lean in and tap her shoulder. Sunderson got up quickly and followed Elli down the aisle to the back of the sanctuary.

Now what's happened? Eden stood up with everyone else but didn't even try to join the singing. She had chosen her seat well. The last seat on the far left of the sanctuary gave her freedom to turn to see a reflection of Sunderson and Elli in serious conversation in the glass partition between the pews and the narthex. Elli gestured over her shoulder, out of the church. Sunderson bowed her head a moment, then turned and looked around, searching the people in the three-quarters-full sanctuary. Eden listened to gut instinct and stepped out of the pew. Troy started to move to follow, but she gestured for him to stay. Kai and Saundra were sitting beyond him and didn't seem to notice.

"Eden, have you seen the Tweeds?" Chief Sunderson whispered when she joined her and Elli.

"They left about ten minutes ago. With the other funeral committee ladies, I think," Eden said after a moment of thought.

"That's right. How could I forget the funeral ladies? Thanks." Sunderson turned to Elli. "Tell them we'll be right there. Maybe fifteen minutes, max."

Elli nodded and hurried out of the sanctuary.

"What's up?" Eden asked.

"Ernie. And a woman who claims she's a partner in their new shop, and has the right to get in. She got into a screaming, slapping fight with Ernie when one caught the other trying to break in."

"Oh boy ..." Despite herself, Eden wanted to laugh. "I'd better come with you. Saundra drove them to church, so they're going to need a ride, and they've asked me to get involved in the whole mess and ..." She gestured at the door.

Sunderson nodded and led the way. Eden explained as briefly as possible the situation with Charlotte claiming the candle shop was her idea, and all the research to protect the Tweeds from the woman's newest scheme.

"Charlotte's back?" Sunderson groaned. "I had a few run-ins with her when I was a kid. Cilla is a saint for not smothering that selfish windbag in her sleep years ago." She paused at the intersection, leading into a wing that had been added to the building just about the time Eden and her cousins had moved to Cadburn. "I'm going to go ahead and give orders for special treatment for our guests." She winked at Eden and hurried back the way they had come.

The Tweeds saw Eden and hurried over to the door to meet her. Telling them took less than a minute. Melba just closed her eyes and shook her head. Cilla groaned and covered her face for a few moments. Eden suspected she was trying not to laugh and cry at the same time. Then they both took deep breaths and snapped into action. They had been helping to wheel carts of all sorts of dishes to a long buffet table set up at one end of the long room. Maybe two dozen tables had been set up, with little vases and hospitality trays of salt and pepper shakers, sugar packets and creamer tubs. Melba took the empty cart through the door into what looked like a kitchen, while Cilla marched out of another door. She beckoned, and Eden followed. She retrieved two purses from a closet full of paper supplies and more purses, probably belonging to the other funeral committee ladies. Melba met them as they headed for the nearest door.

Chapter Ten

"You're a dear," Melba said, as Eden led them to her car. "We don't know what we would do without you."

"You hired me to help out with this mess," Eden said.

"We all know it's more than that." Cilla tapped her arm in teasing reproof.

In the car, they discussed how to handle the situation. They had very little time because traffic was light on the few streets between the church and the police station. Eden found a parking spot only one slot down from the front door.

"What kind of trouble have you two been getting into?" Charlotte wailed when Sunderson led the Tweeds and Eden into the back room that held the cells. "Who is that horrible little man, and why is he trying to break into our shop? What does he want? Why do I have to be here constantly to supervise you two?"

"Stop right there." Cilla's voice had an icy edge that made Eden take a step back. She had never heard her use that tone of voice. She had to look at Cilla to be sure that really was her speaking. "You are going to listen, Charlotte, and there is no arguing, no wheedling, no trying to sweet-talk us, and certainly no rewriting history to suit you. This is our shop, Melba's and mine. Not yours. We do not work for you. The candle shop was not your idea. No matter how much you rewrite history, you will never convince us to make you our partner. So just stop right now. Give up and go away!"

"Cilla ..." Charlotte stared, her bottom lip quivering, sticking out far enough Eden had to wonder if the woman had cosmetic surgery to make it bigger, so it could wobble like a sheet of gelatin. "Why are you talking to me like that? What did I ever do to you?"

"Shut up, Charlotte." Melba sounded more tired than angry.

"You have no right to talk to me like that!" Charlotte shrieked. "You are not my family!" She leaped to her feet with more speed and agility than Eden would have credited to someone of her bulk, and flung herself at the bars separating the cells, reaching as if she would claw at Melba.

"You're a witness," Cilla said, turning to Eden and Elli, who had stayed by the door.

"It's all your idea, isn't it? Locking me out. And buying that chest with company funds and keeping it secret from me. You're planning on selling it and keeping all the profits, aren't you?"

"How does she know about the chest?" Cilla turned to Melba.

"She must have seen it when she was trying to break in," Melba said with a sigh.

"Don't talk like I'm not here!" Charlotte shrieked.

"Like Melba said, Charlotte, shut up!" Cilla got almost within clawing range of the woman's outstretched hands. "First of all, there are no company funds. And even if there were, you have no claim on that money. Did you give us any money to use for the shop? Well, did you? What proof do you have?" she snapped in rapid-fire, while Charlotte's mouth flapped like she struggled for words. "Answer me. Did you give us any money to use toward the candle shop?" She jammed her fists into her hips and glared at the woman.

"No," Charlotte admitted, her tone muted and sulky.

"Exactly." Cilla took a step back and took a deep breath. "And second of all, we bought that chest to use in the shop. To display our candles."

"Oh, but you don't want to do that. Do you know how much money you can get for it? I've been hunting for labyrinth chests for years. I paid nearly a thousand dollars for the last one, and it wasn't—" Charlotte staggered back a step and finally pulled her arms back inside the cell. She glanced back and forth between Cilla and Melba. "Well, it doesn't matter, does it? You never cared about my problems or my plans or all the wonderful, lovely things I could do for you if you'd just use some common sense and listen to me. I know a dozen buyers off the top of my head—"

"Don't you dare even think about selling that chest out from under us." Grit filled Cilla's voice. She stepped closer to the cell, and Charlotte took two steps back, tripping so she sat down hard on the cot. "By some miracle we still don't understand, that is Granny Tweed's labyrinth chest. Nothing in the world can convince us to let it out of our hands now."

"Granny Tweed's chest?" Charlotte lost all her high color. She pressed a hand over her heart. "You're sure?"

"We're very sure," Melba said.

"That's wonderful. It's a miracle! You'll let me look at it, won't you? I had so much fun when we were children, playing with the drawers, figuring out the combinations. For old time's sake, Cilla, you'll let me, won't you?"

"No." Cilla glanced at Melba, who shook her head, and mirrored her.

"But Granny would want you to!"

"No, I don't think so." Melba frowned and stepped up next to Cilla. "In fact … I remember Granny being so upset with you, on your last visit, just two weeks before she died … she gave orders you weren't allowed back in the house while she was alive. She was upset when she found you playing with the labyrinth chest. What were you doing, Charlotte?"

74

"I wasn't doing anything!" She cowered back on the cot. "That vicious old bat didn't trust anybody! Always sneaking around, spying on people, invading my privacy—"

"In her own house? What right to privacy did you have in my grandmother's house, where you had no right to be in the first place?" Melba stepped up to the bars of the cell. Eden thought in another moment she would press her face against them.

Charlotte wailed, stomping her feet and rocking back and forth, making the cot creak alarmingly. "Oh! Oh! How can you talk to me that way? And after I protected our shop from that odious man!"

"That's right," Eden said, and nearly laughed. "Where is Ernie? Shouldn't he be locked up here too?"

"She got him in the face with pepper spray, which he swallowed, not just inhaling and getting in his eyes. And she broke his nose. Right after I got there, he was distracted and trying to pull some keys from her hand while he was yelling at me. First, she tripped him and then tried to push him over the deck wall, into the creek," Elli said. "Slammed his face into the railing. He's at the hospital getting cleaned up. The last report we got, he had a bad reaction to the anesthetic."

"Someone should have pepper-sprayed that menace to sanity years ago," Cilla muttered.

"Umm, ladies?" Chief Sunderson startled them all when she stepped into the cell room. Eden guessed she had been standing out in the hall this whole time. "You might want to watch what you say. Everything is recorded back here." She pointed at the little black boxes hung in several locations along the ceiling. Eden calculated there wasn't a square inch in the cell room that wasn't covered by video surveillance. "Everything has been recorded since Elli arrived on the scene, with her body camera, the dash cam in the squad car, and the security cameras on a couple shops along the street. All on the record."

"Thank you," Melba said.

"Nasty little ..." Charlotte trailed off, her gaze fastened on Chief Sunderson. Eden didn't see the look the police chief gave her, but she was tempted to ask for a copy of the security recording, just to find out.

"Wait a minute," Eden said. "What keys?"

Melba looked to Cilla, who shook her head and reached into her purse.

"You have your keys and the spare keys, and I make sure to keep mine with me. Besides ... how did Charlotte even know we had leased the shop? So how could she get the keys or even know to look for them?" They both turned back to the fat woman, who appeared to be melting into the cot. Or perhaps deflating was a better term.

"Some obnoxious little creature was banging on the front door at nine this morning, wanting to know when your shop was going to open. I was hurt, Cilla. Terribly hurt, that you would go behind my back ..." She trailed off.

"How did you get the keys?" Melba said.

"I know how, and who. The same sneak who was so helpful the last two times Charlotte pretended she lost her keys and needed to get into the house while I was away. Chief," Cilla turned to the police captain, "wasn't that nasty Harrison creature supposed to have all his locksmithing equipment taken away, and forbidden to work with locks ever again?"

"He was," Chief Sunderson said. "Doesn't mean he can't replace all that equipment. He also happens to be a friend of Ernie. What do you want to wager, as soon as he got the call from her, he called Ernie and told him, and he probably made a second set at the same time. I've checked some of the security video from across the street. Ernie was loitering nearly half an hour before he went around the back of the shops. He was probably waiting to get the keys when Harrison finished. Being Ernie, he didn't want to wait until she left."

"That lying little sneak!" Charlotte squeaked. "After all the money I paid him, he turned me in?" She opened her mouth to keep whining, but her glance went to the nearest video camera, and she shut up.

Eden wanted to laugh, but there was something sad and kind of frightening about all this, despite the overtones of farce. Maybe this was all a black comedy?

"Sorry to have to tell you, ladies, but you're going to need to make repairs to the door. Glass was broken in the scuffle."

"Tomorrow," Melba said. "We do have a funeral luncheon to help with."

"That's right! Sarah and her family are far more important than ..." Cilla waved a hand at Charlotte, who squeaked indignantly and sat up, with color returning to her face.

"How can you be so selfish?" she snapped.

"We're not. We're looking after our friends, who certainly—" Cilla tipped her head back and sighed. "This is ridiculous." She closed her eyes. "Lord, did I pray for patience today? Or any time this last week? I did not, so why, I ask, are You teaching me patience?"

That got a snort from Melba and a confused look from Charlotte.

"Leaving you here will keep you out of trouble," Cilla continued. "We have responsibilities. Sarah and her family need us. Go ahead and keep telling more lies to justify your stupid choices, but we're not going to waste any more time on you. I hope Ernie sues you for what you did to him. Serves him right, and serves you right, too. Come on, Melba." Head high, Cilla stomped out of the room.

"But Cilla!" Charlotte wailed.

Eden knew a cue to beat a hasty retreat when she saw it. She let Melba go ahead of her, and Elli brought up the rear. Chief Sunderson stepped away and headed for her office while they made their way through the police station and outside. The Tweed cousins didn't make a sound until they were heading for Eden's car. Then they leaned into each other and let out weak little giggles and staggered for a few steps.

"Are you going to be all right?" Eden asked, wondering if she needed to run back into the station for a paramedic.

"Oh, my, that was a long time coming. And the best part is she did it to herself." Melba dug in her purse. She sniffled and handed a tissue to Cilla, before wiping her glistening eyes with a second one. "Bravo."

~~~~~

Eden stayed with the cousins through the funeral luncheon and the cleanup. She had visions of Charlotte and Ernie managing to post bail, get themselves processed out of jail, and coming after Melba and Cilla. The industriousness and energy of the women on the funeral committee amazed her almost as much as the number of people who came out to support the Fontaines, and the amount of food provided. She offered to help, mostly to keep from getting underfoot, but the ladies all smiled and thanked her and refused, saying that they had a pattern and a rhythm, everyone with an assigned duty. Becca, as the newest member of the funeral committee, sometimes rolled her eyes and mimed wiping sweat from her forehead as she passed Eden from time to time. She had to scurry to keep up with the ladies, many of whom were twice her age.

Eden stayed in the doorway between the fellowship hall and the kitchen, keeping an eye on the Tweeds, and was in the right place to overhear when Lisa Pascal came running to warn the cousins.

Ernie Benders had used his time in the emergency room at the hospital to make phone calls. Dozens. Everyone he could reach. A handful of his cronies were at the Charley Horse, a sports bar that held billiards tournaments on Sundays. Dennis McCoy, a law student clerking at Worter, Worter & McIntosh overheard a group of them laughing at Ernie's predicament and comparing the conflicting stories he had told them. Dennis found Ernie's claims alarming, and called Lisa because he knew she went to church with the Tweeds.

According to Ernie, Melba and Cilla had been there, encouraging Charlotte to attack him. He claimed he had gone there to meet the cousins because they had agreed to let him into the shop to take some things he had put away for safekeeping and hadn't been able to retrieve when Tracy had locked him out. He claimed both Tweeds had threatened his life if he didn't leave town immediately. He told four people they had demanded money from him, or they would falsify more charges against him. Each story had a different dollar amount. According to Dennis, some of the men knew the Tweeds and were either outraged at the foul language Ernie put in their mouths or laughed until they choked. Most agreed that Ernie had to be making it all up, but Dennis still worried. He thought Lisa should warn them, because several of the shadier men at the fringes of the group looked like they were taking Ernie's words seriously.

"I think you should report this to the chief," Eden said, when Lisa finished passing on what Dennis had said. "Ask Dennis to talk directly with her. Maybe you need to press charges. Can Dennis identify any of those men, maybe get them to corroborate what he heard?"

"I can try," Lisa said. "The problem is that any halfway decent lawyer will move to have the report thrown out as hearsay. Those men were all standing around drinking, and they were all pretty much disgusted with Ernie, so they could be considered prejudiced against him, further casting their stories into doubt."

"What I'm worried about is the ones who seemed to be taking his words seriously. How many times does a story have to be repeated before people start believing it?"

"Oh, but the security video is proof we weren't there," Melba protested.

"That doesn't matter if the nasties Ernie hangs out with believe you threatened him," Lisa said. "I'm with Eden. This is serious. You need to be careful. Never go anywhere alone, and try to avoid dark places, or going anywhere at night, quite frankly. They're the type who justify every underhanded, sneaky trick in the book."

"I'm curious, though," Eden said, when an idea that had been lingering at the back of her mind for several minutes now finally moved to the front. "Ernie said he had something put away for safekeeping?"

"Another lie."

"What if it isn't?" She smothered a grin when that got a confused look from all three women. "What if Ernie has stuff hidden somewhere in the shop, and he's so anxious about getting it out of there, whatever they gave him at the hospital helped it slip out, while he's all worked up and knocked off balance?"

"What kind of stuff?" Cilla murmured.

"Considering the rumors that have been going around about him?" Lisa nodded, her eyes narrowing with concern. "I wouldn't be surprised to find things hidden in the drop ceiling or under the floorboards. Illegal guns or ammunition or even drugs. Lots of people agree, there was a whole lot more traffic through the back door of his shop than the front door. I was relieved for Tracy when she finally had a legal excuse to kick him out. The man made the neighborhood unsafe."

"And there was that man who showed up with that delivery and was very unpleasant when he found out Ernie had been gone for a while,"

Melba said. "Do we need to worry?"

"You might want to delay decorating until you get someone to do a thorough search for secret compartments and whatever," Eden said. "Could be expensive, though."

"On the other hand," Lisa offered, visibly trying to be upbeat, "you could find the evidence to finally put that nasty piece of work away, or even that legendary Cadburn treasure that people talk about every few years."

"Cadburn treasure." Melba snorted, grinning. "Just like the ghost of the Cadburn daughter who ran off to fight in the Civil War. Fun stories with nothing but smoke behind them."

Eden started making a mental list of people she could call on who might be able to help, with the right equipment to try to look through the walls and floor and ceiling of the shop without doing a lot of unnecessary damage. Some of those people owed her favors and could be counted on to provide their services at a greatly reduced price, if not free.

~~~~~

Ron and Jake were at the memorial service for Conrad, and they didn't look surprised when Melba asked them to wait a few days before coming back to resume painting. She was surprised, though, when they offered the names of several people who might have the equipment to look inside the walls and floors of the shop, for anything Ernie might have hidden there. Clearly, Eden had been busy asking questions while they were finishing up with the luncheon.

Eden also must have talked to Diane because she suggested the cousins had enough to deal with, they didn't need to stay for the cleanup. That suited Melba just fine.

And that was how they arrived home in time to catch Charlotte coming up the stairs from the basement to get into Melba's side of the duplex. There was no mistaking the heavy clumping of her footsteps. Just how did a woman walking on such thin, high heels make such a loud banging sound, more like a man in mud-crusted combat boots?

Melba paused in the open door of her kitchen to listen, just to be sure, then gestured for Cilla to continue entering through her own kitchen door. She tiptoed through the kitchen to the basement door and turned the little knob inside the doorknob to lock it.

Just in time. The footsteps clumped to a stop on the top step, then the doorknob rattled slightly. A loud intake of air sounded from the other side of the door. Melba held her breath. Low, growling curses erupted, totally shredding the image of a delicate lady that Charlotte still tried to project. A wail rose from Cilla's side of the duplex. Charlotte's growls got louder. She clumped down the stairs again. Melba shook her head and quickly made her way to Cilla's back door.

"What happened?"

Cilla glared at her and stomped over to the basement door and locked it. "Come on, I need your help."

"What did she do?" Melba stepped into the kitchen.

"She didn't clean up after herself, for one thing. I need you to help me check her luggage, and then her car, to make sure she doesn't leave with whatever she found."

Melba followed Cilla into the living room and caught her breath. Cabinet doors hung open. Upstairs, the contents of the linen closet spilled down the short hallway between the bedrooms and bathroom. The folding ladder to the attic was halfway down, stuck where it always caught. There was a trick to getting it to fold up smoothly, and clearly Charlotte didn't know it. The cousins had to duck to get past it.

Cilla's bedroom had been ransacked, the blankets twisted sideways half off her bed, with the under-bed storage boxes pulled out. The accordion doors of the closet hung halfway open, and some clothes had fallen off the hangars. Storage boxes tipped sideways, sitting on the floor.

The guest bedroom didn't look any better. Cilla hauled one of Charlotte's four suitcases up onto the bed and yanked hard on the zipper tab to open it. From the kitchen, a muffled wail filtered to them, accompanied by thudding on the door.

"Think she can knock it down?"

"Let her." Cilla snatched up Charlotte's purse, sitting on the floor by the nightstand. "I'll just hold her credit cards hostage until she pays to have it fixed."

"That won't work."

"Why not?"

"Doesn't she usually come to visit when she's running short on money, or even hiding from a collection agency?"

"Yes. Unfortunately." Cilla glared at the open suitcase. "You start on another one. I want to know what she's looking for before she breaks the door down."

Chapter Eleven

Charlotte's suitcase was just as messy as the closets and cabinets she had ransacked, and Melba was disappointed they couldn't return the favor. They found nothing in the first two suitcases except dirty laundry. Her purse was a different story. Cilla found three sets of keys. She had Melba test them on the front and back doors, while she checked the hiding place in a teapot on the top shelf of her china cabinet, where she kept her spare keys. Sure enough, Charlotte had taken her keys. They had no idea what the other two sets were for. Probably other relatives whose homes Charlotte believed she had the right to come and go as she pleased.

Melba got on the phone to the police station, to find out when Charlotte had been released, and what kind of charges they could file. They couldn't charge her with breaking and entering because Cilla had let her into the house in the first place. Since she had never given Charlotte a key, chances were good she had left the house unlocked when she went to investigate the shop and had her scuffle with Ernie. Melba was still waiting on the phone for the officer on the front desk to find a superior to answer her question, when a gentle knock came on the front door.

Ted Shrieve leaned wearily on the doorpost when Melba opened it. "Did you lock that loony in your basement?" he asked, before she could greet him.

"She called the police?"

Charlotte, naturally, accused them of tricking her to go into the basement, and insisted they had ransacked Cilla's side of the house to frame her. She shrieked and wailed and insisted Ted haul them both away. But first, he had to take her to the hospital to have a doctor treat her for the assault on her poor, delicate, sensitive nerves.

The wails stopped short when Cilla held out the three packages of keys. She went pale. Then she flushed red so Melba thought she could feel the heat from the other side of the room.

"You had no right to go through my personal possessions!" she snarled.

"Just like you had no right to tear apart my house, or to go into Melba's side of the house," Cilla said, her tone as quiet as Charlotte's had been loud.

"But Cilla, you don't understand—"

"No, and I don't want to. You lie and you sneak and you try to make everyone pay for your mistakes, and I am sick to death of it. I'm calling Avery and Gladys and all their children, and I am going to tell them everything you did, so don't even try to tell more of your lies to make me look bad. You brought this on yourself, Charlotte. Get out of my house and never come back!"

"But—but—but I have nowhere else to goooooooo!" Charlotte wailed, and took several steps with her arms spread wide, clearly intending to fling herself on Cilla.

Ted stepped between them with his most stern glare. She stopped with an audible click and went pale, so all her heavy makeup looked like a dirty, thick mask.

With Ted watching, recording what they did, and making Charlotte watch, they searched her other two suitcases. Cilla went white when she pulled out a handful of papers from the bottom of the overnight bag. Melba caught her breath when she saw Cilla's name and address on the top paper. It was her gas bill. Cilla's hands shook as she sorted through the paperwork and found copies of all her regular bills: electric, water, gas, insurance, and three credit cards. Melba didn't have to think hard to imagine all the damage Charlotte could do with that information. She could destroy Cilla's credit rating. She could put all sorts of charges on Cilla's cards. She could borrow money. It wasn't any stretch of the imagination to guess she had been intending to do the same to Melba if she had been able to get into her side of the duplex.

Ted thought of checking Charlotte's phone while she was packing up her luggage and sniffling and whimpering repeats of, "But Cilla, you don't understand." Charlotte squeaked and went completely silent when he demanded to know her password to get in. She gave it when her teary-eyed, pleading looks to Cilla got no mercy.

Charlotte had taken pictures of all of Cilla's paperwork. That meant she was thinking far enough ahead to know she needed backup. Ted checked her email and her texts, to make sure she hadn't sent that information to someone else already. Fortunately, she hadn't.

Ted verified they wanted to press charges and led Charlotte out to his cruiser, to go back to jail. He ignored her protests that she hadn't done anything wrong, that it was all a silly misunderstanding, until he reached to open the back door. Then he couldn't hold onto his stoic, on-duty mask, and grinned at her. Charlotte went white and shut up, and all the fight seemed to go out of her.

Cilla made sure she understood that her number was blocked on her and Melba's phones, so she should just forget about ever calling them. Then she asked Ted how long it would take, and how much it would cost, to have a restraining order taken out, so Charlotte would never come into Cadburn Township. Forget that. She wanted to prohibit her ever coming into Cuyahoga County. Ted's lips and jaw muscles twitched, but he managed not to laugh or grin. Melba felt sorry for him and admired his self-control. He had to drive Charlotte to the police station, after all. He promised he would send another officer to come drive Charlotte's rental car to the police station. Just before he pulled out of the driveway, he let the cousins know he had called Eden.

"This doesn't make sense," Eden said, after she helped the cousins document the mess in the house and clean up. "If she was just looking for paperwork to steal from you, why tear apart cupboards and your closet? In fact ..." She frowned as she turned to look at the milk crates tucked under Cilla's little desk in the kitchen. They held hanging files, with neatly labeled tabs for years and functions. "She didn't make a mess here, when she got what she wanted. So what was she looking for, and why was she so desperate to find it, she made a mess and didn't clean up right away?"

None of that mattered. Melba wanted to wash her hands of the whole ugly mess and never have to think of Charlotte ever again.

David arrived when they were almost finished cleaning up Cilla's side of the duplex. Melba heard his car pull into the driveway as she was stepping away from the garbage barrel. Some of Charlotte's ransacking had turned destructive, probably in desperation, or her usual nastiness when she couldn't find what she was looking for. She looked up and shielded her eyes, and shivered a little, though she didn't know why, when he just sat there a few moments. She headed for the back door. David could come inside when he felt like it. She wasn't going to wait for him. She braced herself for a repeat of his usual insistence that they needed a home security system, probably with a little bit of lecture thrown in.

"Eden, could you do us a big favor?" she said, and closed the door with a little more force than necessary.

"Always." Eden paused in tying up a bag of paperwork. She had offered to take it to her office and put it through a shredder. Cleaning up after hurricane Charlotte had revealed just how much paperwork Cilla and Melba both had lying around, with potentially dangerous information on it.

"Our cousin's son is going to come in here any moment and try to pressure us to let him install a home security system. Could you help us with a little white lie," she hurried on, when Cilla shook her head and rolled her eyes and groaned, "and act like you're handling that for us?"

"Actually, that's a very good idea."

"I'd much rather trust that work to you," Cilla hurried to say. "David is so hyper about his fancy high-tech stuff, I always feel like the robots are going to take over any day now."

Eden laughed. David's footsteps thumped on the back porch steps, cutting off whatever she had been about to say next.

Melba felt a few flickers of guilt when she opened the door and saw the concern wrinkling David's face. That faded when he got somewhat huffy at finding Eden there and learned she was an investigator and was helping them. He backed down when Eden asked how he heard about the ruckus with Charlotte.

"Charlotte's around here?" He shook his head. "No, I came by because I heard about the break-in at your shop."

"How?" Eden said.

He glared at her. Took a deep breath. Looked away.

"Okay, I've got a buddy who's starting up a legal practice. That slug, Ernie, called him, because the shyster lawyer he usually goes to doesn't want anything to do with him anymore. We were hanging out and I overheard some of the story and put things together and ... doggone it, Aunt Mel, this is getting really serious! I've got to head out of town for a few days, but when I get back, I'm fitting you out with the best security system I can put together. Here at your house and at your shop."

"Already on it," Eden said.

"What do you mean, you're on it?"

"My team and I have the preliminary work done. It's just a matter of waiting until our gear arrives. Special order." She rattled off what sounded like gibberish to Melba, but obviously David understood the manufacturer and model names.

She had the oddest feeling he was impressed and irritated at the same time. She suspected some of her frustration and irritation with his father colored her feelings about David, but Melba was in no mood to let guilt override her judgment. He left, after making promises that sounded almost like threats, to check on the quality of Eden's system once it was installed. He wanted to have access to it, so he could check up on Melba and Cilla.

Eden had a wonderful talent for managing not to commit to anything, while being pleasant and deflecting and deflating her opponent's demands. She laughed after David had finally left and Melba told her she had potential to be a great politician.

Tuesday, October 4

The Tweed cousins stayed away from the shop, more on the chance that Ernie would show up and try to get in again, than because the broken window needed replacing, the painters couldn't come back for a few more days, and there was crime scene tape strung across the back deck from the door to the railing. Monday, Eden let them know she had been given copies of the police report, and access to the server with the stored body cam footage, and Tracy had done the same with the security camera footage. The date stamped section had been designated to be held until marked as no longer needed, so no risk of it being erased by accident or the normal routine of clearing records.

Troy and Rufus came by Monday morning to get the dimensions of the rooms and take pictures of the angles available from the windows, looking out onto the yard all around the duplex. Eden and Rufus intended to design the new security system to take care of the house inside and out. She especially wanted to pay attention to the barrier of trees between their backyard and the parking lot of Saundra's apartment building, since Heinrich had noticed people getting through. Melba played with the idea of getting some kind of fence, but at the same time she liked the convenience of Saundra and other friends being able to take a shortcut from the apartment building to their house. Besides, there was all the fuss and legal rigamarole of figuring out boundaries and just where their property ended and the apartment building's started. And it wouldn't do much good to have a fence just on their property if the neighbors didn't fence the back of their property too. Any determined intruder could just walk around either end. Maybe it was just a waste of time considering it. And, she had to admit, she felt even less secure just considering it. Maybe that was the main reason she had always resisted David's regular recommendations that they get security for the house.

What did make her feel more secure, though, was learning that the security system would be tied into her and Cilla's cell phones. No one would see the videos inside and outside their home unless they chose to send a link to Eden or the police or anyone else they chose. That had always bothered her about David's recommendations. He would hold the strings, as it were, to their security.

Then she and Cilla had more important things to gnaw on and worry them.

Ron at Lumberville called Tuesday morning to verify a phone message left late the night before, cancelling the contract for their painting services. He had saved the message on the answering machine since he didn't recognize the voice. Whoever it was claimed to be a niece he had never heard of, saying family problems would delay the redecorating of the shop for at least a month.

"First of all, Ron, write this down for future reference," Melba said, after he had played back the message for her. The words were barely coherent, the voice unfamiliar. "None of our relatives are involved in the shop, so if anyone calls giving you orders, they're lying."

"Yeah." He let out a gusting sigh. "Kind of figured. That Ernie is a real slimebag. He played that kind of trick on us, only it was someone claiming to work for him, telling us we got the work order all wrong, so he could get a refund."

"I don't suppose you have any way of tracing that number back, to find out who called?"

"I'll try."

"You're a good friend, Ron. We both appreciate it."

"That's just going too far," Cilla fumed, when Melba told her about the call a few minutes later. "You know what they're doing, don't you?"

"Besides trying to drive us crazy?"

"Nobody is at the shop. It's the perfect time to break in."

"I'll get the car." Melba strode across the kitchen to get her purse and snagged her car keys off the rack on the side of the lower cabinet.

Cilla called Eden, who called back while they were waiting at the traffic light to turn left on Apple. She would meet them there. Melba saw her crossing the street to head up the bridge over Cadburn Creek when the cousins crossed Center. She honked and Cilla leaned out the window and gestured for the younger woman to get in. She had her tablet with her and tucked it inside her jacket as she ran across the street to meet them.

"I see him," Eden said, when Melba pulled into the deck behind the shops. She leaped from the car while it was still turning and raced down the deck toward their shop back door.

"See what?" Melba said.

"I thought I saw someone running down that way." Cilla gestured toward their door, which wasn't visible from that angle.

When they caught up with Eden, she was on her phone, bent over and studying the doorknob and the doorframe. Some sort of short bar tool lay on the deck, and there were fresh gouges in the frame of the door, and in the paint on the door itself. Eden glanced at the cousins, then murmured a response to the person on the other end of the call. She held up her phone and snapped a few pictures of the door. Then she said, "On their way," and ended the call. She flipped and tapped through a few screens, then sighed and put the phone in her pocket. "Good instincts. I didn't get enough to recognize who it was, just someone in jeans and a black hoodie, with the hood pulled up. A big guy. Dispatch is sending an officer to check things out. They're also notifying Tracy and the security firm. Not that it'll do much good." She gestured.

Melba caught her breath, seeing several wires hanging from the eaves of the back of the building. She looked straight down and saw the broken pieces of what had been a security camera.

"That makes things more serious, doesn't it?" Cilla murmured. "Someone who knows to look for a camera and can reach high enough to break one."

Ted Shrieve took the call to come process the attempted break-in. Melba felt somewhat guilty, because he seemed to get the lion's share of calls relating to their shop. Then again, someone had to get the information for Tracy's insurance claim.

While she was there, Eden examined the labyrinth chest, making notes of identifying marks and measurements and taking pictures, to do more research, to help decode the puzzle box aspect of the chest. Until they could find the key for the chest, that was the best they could do.

Wednesday, October 5

At 6:50 Wednesday morning, Cilla banged on the wall, the sequence meaning she was coming over. Melba hurried to unlock her kitchen door. Another black mark against Charlotte. Now they had to keep their doors locked until they were sure she had left the state. Melba reached for the coffee pot, which had just finished dripping, and snagged a second mug from her cupboard.

"No time," her cousin said, waving an arm she was in the process of sliding into her jacket. "Fiona called from the station. Someone is trying to get into our shop. We've got maybe ten minutes to get there and catch them in the act. Come on!" She snatched Melba's purse off the shelf next to the microwave and headed for the back door.

Fortunately, Melba was already dressed for the day, otherwise she would have been hurtling down Overlook in her pajamas. Cilla explained as she drove.

A locksmith in Strongsville had called to report a request for him to open the locked door of their shop. He found it suspicious, since Cadburn had two locksmiths, within ten minutes of downtown. Most of the locksmiths in the county had a general agreement to notify the police when they got calls to open homes or businesses or cars outside their general service area, and outside normal business hours. The early morning hour was the first sign that something might be wrong. The second was the story the young man told. He was supposed to do some work in his uncle's shop, he had lost the key, and didn't want to get in trouble for that and not getting the work done on time. When the Strongsville locksmith offered the numbers of the Cadburn locksmiths, starting with Lumberville, the caller claimed they were friends of his uncle. He didn't want to be tattled on, he just wanted to fix the problem. If this locksmith didn't want the work, he'd call someone else.

A smart locksmith stayed on the good side of the local police, simply to avoid being a suspect in burglaries that were too clean. The Strongsville locksmith called the Cadburn Police, and got Fiona, who was dating Ted Shrieve and knew some of the mess surrounding the cousins' shop. She called Cilla and promised Mike Wilcox, who was currently patrolling

Creekview, would be waiting.

"You know what I want to do?" Cilla said, as Melba turned down Apple. "I want to be hiding in the dark and wait until they get the door open and then jump out and catch them."

"I want to get pictures as proof." Melba gripped the steering wheel harder and fought the temptation to speed. They were in a twenty-five zone, after all. They didn't need to get pulled over for a speeding ticket when they had to get to the shop before the locksmith and his lying client arrived. Was this Ernie? Was this the would-be burglar from yesterday, making a second attempt?

Mike, a friend from church, was waiting by the back door of the shop when Melba and Cilla pulled into the parking deck. They got inside, and Cilla had time to share her idea for surprising and catching the would-be intruder, before a dark blue pickup with Delveccio Locksmith painted on the side pulled up in front of the shop door. At this time of the morning, there was practically no traffic on Creekview. Melba thought about Valerie's security cameras and wondered if they had been adjusted yet so they didn't cover the shops across the street. Eden wanted to get the security system for the duplex installed first, because after all, the rest of the shops on Creekview had enough cameras to provide security. Right now, Melba wasn't so sure of that.

The locksmith got out of his truck and stepped up onto the sidewalk. He looked down the street, then up the street, then paced several times up and down the length of his truck. Clearly an impatient waiter.

A dirty white truck drove past. Then a patrol car. Melba silently urged the officer inside to get out of there. Whoever had hired the locksmith wouldn't stop if he thought he would be confronted over just why he wanted into the shop. A brown sedan slowed as it passed the locksmith's truck but didn't stop.

"Thar he blows," Mike said.

That struck Melba silly, so she nearly choked fighting giggles. With that dark green van pulling up in front of the locksmith's truck, they couldn't afford to frighten away the client. Not before they figured out who he was, who he was working for, or what he wanted. A young man in faded-white jeans full of holes climbed out and hurried up to the front door, waving for the locksmith to join him.

"Recognize him?" Mike asked.

Chapter Twelve

Cilla and Melba both studied the young man, who paced a little, checking his watch and looking up and down the street as the locksmith got to work. They looked at each other and frowned, then looked back out the window again.

"No, sorry," Melba whispered.

"I'm not," Cilla said a moment later. "If we recognized him, then one of our friends is turning against us. I'd rather a stranger be adding to the whole puzzle, if you don't mind."

"Makes sense to me." Mike gave them both a grin. "Even if it doesn't make my job any easier."

They waited, listening to the locksmith work. The ticking and clicking of the mechanism of the lock was loud inside the darkened shop. The door creaked, pushed open a few inches. The locksmith and the young man talked, their words muffled by glass and brick and distance, but she overheard something that sounded like "credit card" and "cash." She guessed the young man wanted to pay cash for the job, but the locksmith would only take a credit card. That was smart. It left a trail of evidence, if a job opening a door turned out to be assisting in a crime. She took a moment to feel sorry for the locksmith, who had to be careful about ending up on the wrong side of the law when he was just trying to help people.

Finally, the young man got loud enough Melba heard him insist that he didn't have a credit card, he lost it, and the locksmith would have to take his money or not get paid at all. The locksmith walked a few steps down the sidewalk, so he was fully visible in the display window. He glanced inside, maybe looking for the promised police backup, then held out his hand. The young man slapped several bills into his hand, snarled, "Don't need no receipt," cursed a few times, and stomped to the door.

It swung open hard and fast, and almost banged against the wall, but the young man caught it in time. Melba and Cilly moved back from the door, nearly tripping over each other, to move to hide on the other side of the labyrinth chest. Mike stayed by the door, watching the intruder.

He didn't come into the back room. Melba started to lean out, to look for him, when a loud thud, then a crackling sound came from the front room. She darted out from behind the chest in time to see Mike dash through the door. He crossed the front room in five long, running steps, yanked the new key out of the lock, and shoved the front door closed before turning and yelling, "Police!"

Melba and Cilla stopped in the doorway from the back room, just in time to see the young man turn around from the hole he had been cutting in the wall. Strips of what looked like thick paper, maybe old wallpaper, hung down where he had pulled them loose. The young man gaped at Mike, then lunged across the room, aiming for the door where Melba and Cilla stood.

His eyes got wide, and he let out a yelp and skidded, trying to change direction. The utter terror on his face struck Melba as both pitiable and amusing.

"That's far enough," Mike said.

Melba called Eden while Mike went through the formalities of handcuffing the young man and leading him out onto the deck behind the building to his patrol car. She and Cilla waited, staying in the back room, until Mike came back and took pictures and wrote up the report. By that time, Eden had arrived. She walked up to the cuts made in the paint and wallpaper and drywall and leaned close enough her nose almost touched the lower horizontal one, then the vertical.

"Mike, is it okay if we start digging, or does someone official need to do it?"

"Well, it's Tracy's property, but the ladies here are renting, so it could technically be their property, their responsibility, but ... I guess it depends on what you find," Mike answered after a few minutes of thinking and rubbing his chin.

"Did the burglar say anything yet?"

"He's scared of whoever sent him. Sweating up a storm and shaking and clenching his teeth like he's terrified of letting a word out." He shook his head. "Let me hand this guy over at the station, then I'll come back and be an official witness. Chain of custody and all that."

While he was gone, Eden examined the cuts in the wall more closely, taking pictures and measurements. Then she handed her phone to Melba to record video while she pulled strips off, examining the chunks of what looked like plaster, and different layers of paint. Some of the paint and wallpaper peeled off easily enough, until she got about four inches in from the cuts, in all three directions. To get at the upper cut, she had to use one of the ladders left behind by the painters that hadn't been stolen by Ernie when he vandalized the place last week.

"My guess is that someone hid something in this wall maybe two phases of redecorating ago. That kind of makes sense."

"How?" Cilla said. "Does it give us an idea who hid something there?"

"I'd guess either Ernie, or whoever was renting the space before him," Eden said. "When I got stalled on researching labyrinth chests, I did a little digging into the history of the shop. Tracy only became the landlord about four years ago. This strip of shops was owned by a Rupert Monroe, basically an absentee landlord who exchanged superintendent duties for rent to the former tenant of this shop. He dealt with tenant problems and was supposed to fix things." She shrugged. "Not much help, except as a place to start."

"I remember Tracy saying something about Ernie redecorating without permission," Melba said. "What if he hid something in the wall? He'd need to cover it up, and it wouldn't do him much good to hide something if he had to get her permission to change things."

Allen Kenward arrived then, taking over from Mike, who had to get checked by a doctor. His prisoner turned violent when he removed him from the patrol car at the station. Kicking and biting and writhing, he hit Mike in the nose with the back of his head, bit him on the wrist and tore the skin on two fingers.

"Got the chief wondering what he was looking for, that he's so terrified of being identified and charged," Allen said. He had a police department video camera, several large evidence bags, and gloves for himself and for Eden.

"I'm starting to get a very bad feeling about this," Cilla whispered, as she and Melba stepped back and let the professionals get to work.

Allen agreed with Eden's assessment of how many times the shop had been redecorated since the wall had been cut into and papered and painted over. He had a scanner used for finding studs in walls, to essentially locate solid objects behind the wall. Eden held the video camera while he carefully peeled off several layers in one clump, revealing the lines where the drywall had been cut out and replaced or badly patched with plaster. He remarked that indicated this particular spot in the wall had been opened enough times to damage the drywall. He drove several metal paint stirring rods into the center of the drywall, using them as handles to lift the plug out. Boxes fell out, hitting the floor with hard, clattering thuds. One box broke open, and brass-colored objects the size of Melba's index finger scattered across the floor.

"That's not good." Eden lowered the camera to get a closer shot of the items.

"Ya think?" Allen shook his head, lips flattening in a thinking scowl. He took a deep breath, then looked right at Melba and Cilla. "Ladies, I'm going to have to ask you to step back. This is turning official."

"Those are bullets, aren't they?" Cilla said.

"Pretty nasty, heavy-duty bullets," Eden said. "Stop recording?"

"No, we can't afford a break, not until we get more people in here to take over."

"Shall I call Chief Sunderson?" Melba said.

"That'd help, thanks." He took another deep breath and stepped up to the opening cut into the wall.

Melba watched him and Eden work while she called the station. Allen removed more boxes of ammunition. Then he got up on the ladder to look down into the wall where the drywall was still intact. Just a few breaths after Melba finished the call, he pulled a rifle up and out.

She could guess, just from watching all sorts of military movies and police procedural television shows, these weren't hunting rifles, but dangerous weapons. Assault rifles, with all sorts of extras attached to them. By the time Chief Sunderson and two crime scene investigators walked up the street, Allen had pulled out four rifles. Each one, he put down on a sheet of plastic left by the painters. Eden recorded close-up details with the camera, getting all sides and angles. Melba tried not to listen as the four officers discussed what Allen had found already and continued to pull out, but she heard words like "armor-piercing points" and "automatic" and "magazines" and other words that simply didn't belong in her candle shop in Cadburn Township.

"I can understand why that boy we have in lockup is refusing to cooperate," Chief Sunderson said. "He's probably terrified for his life."

By this time, morning traffic had picked up on the street and someone noticed the police activity and someone else must have called Tracy. She came running, and nearly face-planted against the locked door when she tried to open it. Chief Sunderson signaled for her to be allowed in, then led Tracy into the back room, where Melba and Cilla had been waiting and watching, and the four of them went over the sequence of events.

"Do you think it was Ernie?" Tracy asked. "It could have been Harwood Diben, the previous tenant. He was spitting furious when I bought the strip and told him to either pay rent or get out. He did a lousy job as superintendent, nobody was happy. Half the units were empty. He insisted that I had to keep him on, but there was nothing in the paperwork I signed guaranteeing anything. I thought I was going to have to hire someone to drag him out, or he'd burn the place down just to spite me." She caught her breath, eyes wide and shadowed.

"What?" Sunderson prodded, when she stood still and silent for several long moments.

"He changed his mind ... I was so relieved when he stopped fighting me, I didn't even question, but ... he turned cooperative right after Ernie expressed interest in taking the shop. And then a couple of times, I thought I saw him here, talking with Ernie, but I never got close enough." She shuddered. "I never wanted to be anywhere near that man."

"I'm going to need all the information you have on him. And on the previous owner," Sunderson said. "Whoever hid all that in the wall ... Sorry, ladies, but until we can be sure nothing else has been stashed here, you're going to have to keep delaying working on the place."

"That's fine," Cilla hurried to say.

"Could we move the chest out, first?" Melba asked. "We can at least start refinishing it, and I think I'd feel a lot more secure having it in my spare bedroom than sitting here, where apparently anyone can get in, despite all the new locks!"

Friday, October 7

By Thursday night, the outside cameras for the duplex had been installed. Melba felt rather silly, and yet at the same time somehow excited, when Eden and Troy came over to install the cameras under cover of darkness. It wasn't much good to let people know that security was being installed. While yes, that knowledge might keep some criminals away, the really nasty ones would consider it a challenge for them, and watching the installation would show them where to look to break or disconnect the cameras. The advantages of the system Eden and Rufus were still refining was that the cameras were small and made to be disguised.

Feeling much more secure, the cousins spent all day Friday driving from one supply store to another, checking on prices for what Cilla called the "fiddly bits," the colors and scents and tiny items to decorate their candles, and the containers to hold them. They already had accounts with several suppliers for various grades of wax, depending on the complexity of the candles they intended to make. The next item on their list was to design labels, and finalize the logo for their shop, to go on their bags, receipts, and the sign out front. They were still working on that with Becca and were grateful to have her dealing with the printers and sign maker. They agreed that they might know candles, but other details of the business, what Becca called branding, were a few steps beyond them.

Allen called them while they were on the road, coming back from Columbus, to let them know the investigation had finished in the shop. Metal detectors hadn't come up with any more items hidden in the walls or the floor, but the simple tactic of stomping on the wooden floors had uncovered three compartments. Those had been opened, found empty, and swept for trace evidence of what might have been stored there. The shop was cleared for them to come back in and resume redecorating. He apologized for the damage to the wall and the floors, which would require repairs before they could resume painting and refinishing. Chief Sunderson had authorized reimbursing Tracy for the repairs. He added that a team from Lumberville was at the shop, patching the wall, and Tracy had agreed that the repairs would be made in such a way that the wall compartments and floor compartments could be easily opened again, for future investigation. Just in case Harwood Diben was found and charges filed.

"What if you discover that Ernie put the guns there, and he was hiding things in the floor?" Melba asked. She was driving, but Cilla had put the phone on speaker and turned up the volume so they could both hear what Allen had to say.

"We're working on that. And I'm sorry, ladies, but that's all I'm allowed to say right now. It's an open investigation. The captain apologizes for the inconvenience, now and in the future. And if you see Ernie ... well, frankly, and this is my own advice and my opinion, hope that you see him before he sees you, and then run like unholy heck. That man is wacko, and the word on the street is that you two have been threatening him. Like, broken bones and black eyes."

"Of all the idiotic things!" Cilla gasped.

"Anybody who knows you knows it's impossible," Allen hurried to say.

"Well, you have to admit, you did pound him good with your purse," Melba said.

"All I'm asking, ladies, is that you don't give him any excuse to haul you into court."

The cousins agreed to come to the station to look over the reports. They fell silent once Allen made his farewells. Three exits later, nearly to the Sackley Road exit, Cilla took a deep breath, then exhaled loudly.

"Well, we need to get to work, don't we? Not that we've lost too much time, but it looks like we've been pushed backwards in our schedule a few days."

They made plans, and by the time they pulled into their driveway, they had decided to make Saturday a celebration as they resumed setting up the shop. They called Eden, knowing she had received the report, and asked her and Becca to join them at the shop the next morning. Eden laughed and agreed that a celebration workday would be just the thing to thumb their noses at the ones who were getting in their way. She reported she had found some interesting data on labyrinth chests. She would bring it to the shop, and they could decide there how to proceed. Before she hung up, Melba invited her to bring Kai and Troy along to join the celebration.

"The next step is to figure out if we want to start stripping that paint off and refinish it before we start working on the puzzle," Cilla said.

They went to Melba's spare bedroom, where the labyrinth chest had been moved. Common sense said to put it in the garage to do the refinishing, but rainy weather was predicted. Melba cringed at the thought of exposing the chest to the damp. When it was time to refinish, if they did refinish, they would have to hire somebody to move the chest for them. For now, she preferred it safely indoors, where it was warm and dry.

They stood in the doorway, studying the chest in all its swirling colors glory.

"We might need to remove that paint to get compartments open. If someone who didn't know what a labyrinth chest was did the refinishing, they could have sealed up panels that were meant to move," Melba said after a few moments of contemplation. "Which is sad, when you think about it. The more I look at that thing ... it kind of grows on me. And it will certainly be a conversation piece in the shop."

"Which is what we bought it for in the first place."

Saturday, October 8

They resumed discussing how complicated refinishing the chest would be when they headed for the shop early the next morning.

Cilla chuckled over how early they had left the duplex. Melba had had a restless night and kept getting up to make notes of ideas. She even had a dream where she and some of their younger cousins had worked on the chest, getting all sorts of panels and compartments to pop open all over it. Cilla admitted that she hadn't slept well, either. She finally gave up, got up to make breakfast, and then got distracted with more than a dozen emails that had come in from her mother's side of the family. All of them were dealing with Charlotte. She wanted sympathy for Cilla taking over the candle shop that she still insisted was her idea, and how cruel Melba had been to her. Cilla spent more than an hour answering the emails and setting the story straight. All but one of the relatives were laughing at Charlotte, because they knew her tendency to rewrite history in her favor. The one relative who wasn't laughing had no sympathy for Charlotte, either, but he blamed Cilla for triggering her current rampage.

When Melba finished setting up the bookkeeping program for the shop and called over to Cilla to ask if she wanted to head over early, she was more than ready to take a break. And starving.

"I was going to make a comment about the early bird getting the worm," Cilla said with a chuckle, as they pulled out onto Overlook. "I'm hungry enough to feel sorry for birds, that they like to eat worms."

"That does it," Melba said, in response to a cat-like rumbling in her stomach. "We're both starving and too excited to have the sense to eat breakfast. We're stopping at Sugarbush, first."

That early in the morning, they could park on the street in front of the bakery, which practically never happened. Gretchen was putting a tray of long johns into the display case as they pushed the door open. Vanilla, maple, and chocolate, iced and filled. The rich aroma of yeast dough and frying oil, hot apples, cherries, chocolate, and maple swirled around them and made Melba's stomach hurt even more.

"Split one here, and take more with us?" Cilla proposed.

"Why not? We're celebrating."

Gretchen divided up a chocolate-iced and chocolate-filled long john for them and went back into the kitchen for the next tray of freshly baked goodies. Melba licked the frosting off before taking her first bite. Cilla sucked the filling out first. They had been doing that since they were children, going on excursions into town with Granny Tweed. Back then, Sugarbush had been under another name and owner, but in the same location.

Charli Hall and Saundra Bailey came in while they were waiting for Gretchen to return from her second trip into the kitchen. They were planning to spend the day doing a massive research campaign for a new suspense series Charli wanted to propose to a possible new agent. They needed provisions to get them through the day. Brainstorming was demanding work, after all.

When they heard that the Tweeds were allowed back into their shop, Charli and Saundra both wanted to know all the details. Specifically, the facts, as opposed to the rumors. Melba was dismayed to learn the stories about having a knock-down, drag-out fist fight with Ernie were even worse than Allen had said. She didn't know whether to laugh or cry, when Charli hinted at some of the truly nasty things the gossips claimed she and Cilla had said when they threatened Ernie.

Chapter Thirteen

"Don't worry," Charli hurried to add. "Nobody who knows you believes a word of it. Most of the people I've heard talking about the whole mess agree that those words are Ernie's, not yours. His grasp on reality is getting slipperier by the hour. Some of the rumors I've heard about the smells that came out of his shop ... yeah, brain damage from toxic fumes is believable." Then she asked if she could see where the police had opened up the walls and floor. It would be good research for a future story. Melba was glad to invite them to join the celebration.

The four of them were debating whether to get three of each of their favorite flavors, or four, when Troy walked into the bakery. He made a disgusted sound, earning a chuckle from Gretchen, who waited with a large box on the counter and tissue in her hand for handling the donuts.

"You two sure make it hard to surprise you," Troy said. "Gretchen, their money is not good this morning."

"Troy, please—" Melba began.

"You want to get me in trouble with Eden? She sent me in here with orders to treat you two. It's too early in the morning to get the stink eye from her. You don't have to live with her, I do."

Cilla declared that since Troy was buying, he would have to pick out the flavors. He made them laugh when he declared he was going to take the lazy way out and get two of everything. Not just two of every donut, but every scone and fritter. Then he made a show of staggering under the weight of the three crammed full bakery boxes and thanked them profusely when they insisted on driving him, instead of letting him walk all the way.

They drove behind the shop to park on the deck, just in time to see Eden and Kai getting out of Kai's car, carrying trays of sealed cups. Charli and Saundra pulled in less than a minute later. Troy recited the inventory of baked goods as they walked along the deck to the back door of the shop.

"Huh." Charli frowned at the door.

"What?" Troy angled his head to put his chin on top of the stack of boxes and looked where she looked.

"That's odd." Eden stepped ahead of the others and reached to pull at a strip of yellow fluttering in the morning breeze.

Melba recognized the crime scene tape, just long enough to read "OT CRO." One end stuck in the frame of the door. She glimpsed more yellow from the corner of her eye and turned to see more tape caught in the metal bars of the fence surrounding the deck, which allowed for a nice view down into Cadburn Creek.

"But Allen said we were allowed back in," Cilla said. "Didn't he?" She turned to Melba.

"That's what he told me when he called yesterday," Eden said. "I just find it odd that the crime scene tape is still here. They should have cleared it away."

"Maybe they were planning on coming this morning. We are rather early," Melba offered.

"That makes sense. So why is it torn down, but not cleared away?"

"Maybe some kids were out running around back here, trying to find a way down to the creek. There are those stairs further down by the bridge," Charli offered, pointing toward Apple and the bridge. "Some kids can't keep their hands to themselves, they have to break something, defy the law in little ways."

"Think we need to tell Allen?" Kai said.

"Someone will know, one way or the other," Saundra said.

Melba shook her head, realizing how ridiculous they looked, just standing there, most of them with their arms full, looking at the locked door. She stepped up, digging in her purse for the key. She opened the door. The crime scene tape fluttered for a moment in the breeze, then wafted away to the left. She wondered if she should have tried to catch it, then shook her head and stepped into the darkened back room of the shop.

"What's that smell?" Saundra said, third into the shop after Kai.

Melba sniffed, expecting something like sawdust or maybe mildew. Allen hadn't told them the condition of those hidden compartments in the floor, but she could imagine them being sealed up and damp and growing mold or more disgusting things. The aroma was sharp, chemical, and hot.

"Stop." Charli reached out to catch Troy's shoulder. She missed. He headed for the worktable tucked into the corner of the back room to put down the bakery boxes.

Fury pulsed two sharp knots in Melba's temples. She had a clear image in her head of that idiot, Ernie, breaking into the shop and doing something nasty, to get them back for discovering his cache of guns and ammunition. She stomped across the back room, to see what had been done to the shop. This had to stop now.

"What?" Kai said.

"Smells like gunpowder." Charli spread her arms to stop the others from going any further.

"Why would they use gunpowder to search ..."

Melba got four steps into the front room and stopped short at the sight of the long rectangular hole in the center of the floor. Allen had said the floor had been patched. What was going on? With the shades down across the front of the shop, she could very easily have stepped into that hole if there hadn't been light coming in the back window.

"Why are the shades down?" She turned to look across the front of the shop. Melba very clearly remembered having those shades installed, but they hadn't been unwrapped. They still had to have the plastic removed before they could be opened. Yet they were down. She didn't think the police would have done that. In fact, she could remember the crime scene people putting up plastic drop cloths across the windows before they got to work, to control the dust and protect the investigation from onlookers.

"Shades?" Cilla stepped up to the doorway behind her.

"I don't think you should go any—" Eden stepped past Cilla and stopped short. She took a deep breath. "Melba, please come back in here. I'm calling Allen, since he seems to be the lead on this."

"Why would—" Cilla caught her breath, ending on a little "oh." Melba turned to see her point to the far corner of the shop, at the wall the young man had cut into.

At first, she thought it was just a bundle of rags and drop cloths left by the police. No, that was dirty hair. Dirty gray hair. Eden's hand on her shoulder, to lead her back to the other room, startled her. She twisted free and took a few more steps, barely remembering to avoid the hole in the floor. Even in the shadows, that scowling bug-eyed expression and five-day growth of beard were too clear, Along with the unwashed clothes odor, and something she suspected was blood. A dark puddle spread out from under the body.

"It's Ernie," she said. Later, she could almost laugh at how calm she became, the moment she saw him. And maybe feel a little guilty that she didn't feel a flicker of compassion. Despite his nastiness, he was a lost soul. If not compassion, then she should have been furious because this was going to cause another delay in getting the shop ready for business. How were they going to make the grand opening at the fall street festival, if all these complications kept occurring?

She felt nothing right that moment. Was this what it felt like to have been pushed past the point of "too much"?

~~~~~

When Eden called Allen Kenward, rather than go through the dispatcher, he was across the street, processing a break-in. Tracy's office for Creekside Shops had been vandalized. By the time she followed him across the street to Brighten Your Corner, in response to the call, she verified what had and hadn't been taken. Her computer was still there, the box of checks waiting to be deposited, her iPad, and other items that could have been carried away and sold for easy cash. As she told Eden while Allen began processing the scene, it looked like the burglar had been frightened away by her arrival before he could do more than make a mess. The new alarm for her office was part of the security package she was upgrading for the shops. Something triggered the partially installed security system. It wasn't supposed to be activated for three more days, but it had rung and alerted her and the police department at 5am.

Just before Eden called Allen, Tracy had excavated the piles of debris and paperwork spilled across the floor and found the box she used to organize all the extra tenants' keys. The compartment for the keys for Brighten Your Corner was empty.

"So ... what?" Eden said, while she and Tracy and Allen stood a good three feet back from the body.

She glanced over her shoulder at the back room, where Saundra and Charli were keeping watch over Melba and Cilla. Her admiration for the two elderly cousins had doubled in the last half hour. They were calm, but more important, they didn't try to poke at the surroundings. Not like that mess when the dancing club had discovered Conrad's body just a few weeks ago. With all the crime investigation shows on TV nowadays, nobody in the entire state of Ohio could claim they didn't know that crime scenes and dead bodies should be left alone to prevent destruction of evidence.

"You think Ernie broke into your office," she continued, "stole the keys, and accidentally finished configuring the alarm system while he was trashing the place?"

"Considering some of the nasties he used to hang around with? The kind more likely to stab a pal in the back than pat him on the back?" Allen shook his head, went down on one knee and reached to touch Ernie's bare ankle. "Still got some warmth in him. Warmer than the air in here. The timing is right for the alarm going off. I still can't see him fussing with the electronics, though."

"I can see some of the jerks he hung around with playing with the alarm," Tracy said. "Someone with enough training or experience to recognize the alarm system and try to sabotage it. But activated it instead."

"How about whoever owned that last cache of weapons and ammunition, setting him up to take the fall?" Eden said, lowering her voice. "Someone who figured he's useless to them, and took him out to keep him from identifying them?"

"From some of the rumors..." Allen nodded, then closed his eyes and rubbed his temples for a few seconds. He wobbled as he got back up on his feet. "Not my idea of a good way to start the day."

"Yeah, and today was supposed to be a celebration."

That earned a snort from Troy, who stood by the front door, keeping watch. Kai matched him by the back door. Both of them focused on the four women in the back room. Charli stepped through the door, holding out her phone. Eden groaned, hoping she wasn't about to do what she thought the local suspense writer was about to do.

"I've got Carson Fletcher on the phone," Charli said, relieving Eden immediately of the fear that she was going to try to take pictures of the dead body. All in the name of research for her next novel, of course, but still, a violation of police procedures and privacy. Even if it was that stinker, Ernie Benders. "From what Saundra and Kai have said about how you work, I figure this just went way above your pay grade. He's got a lot of experience with ..." She grimaced and fluttered her fingers at the body. "He's willing to help."

"Actually, yeah." Eden let out a sigh and summoned a smile. "Thanks." She reached for the phone, then glanced at Allen.

"Good idea. I'm going to call this in. Some things are above my pay grade, too," he said, and turned to put his back to the body as he pulled out his phone.

"Hi, Carson," Eden said, raising Charli's phone to her ear. "Appreciate the help."

~~~~~

Saundra drove the Tweed cousins back to their duplex, with Charli following in her car. They had left Charli's car at her apartment building, so she didn't have far to go, just around the corner. Clearly, their day of goofing off and brainstorming was canceled. Melba and Cilla were certainly taking all the shocks calmly, but Saundra feared something would become the last straw any moment now, and they would need someone to look out for them.

Charli very clearly had the same idea. Once she had parked Saundra's car, she hurried across the backyard and sailed through the back door of Melba's side of the duplex, through the kitchen and into the living room. She carried the bag of treats she had brought for their brainstorming day. Including the holiday spiced tea she had been raving about to Saundra. It was only available November and December, and Charli always stocked up to allow herself a treat of a cup or two each week through the rest of the year. The Tweeds recognized the box. Cilla smiled, then let out a little gasping sob that was part chuckle.

"Figured we all needed a treat about now," Charli announced. "Everybody up for a bracing cuppa?" she added, twisting her voice into an awful Cockney accent. Every time she used it, she reminded Saundra of Dick Van Dyke playing Bert in *Mary Poppins*.

"You're a dear," Melba said.

"No you don't," Charli hurried to say, as the woman started to get up from the easy chair she had fallen into just ten minutes ago. "I know where everything is. The biggest pot? A huge batch to get us started?"

"You'd better use my soup tureen teapot, then," Cilla said.

"I know where it is," she announced, turning to hurry back through the kitchen.

Saundra winced at a little twinge of envy that Charli knew them well enough she could navigate through their duplex and know what teapot Cilla referred to.

Charli also clearly knew what would help the cousins get over the shock. Once the tea was steeping and she had put an assortment of pastries on a platter large enough to hold a forty-pound turkey, she settled down on a floor pillow by the coffee table and demanded to know the plans for the candle shop. Saundra had been half-expecting Charli to pull out one of her fresh notebooks, bought for today's brainstorming session, and ask for details of all the problems the Tweeds had been having with Ernie. Maybe, Saundra supposed, she really only knew Charli Hall the writer, not Charli Hall the good friend who was willing to give up her precious brainstorming time to comfort two dear elderly ladies who had had a shock.

Melba and Cilla were hesitant at first, because yes, the topic was too closely tied to what had just happened. Soon, though, their voices and expressions brightened. Melba fetched her organizer folder and the box of samples, and the sketches for candle designs. Charli pulled out her notebook and sketched a floor plan of the shop and made suggestions for some unique pieces of furniture that would make good display pieces. She had seen them and made note of them at various secondhand stores she had scoured, as part of her research for a book where antiques and family heirlooms featured heavily in the mystery.

That confession turned the conversation to the labyrinth chest. That necessitated moving from the living room to the spare bedroom to examine the chest. Saundra cringed at the swirling paint job. She had done a little research into labyrinth chests when Kai first mentioned the brouhaha over it, and she found the whole concept fascinating. It was a massive puzzle box, with all sorts of gears inside, like a combination lock. The proper combination of open drawers, in the precise positions, in the right sequence, would in theory pop open hidden compartments. She winced when Cilla mentioned one conversation with a cousin who had suggested just taking apart the chest. Demolishing it down to its component pieces, to find all the lost treasures the many Tweed cousins had hidden in it over the years, and then couldn't figure out how to retrieve again. By now, a number of relatives had mentioned the final treasure hunt their grandmother had promised to put together for them but had never materialized.

"A treasure hunt?" Charli said, drawing the words out slowly.

"Oh, now you've done it," Melba said. Her smile seemed genuine enough to Saundra. "We'll have a story with treasure hunt clues in old pieces of furniture by next year."

"Shows you know nothing about the publishing industry," Charli shot back and grinned. "Takes more than a year for any of my books to get to the stores once I've turned it in. And I've got to brainstorm and outline and research and write and revise and polish the wretched thing, first." She gave an exaggerated shudder.

The conversation slid back to the labyrinth chest, and the dismay and arguments that swept over the family, when it was discovered missing right after the funeral.

"I'd be interested in how much the thief got for the chest when it was first stolen, and how you managed to get it for such a bargain price," Saundra said. "The little bit of research I did says some labyrinth chests have sold for thousands of dollars."

"Come to think of it, Charlotte did make a fuss over it, when she saw it." Cilla shuddered. "I can imagine her trying to break in and take it, if she finds out it got moved here."

"Yes, and there's the whole mystery of who took the chest from the house without anyone's knowledge or permission," Melba said.

"That we know of," Cilla corrected her. "It's a little too big for one person to pick it up and haul it away. It was a group effort. One greedy snot among our cousins' children, yes, but three or four?" She sighed and seemed to deflate a little. She tipped her cup to look inside. "Refill please, Charli dear?"

"I'm going to start a new pot, and get a new batch of goodies out," Charli announced. Saundra beat her to the teapot and tipped the last of it into Cilla's cup. There was just enough to refill Melba's cup too.

The doorbell rang while Saundra was dumping the used tea from the infuser ball into the trash. She barely heard it over the running water filling the tea kettle. Charli leaned back, trying to see through the kitchen door into the living room.

"Uh oh," she murmured, and flashed Saundra a grin. "Eden and Carson." She tipped the last box of donuts onto the platter. "Hurry up. We don't want to miss any of this."

Saundra barely got the tea kettle square on the burner before scurrying back to the living room on Charli's heels.

"No easy way to handle this, so we'll just start with the big problems and work our way down the list," Carson said.

Somehow, from the deep tones of his voice, Saundra had expected him to be a big man, granite-faced, square-built, with lots of lines of experience. He was more like a well-preserved Pierce Brosnan incarnation of James Bond. Far too young to be as skilled and successful as Charli claimed.

"Evidence says that you two lured the victim to the shop," he continued after a moment.

Carson stayed standing. Saundra couldn't decide if that was politeness, or an effort to distance himself, keeping this official.

"How?" Melba said after a few moments while she and Cilla exchanged glances. Her voice was quiet and calm, dignified.

"The coroner found printouts of emails from you in his jacket pocket," Eden said. "He printed out the whole thread. Lots of back and forth between the three of you, him making accusations and you shooting him down. I don't believe it for a second, because you wouldn't put up with the language he was using, you'd just refuse to respond."

"It doesn't matter if you believe they're fake or not," Charli said. "If there's someone in the chain of the investigation who believes you did it, we'll need to convince a jury that you were spoofed, that someone else set up Ernie to lure him there and kill him and make you take the blame. I mean, think about it, why would he bring printouts of emails with him to have an argument with you?"

"We did think about it." Carson winked at Charli. "Keep it up, and I'm gonna make you get your license and go full-time. Forget about this writing gig that's making you so miserable."

"Yeah, yeah, try another line of sweet-talk," she muttered. Charli visibly fought a grin for a few seconds. Then she got serious again. "Who can you get to dig into the email and find out who set them up?"

"I'm putting Rufus on it," Eden said. "Once we get the official okay from Sunderson, to open up the evidence."

"We're going to need your cell phones, too," Carson said. "Funny thing, but the password on Ernie's cell phone was turned off, making it easy to get in and read everything. Which doesn't fit with his reputation as a nasty, secretive paranoid. But they found a whole string of texts from Melba, supposedly, taunting him, telling him he was late, asking if he was scared of the dark, or just scared of facing two little old ladies."

Chapter Fourteen

"We don't text," Melba said. "We don't use our cell phones for anything except phone calls."

"And the GPS," Cilla added. "Anything we do on the Internet is done from home. The phone screens are just too small to read clearly."

"We're going to need to get into your computers, too," Carson said. "To prove you didn't send those emails."

"Sorry, but getting into their computers won't really prove anything. Just that they didn't do it from home. They could use a computer at the library or an Internet café or a dozen other places," Charli said.

"Why would someone go to all the trouble to lure Ernie to the shop to kill him?" Saundra said, asking the question that had been crystalizing since Carson and Eden arrived.

"The easy answer is to frame Melba and Cilla," Carson said.

"Probably the same person who's been spreading all the tales about threats and fights between them and Ernie," Eden said.

"What I find interesting is that he believed he was meeting you two ladies there." He finally sat down.

"You mean, someone didn't lure him there and then plant the evidence to frame them?" Charli held up a hand, stopping him when he opened his mouth. "Hold that thought. The water's ready. We're gonna need a lot more tea."

Carson was eyeing the last maple long john when she came back with the teapot, which was just as Cilla called it, the size of a soup tureen. She walked carefully, holding it with two hot pads, and set it down on the trivet in the middle of the coffee table.

"I believe the printout of the emails was planted evidence," Carson said, after taking a bite of the long john. He had the enviable ability to talk with his mouth full without spitting, the bite of donut tucked neatly in his cheek. "It wasn't enough to lure Ernie there. You two were targets as well. Some of the things Ernie said in the texts that started about four this morning make me think he was surprised you contacted him."

"I think the fact that the fake you told him he had to get keys to get into the shop, instead of telling him the door would be open, is strong enough evidence to clear you," Eden added.

"But the strangest part is the phone call Ernie was on, while he was waiting for you to show up." He chewed a few times and reached for the cup Charli had filled for him. Saundra noted that she put in both cream and sugar for him. Carson paused after the first sip and looked into the cup. "Didn't expect that... Anyway, phone call. He was on the call for a good ten minutes, leaving a message for the lawyer he wanted to file liens against you and Tracy. Yeah, we listened when Allen called the guy to ask what they talked about. He was adamant they didn't talk, that he's strict about office hours. Allen recorded the whole conversation with his permission. According to the lawyer, Ernie was spitting mad. Supposedly you two had been harassing him for the last couple of months, taunting him that you had gotten him thrown out of his shop, and now you were keeping him waiting, after forcing him to come to the shop to pay you off because you had all sorts of blackmail to use against him."

"We never!" Cilla blurted, going pale.

"Just more reason for getting into your email and phone records, to prove you didn't have any contact with him, that the threats were never made, and you didn't ambush him in your shop."

"That black eye when you clobbered him with your purse is working against you," Eden said. "Along with all the rumors, spread by people eager to get back at Ernie for all the trouble he's caused over the last few years. Someone with a real grudge against him took advantage of it, used it to reel him in, get him worked up to distract him, and try to put all the blame on you."

"So what are we going to do?" Melba said. Saundra suspected her even, calm tone had a strong foundation in weariness, maybe shock, rather than solid peace of mind.

"It's going to take a while getting our hands on everything that the police are preparing to subpoena right now," Carson said. "Cadburn just doesn't have the technical manpower to handle this kind of investigation, so they'll have to send it out to a bigger crime lab. That will add to the time it takes to investigate. We have to wait to get our chance at investigating and taking things apart."

"I'm going to kick myself for this later," Eden said. "Kai actually suggested it ... Saundra, could you ask your friend Nick if he could pull some strings, use whatever connections he has? He was a big help with the Fontaine problem."

"Sure. I'd be glad to." She fought down a chuckle, imagining Nick's smug reaction to the request, and suspecting just how much Eden resisted the idea.

It was proof of how important the Tweeds were to her, that she would put aside her misgivings and mistrust of Nick, to ask for his help. And to be honest, Nick deserved the mistrust. He positively delighted in keeping secrets, in knowing details that he wouldn't share with anyone else. There were times Saundra regretted reporting that Eden and Charli both had what certainly looked like Venetian glass heart lockets. She wouldn't put it past him to steal those hearts someday, if she didn't make any progress in getting a closer look to verify they were the genuine article. And hopefully get a look inside them.

While Saundra made her call, Eden explained to the Tweeds the part Nick had played in dismantling the scheme of Conrad Price's identical brothers before they got away with murdering him. Nick had used his connections to save time and reams of paperwork, to get into records and reveal facts that helped trap the guilty.

Saundra had to leave a message for Nick, which suited her just fine. She would rather negotiate in private for his help.

"I'm out right now, but I should be home this evening," she said, finishing up the call, when a banging began at the back door.

Charli got up and took a few steps toward the kitchen, probably at the right angle to see out the back door. Then a wailing sort of voice joined the banging. Cilla moaned and bowed her head into her hands.

"Is that...?" Eden didn't finish the question when Melba sighed and slouched in her chair.

"Charlotte," Cilla said.

The kitchen door slammed open and a heavyset woman stomped her way inside, through the kitchen, hitting the doorframe and walking crooked a few steps.

"Sorry. Forgot to lock the door," Melba muttered.

"What have you done?" Charlotte wailed as she entered the room. "You lost it, didn't you? Why didn't you take better care of it? What are all those police doing at our shop? How could you betray me—"

"Lost what?" Cilla snapped. Saundra had never heard her voice go so icy and sharp before. "And for the last time, Charlotte, the candle shop is ours, not yours. It will never be yours!"

"But Cilla—" The wail turned into a whimper, and the woman's bottom lip stuck out a good inch, quivering, as her eyes filled with tears.

"Nobody betrayed you, Charlotte." Melba levered herself out of the chair and moved over to stand beside Cilla's chair and rest a hand on her cousin's shoulder. "Whatever you think we lost, it isn't. There was nothing to steal from the shop. Which you had no business going anywhere near."

"I have every right to go there. I've decided to investigate what happened to Granny's labyrinth chest. I need to examine it. There could be dozens of valuable clues inside it."

"The chest wasn't stolen, if that's what you were whining about."

"I couldn't see it. Those stupid police wouldn't let me in to make sure it was all right. They didn't believe me when I told them I was a partner in the shop."

"That's because you aren't." Eden got up and moved over to stand on Cilla's other side. Her cool tone and the steel in her eyes had a quelling effect on Charlotte, to Saundra's relief.

"Just who do you think you are, telling me—"

"We told you on Sunday. She's the investigator we hired to track down the trail of the chest," Cilla said. "Charlotte, just go away."

"She is no investigator! She's a poseur, a con artist, trying to milk you for thousands of dollars to do the work that I'm offering to do for free. Out of the kindness of my heart. Because you are my favorite cousin."

"What kind of investigator doesn't know how to listen?" Carson said. He leaned back in the couch, one knee crossed over the other, and looked amused rather than irritated.

"A good investigator knows how to ignore useless details and focus on the valuable clues," Charlotte snapped.

"Oh, really? How long have you been an investigator? Which division of the brotherhood do you belong to? The FSC? The PIAA? The CDW?"

Saundra caught Charli covering her mouth, her eyes sparkling with amusement. She had a very strong suspicion that the initials Carson was throwing around were all made up.

"I don't have to answer those questions. You have no right to question my credentials," Charlotte responded after a long pause. Her nose went up at a haughty angle and her tone went chilly.

"As a fellow investigator, actually, I do."

"An investigator? You?" She raked him with her gaze, then snorted. "Another poseur. They're setting you up to cheat you. They'll probably run off with the chest when your back is turned, just like—" She stopped with an audible click, her eyes bugging at the leather credentials folder Carson now held out. "What is that?"

"Proof I'm a licensed investigator. I showed you mine, now show me yours." Carson smirked, while Charlotte went pale, then flushed red.

"You—I—that's—" She let out a huff and turned her back on him. "That's just typical of you, Melba, hiring such a vulgar creature, getting him involved in family business."

"Tweed family business, not yours," Melba said, her tone cheerful.

"For the last time, Charlotte," Cilla said. "Go away. You're not wanted here."

"Well, I never!" Charlotte turned, wide-eyed, glistening with the threat of tears again, staring each of them in the face. She flushed redder when her gaze locked with Carson's. He waved his credentials folder at her again. With a shriek, she turned and dashed with heavy footsteps for the door.

Charli followed her into the kitchen. The door slammed a few seconds later.

"Wow," Charli said, coming back into the living room. "You don't mind if I use that in a book someday, do you?"

"Nobody will believe it." Carson shook his head, laughing.

~~~~~

"So, what do you want to call your home decorating business?" Nick said, when Saundra answered his call that evening.

"Huh—what?" She thought for a moment about claiming that the caller had the wrong number, but that rich, teasing note in that smooth baritone voice was far too familiar. "Have you been drinking?"

"Depends if chocolate milk is now considered an intoxicant."

"Nick..." She closed her eyes. Nearly eleven at night after a very long day made her too tired to laugh. "What are you up to now?"

"Remember that house hunting trip you dragged me on, a few months ago?"

"I dragged you?" Something more potent than caffeine shot through her. She didn't know if she should be grateful, because she certainly needed all her wits when it came to Nick when he was up to something. Maybe she should be irritated, because just minutes ago she had been looking forward to dropping into bed. After some earnest prayers on behalf of Melba and Cilla. "You dragged me, and it was all a ruse to get me away from my apartment so you could set up a trap. You're even worse about rewriting reality than Charlotte."

"That would be Charlotte Westover, Cilla Tweed's cousin, but not Melba's. How is that overdressed windbag?"

"Nick..."

"You're getting repetitive." The laughter left his voice, which was comforting. She actually preferred him serious and even angry. Nick West in a teasing, mischievous mood was dangerous and unpredictable.

"What do you want?"

"I need your help setting up my new house. Not any of the houses we looked at, by the way."

"I thought you were joking about settling down around here." Saundra dropped down on her couch, facing the balcony. Nick's call had caught her just as she came home from the Tweeds' house. She turned to check that she really had closed the apartment door before she dug her phone out of her purse.

"Considering I've never had a house of my own before, yeah, I can see that." A gusting sound conveyed a hint that maybe, just maybe, Nick had had just as busy and draining a day as she had endured. "Believe it or not, that's why I wasn't available to pick up the phone the first dozen times you called. Out looking for something to fill the place."

"I only called once, you jerk." She laughed, surprising herself a little.

"Are you happy now? You've finally found something I'm

completely incompetent at."

"I'll believe that when I see it."

"You will. Since this problem with the dead body and all those nasty rumors about a pair of really nice ladies doesn't involve you. Except as a friend," he hurried to add. "I've got to charge you for my highly valuable time. You can help me with things like furniture and bedding and whatever to make this place livable."

"You're serious." Saundra considered pinching herself, to make sure she wasn't dreaming this whole conversation.

"Totally."

"How do you know about the rumors?" She wouldn't admit it, but she was grateful. Nick had a strong sense of justice, and he would help the Tweeds just because they were victims. She hoped, though, that the fact they were her friends would prompt him to work harder.

"Anybody who gets close to you, and your friends at the coffee shop, they're going to get watched. Besides, Pastor Roy asked me to look into things when the whole mess started with that wacko. I got hold of the inventory of that interesting cache taken out of the wall. I'm arranging to have some specialists scan and swab the other hiding holes in the floor, to get an idea what else has been hidden there."

"Are they in trouble?" Now she shivered, despite the day having been comfortably warm, so she didn't even need her sweater when she walked home.

"Someone's gone to a lot of trouble to frame them for the murder. What I find interesting is that they set up the frame like someone would on a slightly better than half-baked crime drama. Slightly clever, but still sloppy. And several steps away from reality, so the mastermind isn't a pro. Makes me wonder if the frame job is aimed at them, and the dead body was just a convenient prop, or he was the target, and the ladies were unlucky enough to be convenient patsies."

Saundra wanted to snap that the difference didn't matter, her friends were in trouble, period. The reasons didn't matter. But she knew Nick well enough to trust his judgment. The motivation for the framing or the murder, or both, made a big difference in determining the kind of people they were dealing with, and how to handle the investigation.

"Okay, what do we do first?"

"I'll pick you up for church in the morning, and you'll introduce me to the ladies. Then we'll have lunch and do some furniture shopping."

"Furniture shopping." She waited for him to laugh and admit he was joking.

"Starting with the local used furniture shops."

"Okay." Saundra knew what he would ask next, though she couldn't figure out why. What did the labyrinth chest have to do with Ernie

Bender's murder and someone trying to frame the Tweeds for it? "Yes, I know where they bought the chest."

"What chest?" Nick chuckled. "Downstairs, 8:15 sharp."

"Eight-fifteen sharp," she echoed. She knew better than to retort that the service started at nine, and it only took ten minutes, max, to get from her apartment to Cadburn Bible Chapel. Nick had plans, and she wasn't going to give him the satisfaction of asking.

Sunday, October 9

"Do you happen to know a Valerie Carter, setting up a public relations firm across the street from the candle ladies?" Nick said, before Saundra finished buckling her seat belt the next morning.

"A couple people have mentioned her. Becca is helping her get things set up. You could probably hack her computer and get all the information."

"*Moi?*" He flashed her a grin and shifted his car into gear. "She's out of town. Would Becca happen to know when she's due back?"

"Why?"

"The security cameras at her new place have been pretty helpful before. Our friendly Captain Sunderson has been stalled on getting permission to access that data. The judge who usually signs the orders is out of town. It'd save time if we could just ask this Valerie to give us her passwords and go into the system legally."

"As opposed to your usual methods?" She chuckled when Nick gave her a sideways glare. A few seconds later it morphed into his usual grin.

He switched to updating her on the latest news from her Aunt Cleo, which wasn't much. Which was normal. What mattered was that Cleo was safe, she was healthy, and she was taking a short break with some friends in Ireland who were having great success with the rootings Saundra had sent them two years ago. After all this time tending the plants for Cleo, Saundra knew better than to ask what the plants were, and what her aunt and her associates expected from them. She had played with the idea of downloading one of those plant identification apps, on the off chance they would work better than her sporadic searches through hundreds of botany websites. The problem was that if the secrecy surrounding the seeds that came from the Venetian glass heart was as dire as she suspected, a misstep that resulted in posting even one photo of the plants on the Internet, to try to identify them, might bring the wrong kind of interest focused on her.

"With all your connections, you can't track down Valerie's cell phone and just call her?" Saundra asked, as Nick pulled into the parking lot of the chapel.

"Just how prone would you be to turn over security camera video to a total stranger? A friend asking will get faster cooperation and fewer questions." Nick clicked his tongue. "I'm surprised at you. Thought I trained you better."

"Keep it up," she murmured, which earned a chuckle from him. "You're putting a lot of power in my hands, asking me to help you with paint and wallpaper and furniture. I can set you up to be miserable for years to come."

Another chuckle. "Yeah, I trained you well."

Saundra muffled several retorts. Then she spotted a familiar green sedan, and a moment later, the driver getting out. "Your lucky day." She pointed. "Becca at three o'clock."

Nick didn't join her in the sanctuary until after the first hymn. He winked at her as he slid into the pew, where she sat with Patty. So, mission accomplished. He had gotten hold of Valerie, after Becca called and gave her a heads up that he was calling, and legitimate.

Chapter Fifteen

Nick made Vintage House his and Saundra's fourth stop. At every secondhand and antiques store, Nick showed the clerk or owner multiple pictures of various styles of labyrinth chests. Several people showed great interest, either never having heard of such a piece of furniture or wanting to examine one. Two people directed them to the Vintage House. One offered Nick copies of research he had done on decoding the puzzle of the chest.

"You might find this interesting," Nick said, on the drive to Vintage House. "I got an email this morning from a friend who was tracking Charlotte's finances. She's been making a habit of hitting antique stores and secondhand furniture stores, and haunting museums that specialize in furniture. Four years ago, she got arrested and fined quite heavily for climbing over a half-wall around a display featuring a labyrinth chest. There was quite an argument with the curator, who claimed she broke a drawer, trying to force a hidden compartment open. Charlotte claimed it was already broken. She tried to sue for the splinters in her hand."

"That sounds like Charlotte." Saundra shuddered. "Suddenly, her demands to look at Melba and Cilla's chest feel kind of ominous."

"She's also invested large sums in buying labyrinth chests. Usually with borrowed money she tries not to pay back. Did you know they're worth quite a lot of money, to the right people?"

"Something tells me Charlotte isn't the right kind of person."

"I trained you so well." He chuckled when she gave him a withering look. A few seconds later, they were both grinning. "Actually, Charlotte could have paid back that money and made a tidy profit if she had sold the chests, but she has this bad habit of breaking them, or at least damaging them so no one is willing to pay what she paid."

"She's looking for something ..." Saundra caught her breath.

"You thought of something."

"The treasure hunt. Charlotte got in trouble, sneaking around shortly before Melba and Cilla's grandmother died. She was working on a treasure hunt for the family, but no one ever found it. What if Charlotte hid the information or clues or whatever in the labyrinth chest ... and she's been trying to find it all this time?"

"Why would she hide it?"

Saundra used up the rest of the ride to Vintage House sharing some of the stories Melba and Cilla had told Carson Fletcher the day before, after Charlotte had invaded. Just to give him an idea of what kind of distraction or obstacle she could be, if she insisted on playing at being an investigator. What Saundra found interesting, and from his intent expression, Nick did too, was how Charlotte kept trying to be considered a Tweed. Except when it wasn't convenient or profitable for her. Whenever she didn't want to do something, like attend church with the family, her first response had always been, "I'm not a Tweed, you don't have authority over me."

She had been banned from Granny Tweed's house several times in her childhood and teens, when she destroyed things the cousins wouldn't share with her. If Charlotte found out about the treasure hunt, and then learned she wasn't going to be included, she more than likely hid the information to punish everyone else.

Nick agreed with her theory, without any smug comments or his trademark smirk. That chilled Saundra, because he was taking this so very seriously. That was a bad sign, for the Tweeds.

Saundra was disappointed, but not really surprised, when they learned that the shop that sold the chest to the Tweeds had bought it from another shop, in Cedarville. Nick had her call the shop while he brought out his laptop computer and got to work researching the place. That call led them to an estate liquidation company, which wasn't open on Sunday. Nick got into their online files after only about ten minutes of tapping and scowling. She refused to ask how he did that.

The search ended, after he must have flipped through and read a dozen pages, with a grunted, "Huh," every once in a while, and a cocked eyebrow as he scowled at the screen. Saundra waited. He tapped some more. He had the computer perched on the console between them. To see the screen and try to figure out what he was doing, she would have to kneel on the seat and look over the top of the computer and down and read upside down. She was very good at that. Or she could snatch the computer away from him and try to read the important bits before he snatched it back.

Neither option was a good choice and might end with her being shoved out of the car on the side of the road, and Nick speeding away. They were in North Olmsted, not that far from Cadburn, but a long walk if she couldn't find her way to a bus route that wouldn't take her on a long detour. She didn't even want to consider calling Kai and asking him to rescue her. He would do it, but the embarrassment factor stopped her. Besides, Nick seemed to be making progress. If Saundra wanted access to that information, she had to be patient. But she had waited long enough. Time for him to share with his partner.

She had never had to play the "don't make me tattle to Cleo" card, and she hoped she never had to. The situation hadn't gotten dire. It was just a mystery over a chest that never should have gone missing. Still, that frown and the intensity of Nick's concentration, the way his shoulders hunched as he read and the notes he tapped into his phone, indicated this was getting interesting. This could be fun. She hoped.

"We're going to the Mug to report what we've found so far, aren't we?" It was stated as a question, but she made her tone of voice turn it into a statement of fact.

"Oh, absolutely. After you approve some of the things I picked out. What looks good online might be ugly as all get out in the light of day." Nick grinned and snapped the lid of his laptop closed.

"What you picked out. Online." Saundra shook her head and smoothed her expression into something blandly amused. She wouldn't give Nick the satisfaction of irritating her. "You know, we'd get a whole lot more done, faster, if you wouldn't keep playing all these mind games with me."

"Hey, gotta keep you on your toes, Babycakes."

"Babycakes!" She punched him as hard as she could in the bicep. It was a good thing he hadn't pulled out of the parking space yet.

Nick snorted and grinned, then mouthed, "ow," and rubbed his arm. In what had to be paybacks, he took them to two more stores, checking out backsplash tile, flooring, and curtains before he finally headed them for Cadburn and Book & Mug.

With one final stop. At the townhouse in the same neighborhood where Charli Hall lived. For a few seconds, Saundra feared Nick was going to park three doors down and break into Charli's townhouse in broad daylight. Instead, he stepped over the bumper and walked straight to the closest door and pulled keys out of his pocket. He opened the door and turned to look at Saundra, who hadn't unbuckled her seatbelt yet.

"Well? The faster we're done here, the faster you get your cappuccino. Anybody ever tell you what a grump you are if you don't get your daily dose of caffeine?"

She wished she had something to throw at him. Muffling a sigh and struggling to keep her expression neutral, she slid out of the car and followed him into the townhouse. It smelled of fresh paint and new carpet. The kitchen had been entirely gutted, with only empty slots for the appliances. The sink and the body of the cabinets looked brand new, waiting for the countertops to be installed. Saundra struggled for a few moments, sorting through her memory of all the materials and samples he had showed her in the different stores. She wasn't about to admit that by this time she hadn't been paying much attention to what went where.

Nick seemed genuinely interested in her opinion and input. She didn't know whether to be touched or worried that he might be playing a trick on her. Why did he choose Charli's neighborhood? Why Cadburn at all?

~~~~~

"Spook alert," Troy said, pausing at the end of the counter to deposit an espresso mug in a bus pan. He gestured with a tip of his head toward the door.

Kai frowned and turned to look where Troy had gestured. He understood and frowned a little more as Nick West followed Saundra through the front doors of Book & Mug.

Was that guy ever going to leave town? He didn't care if he got the "big brother" speech from Nick during the whole mess with Conrad Price and his brothers. Kai wanted him gone and the air space around Saundra clear of him for a while. Was a few years too much to ask?

Then Kai grinned, realizing how ridiculous he sounded, even to himself. Was he that serious about Saundra already? It wasn't like they had had much in the way of official dates.

"Can we go up?" Saundra said, reaching the counter a few steps ahead of Nick. "Eden asked for some assistance, and we've done a little work." She rolled her eyes, prompting a snort from Kai.

He must not have controlled his expression very well, because Nick's eyes narrowed, and he gave Saundra a sideways look when he joined her at the counter.

"Does she know you're coming?" Troy leaned into the far end of the counter as if he would shove it across the floor.

Saundra shook her head. "We've been out running errands, asking questions. Found something interesting." She must have seen that glint in Troy's eyes and recognized it as his stubborn, protective streak rising up. "It's for Melba and Cilla."

"Go on. I'll text her," Kai said, and pulled his stairwell key out of his pocket. "This doesn't leave your hand, understand?" he added in a stage whisper that was meant for Nick to hear.

"Yeah, and it's good to see you guys, too," Nick said. He caught hold of Saundra's arm. "Someday, we're all gonna look back on these big boy games and laugh."

"Nope, I don't think so," Troy muttered as the two of them headed for the hallway to the restrooms and stairwell.

~~~~~

Eden had been taking a break from what was turning out to be a long list of places she had to visit in person and people she couldn't talk to until Monday. She had diagrams from the inner workings of several labyrinth chests spread on the conference table. The whole concept threatened to turn into an obsession, or at least a hobby. Duchene was the biggest name in labyrinth chests, but there were a handful of others who were acknowledged designers and specialists in what had actually been a short-lived fad. Only the wealthy at that time could afford them, and most were custom-made, for specific purposes. She wondered just how secure the items hidden in the chests could be, when it certainly looked like their presence and purpose were never kept secret. It was like hanging a sign in the front hallway, advising would-be burglars that a safe of a particular model was in the house. Someone determined enough to take whatever was safeguarded in the chest just needed a few woodworking tools and enough time to disassemble it.

Still, she liked comparing the notes on the various designers, their styles, and the known patterns for the combinations to make secret compartments pop open.

Her phone chattered, signaling a text coming in. She rubbed her eyes, then shoved her chair backward to roll to her computer station and pick it up.

Kai: *Saundra & West coming up.*

She thought a moment, tapped in the thumbs up emoji, and got up. While something about Nick West set off warning prickles down her back, they were nearly identical to the tingles she got when she was on the verge of solving a puzzle. The look in his eyes, in those few unguarded moments when he didn't know she watched him, gave her the sense that he knew something important, but he was waiting for the right timing to spring it on her. She could respect him, because he had proven several times he was an ally, a useful resource for cutting through red tape. He just had a nasty sense of humor, and a very clear need to be in charge of the situation. And yeah, there was that sense he knew something that mattered to her, but he wasn't going to tell until it suited him. Probably not until he could have the upper hand.

Right now, though, he was helping with the whole Tweed puzzle. That had to be why he was coming in here with Saundra. Eden was willing to extend hospitality to an ally and show her appreciation. The fact they had come up with something so soon after asking for that help made her pulse blip a few times. She ducked into her apartment and snagged her nearly fresh pot of dragon tea and the box of raisin-filled cookies she had picked up at Sugarbush last night. She paused to peel off the day-old sticker and reduced price tag. No need for them to know. It wasn't like the bakery would go bad in just a day. She heard Saundra call for her just as she slid a hot pad under the pot of tea. Not that it would do any damage to the simple white plastic tray, but she believed in taking care of her possessions so they would last.

"That's a cat that ate two canaries look if I ever saw one," she greeted them, and nodded toward the conference table. "Didn't think labyrinth chests were such a big thing, did you?" she added, seeing Nick's gaze immediately focus on all the diagrams she had been studying.

"The bubble didn't last long, so I'm not sure how big they were." He tugged aside a drawing that partially covered another, then smiled and met her gaze. "You're good. That's a lot of work in a short amount of time. I'm guessing friendship is a much bigger motivation than a paycheck. And you're not planning on charging them much, if anything," he added, before Eden recognized the tightening of irritation in her chest and jaw.

"Nick, can you please be nice for once?" Saundra said. She tweaked a few diagrams and partially scattered stacks of printouts together into a pile, to make room for the tray.

"This *is* me playing nice." He winked at Eden and tugged a chair out, then put the laptop tucked under his arm onto the table before sitting.

"That's what I'm afraid of," Eden said, earning a few chuckles from him. She couldn't help grinning back. She wasn't sure if she was frustrated or amused to realize she liked the guy, despite the irritating mannerisms.

"We found—all right, James Bond here found something really interesting," Saundra said. She leaned close enough to sniff at the steam rising from the teapot. "And that's interesting, too."

"Smells like lapsang souchong," Nick said. "With something else, coming through the smoke."

"I call it dragon tea. A friend from college came up with it. Lapsang souchong," Eden nodded, confirming his guess, "with a dash of cayenne and ginger."

"To stimulate thinking?"

"Among other things." She stepped back to snag three mugs from the little cabinet holding all the hospitality paraphernalia. "I'm hitting a firewall with the historical society entrusted with Duchene's records. Please tell me you went at it from a different angle."

"We went at it from a different angle," he said, deadpan.

"You have my permission to slap him at regular intervals," Saundra said in a stage whisper.

That got a grin from Nick. Eden poured mugs for all of them, opened the bakery box, shoved it into the center of the end of the table where they had all settled, then sat. He took a slow sip from the mug. One eyebrow cocked, then he nodded, put the mug down, and flipped open his laptop.

"We backtracked the chest to an estate sale company that apparently received the chest from the person who stole it from Granny Tweed's house."

"You have their name? You know that's the thief?" Eden stayed in her chair when she wanted to get up and go stand behind him to read whatever he was calling up on the screen.

"Theory, really," Saundra said. "The person who consigned all the furniture and dishes and quite a nice inventory of artwork to the estate sale liquidators was a Clyde Bancroft. He was the trustee for his stepfather, Jerome Tweed."

"So the stepson ..." She shook her head, gut instinct telling her it couldn't be that easy. "Who do you think the real thief is? Not his stepfather? He wouldn't steal from his own mother. Not if he's the adorable Uncle Jerry the ladies were talking about ... Oh." She settled back in her chair, cradling her mug close under her chin, as she ran through all the stories Melba and Cilla had told her yesterday.

"Sending you everything I copied from the files. Which you will not be able to trace back to me," Nick said with a wink. "Not if this goes to court. Which I doubt it will since all the guilty parties are dead and won't raise a stink."

"You hope," Saundra said. "We found a whole—" She sighed. "Nick found a whole file full of angry letters, and copies of reports revolving around the estate sale for the Jerome Tweed family. Kind of sad, when you consider that everything was put in the stepson's hands, and his wife, his second wife, the stepson's mother, was entirely cut out. With specific instructions not to cooperate if she tried to get involved in the disbursal of the property and funds. An estranged daughter and her conman husband were tangled up with enough legal restrictions to ensure if they even whispered that they were unhappy with their bequests, they lost it all." She shook her head.

"The important detail is that Clyde's mother, Annabelle Bancroft-Tweed—don't you get suspicious of people who hyphenate their names, like they're using their pedigree as a club to get their way? Annabelle Bancroft-Tweed harassed the estate sale company, demanding to see the inventory of what they were selling. She got three lawyers involved, apparently never telling each one in turn that the others had failed to get the information through court orders. Her husband's will tied everything up nice and neat. Makes me wonder if he knew what his wife did, and he was punishing her after the fact.

"Annabelle apparently was looking for one specific piece of furniture, but she didn't want to tell the company what it was. When they wouldn't hand over the inventory, following her son's orders, she tried to break into the warehouse to get a look. She claimed the item was a family heirloom and wasn't supposed to be sold."

"The really interesting part," Nick said, sitting back and picking up his mug again, "is that she was on a list of people who were to be barred from the estate sale. The company made a suspicious effort to document everything surrounding this particular estate sale, all the complaints, all the instructions, specifically the list of people who were to be sent personal invitations to the auction, and invited to a preview before it was open to the public. Nearly every living Tweed was invited." He grinned. "None of them made it to the preview."

"You have to wonder why Clyde was so insistent on his stepfather's relatives being invited," Saundra murmured.

"Oh, no, let me guess." Eden grinned despite herself. "The labyrinth chest was sold at the preview when none of the Tweeds were present?"

"Got it in one." Nick grinned back at her. "The person who bought it was some sort of eccentric who made her reputation going against aesthetic standards, so she repainted the chest and put it in her art gallery until the place went bankrupt. Then it was sold, handled by the same estate liquidation company she bought it from, and eventually made its way to Vintage, where the ladies found it."

~~~~~

Melba looked around the living room, meeting first Eden's, then Saundra's, then Nick's gazes, and ending with Cilla.

"Do you remember being invited to the estate sale?" Eden asked.

"Yes, but we didn't go. We didn't want to run into Aunt Annabelle. We didn't find out until later that she was kept away. Found out directly from her." Melba rolled her eyes and couldn't repress the chuckle that escaped. "You have to understand, she was such an unpleasant, snooty creature. We all wondered why Uncle Jerome married her. Maureen, that's his daughter by his first wife, Laura, despised that woman from the moment she met her."

"Two weeks before the wedding," Cilla added. "We were all sure that if she hadn't been so busy galivanting around the world, pretending to be an artiste and had been there from the moment Annabella started chasing Uncle Jerome, she could have prevented the whole ugly mess. Her father adored her. All she needed to do was curl her upper lip and he would have dropped the nasty snob before things went too far. Well, Maureen lost that war before she could arm herself. She had a hissy fit when Uncle Jerome wouldn't cancel the wedding and took off and married that slick fellow ... what was his name again?"

Chapter Sixteen

Cilla shook her head. "Doesn't matter. They never came to visit. Broke Uncle Jerome's heart, never knowing his grandchildren. We were sure that all the stories of the legal trouble the husband got into contributed to his decline. Fortunately, Clyde was an absolute dear. He more than made up for his mother's nastiness. He was Jerome's support through everything. He deserved to get everything."

"You know ..." Melba sat back, waiting for the disparate pieces swirling in her brain to settle down. "Yes, you're going to suggest that Annabelle stole the chest, aren't you? I completely agree."

"Considering how nasty that woman was, when it came to the chest?" Cilla nodded. "Every time there was a family get-together, you could almost set your watch by how soon she would start screeching about how the children were abusing it. Damaging a precious, irreplaceable antique. She kept insisting Granny Tweed didn't deserve to have it in her house if she couldn't protect it. I remember one time she got into an awful argument with several of the aunts. Aunt Tabitha was just furious. She accused Annabelle of wanting to have Granny committed to an asylum, always hinting around that she wasn't in her right mind. Just because she didn't consider the chest a delicate antique. Annabelle tried to laugh it off."

"I remember coming in on that part," Melba said. "She kept backtracking, changing what she had said, insisting that she merely thought Granny was failing, mentally, and she needed a guardian to look after her. She volunteered Uncle Jerome to take power of attorney or something like that and started talking about moving Granny to a much smaller house. Why should she be burdened with the upkeep of the family house, with all the rooms to clean and furniture to look after?"

"She talked about furniture far too much," Cilla said. "She had her eye on more than the chest, but that was the main subject of her whining."

"So that woman stole the labyrinth chest ..." A chuckle bubbled up from deep inside. Melba imagined the arguments between Jerome and Annabelle when he discovered that his wife had stolen the chest from his mother's house. "Knowing Uncle Jerome, he tried to handle things quietly. To avoid riling up the family, and to protect her. Even if she didn't deserve it. A good dose of public humiliation would have done that woman a world of good. Knowing what a good help Clyde was, the two of them probably hid that chest. Annabelle probably drove herself insane, trying to find it."

"She did get a reputation for scouring the countryside, checking auctions, estate sales, and secondhand furniture stores," Cilla added.

"So all those restrictions on the will and the estate sale were to keep her from getting her hands on the chest once Jerome was gone," Eden said.

"Makes sense." Nick grinned. "Family. Can't live with 'em, can't blow them to kingdom come. Speaking of which, have you heard from your cousins lately?" he added, turning to Saundra.

"As far as I'm concerned..." Saundra shuddered. "No. And the longer the silence lasts, the happier everyone will be. Thanks for ruining my afternoon, by the way."

"You're welcome." He winked at Eden. "If you feel like adopting her or adding her to the family some other way, you have my blessing."

Eden just shook her head. Melba wondered what that was all about. She had the oddest feeling that Eden had tensed up when Nick mentioned Saundra's cousins.

"You might be happy to know that dear Aunt Annabelle got herself into a whole heap of legal trouble, around the time of the estate sale," Nick continued. "She tried to sue the company for removing furniture that she insisted was her personal property. She never got beyond threats, because she refused to identify the furniture. No lawyer would take her on. She tried to ruin their reputation. They countersued for defamation. And won. She headed off to Europe to drown her sorrows on some grand tour, according to the society column. Want me to keep digging, to find out what happened to her?"

"No, thanks. We've got enough drama going on right now without raising the spirits of the gratefully departed." Cilla punctuated her words with a groan and a shudder. Then a moment later her gaze met Melba's, and they chuckled.

"I wonder what ever happened to Clyde," Melba mused. "I think if he's still around, he might be amused to hear what's going on now."

Saundra's groan caught her attention. She looked around to see the young woman shaking her head, looking at Nick, who grinned. His glance flicked to Melba, and he sat up and put on a thoroughly believable expression of innocence. He was one to watch and be careful of, she decided.

"I just so happen to have his last known address. If you're interested," he said.

"Please." She left it at that. Later, she had an awful thought. What if there was more than just friendship between Nick and Saundra? Melba dearly wanted her to end up with Kai. The two of them clicked. They were good for each other.

Definitely, Nick West was someone to watch out for, if only to keep him from causing trouble later for those she loved.

Monday, October 10

Eden called just after lunch. She had finally gotten hold of Valerie, to access the security cameras. The bad news was that someone had stolen the cameras right off the building. The good news was that everything recorded before the theft was downloaded to a wireless storage system on the Cloud. Valerie didn't have that information with her, and she was out of town on a family emergency for at least a week. She would try to remember the password or try to retrieve it but might have to wait until she returned to town, to send the files to Eden. Fortunately, being Cloud storage, there was no fear of the video of Ernie and his accomplice coming into the shop getting written over. Eden said she was trying to gain access to the security videos of other shops on both strips. She had high hopes for Schuster's, across the street from Brighten Your Corner, at a slight angle. With the regularly rotating display of antiques in their front window, they were more than likely to have security cameras. With any luck, their cameras were at the right angle to catch activity at Brighten Your Corner.

~~~~~

A message was waiting on Eden's cell when she finished her call with Melba. Nick West let her know that someone had been trying to hack into the signal between the new security system at the duplex and the hub Rufus was still refining. He promised to send over a patch for the oversight program that would keep intruders from detecting a security system was in place, "but it might take a while, jumping through hoops to get permission."

Then he chuckled. "You're probably ticked and wondering how I was able to get past all your really brilliant safeguards to insert a program that would let me know when someone was hacking into your system. Well, that's part of what I do, *a'mosi*. Those ladies mean a lot to Saundra, so I'm going to be there for them until this mess is cleared up. Calling our friend Allen to give him a heads up. It's up to you if you want to tell the ladies about the attempt this morning. Which apparently happened right after they left on errands. Looks like someone is watching their place. Wonder what they're after."

Eden stared unseeing at her phone after the message ended. Her brain seemed to catch on the foreign word he had used. It implied affection, but in a totally familial way. As in between blood-relations. How did he even know that word? She still didn't know what language it came from. She couldn't find any clue no matter how many translation programs she had used on the Internet.

Nothing was going to convince her to ask Nick West for an explanation.

No, better to focus her mind on other things. Like notifying Rufus there was a hole in their security program they had never even anticipated. Not that she wanted to owe Nick anything, but she would be very grateful to examine that patch program and add it to the system. Nothing had blipped to alert her or Rufus that anyone was trying to break into the Tweeds' duplex, so whoever had been testing the program for the security system had done it from a distance.

This was getting far more curious and tangled than she liked. Eden had the awful feeling that whoever had killed Ernie and tried to frame the Tweeds thought they had found something at the shop. Something they hadn't turned over to the police. Something that person wanted to get back before that happened.

Maybe it was time to call on her old mentor, Rance Harcourt, and call in another favor. Nick could probably dig faster, and had nastier connections, to get past all sorts of official barriers. Eden didn't want to have to owe him any more than she already did. Maybe that was a flaw in her, but until the situation turned more dangerous for Melba and Cilla, she preferred to take the longer, more legitimate route.

~~~~~

Melba and Cilla ran late with their errands, so Melba dropped Cilla at the library for afternoon story hour before she took the groceries home. Saundra flagged her down just as she was about to pull out onto the street again. She turned back, and they chatted about some ideas Mrs. Tinderbeck had for the holidays, setting up a candle corner in the craft shop the library always sponsored, for the children to make Christmas gifts. Melba had nothing frozen in her groceries, so she didn't mind sitting and chatting for nearly ten minutes.

Her phone rang just after Saundra stepped back into the library, and Melba was about to shift into reverse and pull out of her parking spot. Again.

Helen Wright, the neighbor across the street, apologized for bothering Melba, but she had called Cilla first and was worried because she wasn't picking up her phone.

"Oh, no, today's her turn for storytime. She turns her phone off when she's with the children," Melba hurried to tell her. "Cilla's all right. Thanks for checking."

"Well, that's a relief, but I really think you need to get home fast. Some enormous woman is shrieking and stomping around your front yard. First, she was pounding on Cilla's door, then she was at your door.

Then Heinrich came over and told her to go away or he'd call the police." She chuckled. "Don't worry. As soon as I heard the thumping start up, I turned on my iPad camera. As soon as he mentioned the police, she pulled out her phone and shouted she was calling the police and then the fire department and the paramedics, because she's positive both of you are dying from a gas leak or some such idiocy. I can't understand half what she's saying. But oh, my goodness, Heinrich is my hero. He actually got within reach of her and yanked the phone out of her hand and threw it into the street. Then he walked away, and I swear he had the biggest grin on his face. Do you know, Heinrich's rather good-looking when he smiles. Not that he does very often, but still—"

"Is she still there?" Melba interrupted. Despite the awful certainty that Charlotte had struck again, and was disturbing all the neighbors, she had to laugh. Helen was ten years older than her, and had a delightful, mischievous passion for all the new technology. And using it to capture the people around her in their most embarrassing and ridiculous moments.

"Stomping through your flowerbeds, banging on the windows and wailing that she just knew the house was going to kill ..."

"Helen?" She put the phone on speaker, set it into the little cup in the console, and put the car into gear. Ohio law said not to touch the phone, or something like that, but there was nothing in the law about not talking on the phone as she drove. Just as long as she wasn't distracted by touching it, holding it to her ear. The drive down Overview to her street seemed like ten miles instead of ten minutes. "Helen? What happened? Are you all right?"

"Oh, I'm fine. Some man just drove up and he's risking his life trying to get that awful woman to settle down." A pause. "Huh. She's actually listening. Or maybe she's about to collapse, just ran out of breath. Why do women let themselves get so huge?"

"I'm on my way." Melba muffled a chuckle. "You're still recording all this?"

"Oh, you better believe it!"

What was Charlotte up to now? Melba could easily believe she would throw herself at one of their front doors and eventually break it down. How long would that take? Just how long could the hinges and locks stand up to her bulk and the growing desperation she probably felt to get at the labyrinth chest? Why was it so important to her? The speculation that Charlotte had hidden Granny's treasure hunt out of spite, because she wasn't included, seemed more plausible every time Melba considered it. But why would Charlotte care about that silly game so many years later? Whatever Granny had designated as a prize had vanished years ago, divided up between all the children, grandchildren, and great-grandchildren.

When she turned down the short street with the duplex and six other houses, Melba tapped the brakes, wondering for a moment if she had turned down the wrong street. Charlotte's ridiculous, expensive rental car was nowhere in sight. She couldn't imagine the woman parking in the apartment lot and struggling through the backyard to get to the house. Sneakiness was embedded in her DNA, but so was laziness and comfort and protecting her ridiculous spike-heeled shoes.

An unfamiliar SUV sat on the street in front of her house, and as she pulled up and debated pulling into her driveway or turning around, a man walked up the driveway from the back of the house. David. Irritation fought with relief, and a twinge of guilt, too. Melba wouldn't put it past David to have come over here in the middle of the day to try to talk her and Cilla into using his recommended home security system. Or maybe even try to break in, to prove that whatever Eden was installing didn't work.

While it served him right to have to deal with Charlotte, at the same time, he really didn't deserve to have that ridiculous, selfish twit shrieking at him. And considering how good-looking he was, probably throwing herself at him, demanding a knight in shining armor defend her and her "poor, abused, sensitive feelings."

She waved to him as she headed down the driveway to the garage. David followed her. He pulled the back door of her car open before she pulled out her house keys and opened the driver's side door. He gathered up the four bags of groceries and let her precede him to the back door.

"How did you get Charlotte to go away?" she asked, once they were both inside the house and the groceries sat on her kitchen table.

David gave her that crooked smile that always tried to look sheepish but had too much of his father in the expression. It always came across as sly, and Melba always mentally slapped herself for trying to blame the son for the father's flaws. "Well, I told her I had just talked to you both, and you were busy setting up your candle shop and ..." He shrugged. "I promised her I'd get her something she claims she left behind by accident."

"Probably something she tried to steal from us," Melba said, punctuated with a snort.

David raised an eyebrow at that. "She gave me this sob story about an embroidery project she messed up when you were all kids, and Great-granny Tweed helped her fix, and it means so much to her, and if she just has this keepsake, she promises she'll go away and never come back."

"She's been promising never to come back for the last thirty years. Every time she gets her feelings hurt." She settled down at the table and rubbed her forehead, to ward off the headache she knew was about to pounce any moment. Then his words registered. "Embroidery?"

"Yeah, a pillow shaped like a heart."

"When will that ridiculous woman stop wasting time and energy rewriting history, when she knows she won't get away with it?"

"Come on, Aunt Mel, what would it hurt? You and Aunt Cilla have a couple dozen of those things sitting around, gathering dust. Are you really going to miss one pillow? Especially if that's all it takes to make her go away for good?" He leaned down so they were nearly eye-to-eye and gave her what a less charitable cousin had called his used car salesman smile.

"It's the principle of the thing ..." She fought down several unkind remarks. "And you're wrong, we don't have a couple dozen pillows. Certainly not heart-shaped ones. And all of them are precious to us, because we made them with Granny."

"What would it hurt?"

Why, she wondered, was David so sympathetic to Charlotte?

He was up to something. Even if he hadn't followed in his father's footsteps, scheming and manipulating people, and quite frankly putting some smears on the good reputation of the Tweed clan, Melba knew he was up to something.

A sudden vision of David handing the pillow over to Charlotte, and the woman attacking him when she realized he gave her the wrong pillow, nearly startled a chuckle out of Melba. She hoped she controlled her expression.

"You're right, what would it hurt?" She stood up so quickly, David stumbled, backing away so she wouldn't bump into him.

Then again, she thought, as she dug in her purse for her key to Cilla's back door, chances were good Charlotte wouldn't know she had the wrong pillow. How many years had it been since she actually got her hands on that specific pillow she had managed to steal, and Cilla had taken back, so many times they had lost count? Charlotte's grasp on reality and facts was so slippery, she might not be able to remember details. Especially with the way she kept rewriting history. How could she keep any of her ridiculous, false stories straight?

Why was it so important to have that specific pillow?

Melba beckoned for David to follow and stepped out her back door, unlocked Cilla's, and led him to the guest room. It still reeked faintly of Charlotte's expensive perfume that she claimed had been designed especially, personally for her. Why some women thought that an aroma that was almost toxic was attractive, Melba could never figure out.

The day bed had been put back in order, with all the pillows neatly arranged. Six pillows were heart-shaped. Some large enough to use as seats on the floor, others small enough to hide between her hands. She chose one the approximate size of the pillow safely hidden in the closet of her own spare bedroom, the colors slightly faded, testifying to its age. She held it in her hands a moment, trying to remember when it had been made, and who made it. Would Cilla be upset to lose this particular pillow, on the off-chance Charlotte might indeed never come back?

When Melba told her about the trick later that afternoon, Cilla chuckled and commented that they should have tried that switch years ago.

She squeezed it before handing it to David and caught his eyes widening. Almost like panic. What was that all about? Melba's fingers didn't register the slight stiffness in the center of the pillow until it was already in his hands. She remembered the details, now. Granny had called it a keep-safe pillow, instead of keepsake, because there was a slot in the middle of all that thick embroidery where they could hide small items. Such as teeth that had just fallen out, held safe and waiting for the tooth fairy to visit. Or coins. Or pieces of candy. Or other treats. Granny had always put a pillow on each girl's bed when they came over for cousin sleepovers, usually with some kind of clue for the treasure hunt they would enjoy during their stay. Melba nearly asked David to give it back, so she could see what memory had been left in there all these years, never discovered because they treated those pillows with such care. In memory of Granny Tweed.

Almost as an afterthought, as he was heading down the front steps, he asked if they had had any success finding more compartments in the labyrinth chest.

"Oh, no. I'm afraid they've been sealed shut by all that paint. We're going to have to wait until it's been stripped clean before anything will open," Melba said.

"Well, let me know when you do. Might be kind of fun, playing detective," he said, and smiled, his steps almost jaunty as he hurried across the front lawn to his SUV.

Chapter Seventeen

The security video from Schuster's proved to be little help. They now knew what time Ernie came to Brighten Your Corner, using the stolen keys and for some inexplicable reason, despite knowing about the security cameras that had caught his vandalism and invasion, walked in the front door. That did them little good because the person who arrived maybe twelve minutes later wore a dark hoodie, pulled low over his face. The "his" was only a guess because the person was taller than Ernie, with wide shoulders, dressed in jeans and dark sneakers. Colors were nearly impossible to determine in the odd pre-dawn light.

The presumed killer came from behind the strip of shops, but no video cameras showed any cars pulling into the parking deck. Had he come up the other direction, on foot, out of range of the camera? That begged the question of who helped Ernie steal the keys from Tracy's office.

The only benefit of the video was to prove conclusively that despite the hopeful rumors swirling through the township, Melba and Cilla did not kill Ernie.

"Yeah, and a lot of people are gonna be really disappointed, because they despised the nasty old cuss, and it was just more humiliating for him to die at the hands of two sweet old ladies," Troy commented, when he overheard the report that Allen passed on to Eden.

~~~~~

Kai caught fragments of a conversation at one of the long tables that ran down the center of the shop, between the booths and the glass block wall that divided the coffee shop from the bookstore. He hadn't been paying attention, experimenting with some variations on the cider-and-red-hots drink, until he heard "Tweeds" and "Ernie deserved it," and other comments. Were people trying to blame the Tweeds for that filthy old creep's death? Or what was more likely, considering how unpopular Ernie was, they were getting the credit for doing a community service?

Whatever the sentiment or reasoning, if there was any, Kai didn't like having the Tweed cousins implicated in any way. Didn't anybody consider how uncomfortable this had to be for them? Embarrassing? What a bad light it cast on their business before they had even finished painting and installing furniture? He put down the bag of red hots he had been about to drop in the grinder, to turn them into powder and prepared to step out from behind the counter to confront those people. To find out what they were saying, if not set them straight. He wouldn't even mind asking them not to come back, if they couldn't control their mouths and think before they spoke.

"That's enough from you morons," Heinrich growled.

Kai flinched. He hadn't seen the old man come stomping up to the table. Judging by his armload of books, he had been on the other side of the wall for some time.

"Can't you stop and think and use your pitiful excuses for brains for just a second?" Heinrich continued, when the company of gossips raised their heads. Most of the group of nine looked embarrassed, rather than angry.

Kai stayed where he was. A curmudgeon like Heinrich could sometimes get away with saying things that Kai, who depended on good will to keep his business going, would never dare.

Heinrich snapped out half a dozen sentences, changing his tone each time. Kai nearly laughed to realize he was mimicking the people who had said them. Who would have thought the old man could do that? And that he had such a good memory?

"For your information, those two ladies — and I mean *ladies*, who deserve better than you've been giving them just now — they could never do anything like that. And I got proof they didn't. I got proof where the killer came from." He punctuated the statement with two sharp nods.

"Have you told the cops yet?" someone at the far end of the long table said. He sounded more ashamed than belligerent after the tongue-lashing Heinrich had given them.

"Not yet. Not sure yet if I should or not."

"What if the cops think the Tweeds did it? Shouldn't you defend them from ..." The woman who spoke slumped in her seat, visibly melting under Heinrich's furious glare.

"Anybody who'd think for a second they did that, they don't deserve to be cops. Ain't a brain in this entire town if that happens!" Then he turned and stomped to the door, knocking it open hard enough to bang against the outside wall.

Kai leaned on the counter, a slow smile spreading as his mind spun through what he had just heard. He wasn't even going to try to figure out where that outburst had come from, other than Heinrich had a strong sense of justice. And he had been watching from across the creek. Eden needed to know about that, at the very least. She would tell Allen and Ted. They needed to know. Because yes, despite the sloppy frame job, some people would still believe the Tweeds had murdered Ernie Benders.

Tuesday, October 11

"Cilla? Are you all right?" Melba's voice cracked, despite her good indoor library voice, which Saundra wished more patrons could learn.

That tone caught her attention and had her rising from her seat before she turned around to see Melba hurrying to meet Cilla, in the library doorway. The other Tweed looked pale, her wide eyes looked a little glazed, and she held out her cell phone at arm's length. Saundra reached her at the same time Melba did. They each took hold of an arm and guided Cilla to the break room. Melba helped her into a chair at the lunch table while Saundra got a cup of cold water. Mrs. Tinderbeck followed them and stayed in the doorway. The Tweeds had come in today to talk with her about the idea for candles for the library's holiday craft project.

"What happened? What did you hear?" Melba took the phone out of Cilla's hand.

"That silly old ..." Cilla shook her head, seeming to shake away whatever had stunned her. She took a deep breath, then startled Saundra by blushing and hiding her face in her hands.

"Who?" Melba demanded. She clutched her cousin's upper arms. Saundra wouldn't have been surprised if she shook Cilla in another moment.

"We have a date." She took another deep breath. "That was Heinrich." She glanced past Melba, her gaze meeting Saundra's, then went to the break room door, where Mrs. Tinderbeck shook her head, smiling.

"He most certainly is a silly old man," the head librarian agreed. "I'm not surprised he's asked you out, but the timing really is somewhat thoughtless. Half the town knows he's had a crush on you for years, but he's too proud and stubborn to do anything about it."

"No, not me. Well, not just me." Cilla's mouth trembled into a smile. "Both of us."

"Both of us?" Melba echoed. She shook her head. "Like ... a double date?"

"He wants us to come over for dinner, and he'll give us some information on the break-in and the ..." A sigh. "The murder."

"That isn't wise," Mrs. Tinderbeck said.

"Oh, Heinrich is a curmudgeon, always looking for something to complain about, but he isn't dangerous," Cilla hurried to say.

"No, I think she means it isn't wise to withhold evidence in a police investigation," Saundra guessed.

"Exactly."

Eden agreed, when she joined them at the library, in the smaller conference room, an hour later, after the craft meeting. Saundra had called to tell her what had happened, and she agreed to come meet with the cousins instead of asking them to come to her office.

"You know how Heinrich is. He's going to grumble and make all sorts of cryptic comments and think he's being clever and secretive, until you go on that date and he gives you the information. The problem with Heinrich is that he probably can't even spell cryptic, much less be cryptic. He's already dropped hints all over town that he knows something about the murder. The murderer could decide to do something about it." Eden looked back and forth between the Tweeds, who faced her across the conference table.

Saundra stayed with her back to the door, blocking the window in the door. Just in case Twila took it into her head to come snoop. Eden knew how to speak softly, so eavesdropping wouldn't do any good, but with their luck, Twila the snoop knew how to read lips.

"I'm still having a hard time wrapping my mind around the idea he wants to go on a date with us," Melba said.

"It really isn't a date." Cilla blushed, which Saundra found adorable. "He just wants us to come over for dinner. He's probably lonely."

"With good reason."

"Melba!" She slapped her cousin's hand, grinning. "You're right, this could be dangerous if the wrong people hear, but … well, yes, I do know Heinrich. If anyone goes to him, asking for that information, he'll shut up and shut down and be twice as annoying as before. And it's almost applesauce time."

"Excuse me?" Eden's mouth twisted like she didn't know whether to laugh or be confused.

"Heinrich has this enormous … well, it's basically a cauldron. It was his grandfather's, and it's a family tradition for the Founders' Club to set it up in the park out there in the historical village in North Olmsted and make applesauce over an open fire. He spends the whole day, peeling and coring and chopping and stirring. Do you know how many people will be disappointed if Heinrich doesn't bring that cauldron? It's the most delicious applesauce. I don't want to be responsible if he has one of his grumble fests and gives the entire county the cold shoulder for a couple weeks." She shrugged.

"I didn't realize …" Eden shook her head, and grinned, glancing at Saundra. "I mean, I've been to the harvest fest at the village, but I never realized that was Heinrich."

"Probably because that's the only day of the year anyone sees him smile," Melba said. "He really is rather handsome when he smiles. Kind of frightening, if you think about it."

"Melba!" Cilla elbowed her, then they both chuckled.

"So what do you think they should do?" Saundra said.

"No matter who talks to him, asking will just shut him up," Eden said. "He's more paranoid and cranky than ever, after the whole mess with the security cameras over at Windows and ..." She stopped and sat up a little straighter, and her gaze went distant.

"You thought of something, didn't you?" Melba whispered.

"Knowing Heinrich?" She nodded, smiling a little grimly. "He threatened to install his own security cameras, half a dozen, covering every angle. Including across the creek, just to make sure someone can't break into his shop from the back."

"You think he caught video of the murderer?" Saundra said, when the Tweeds just looked at her and held each other's hands.

"I don't know how much good it could do, but he probably caught something he thinks is useful. Heinrich is a grump, but he's an honest grump. He's never made unfounded complaints, just ..." Eden shrugged. "Exaggerated ones. He wouldn't hold you two hostage for dinner plans if he didn't have something he thought was useful to hand over to you at the end of the evening."

"So what do we do?" Melba said.

"How bad will it be to spend the evening with him? It's the both of you, so it isn't like he's going to go full on Casanova with Cilla." That got a blush from the other Tweed cousin. "I'll keep Allen and the captain informed, and we'll be ready for when he hands it over and go from there. And try to get him to keep his mouth shut, will you? We've had enough murders in this town to last us a couple years."

"Starting to feel like Cabot Cove around here," Saundra murmured. Neither Tweed seemed to have heard her, and that was a good thing, because it really was a bad joke. Especially since she knew they both loved *Murder She Wrote.*

~~~~

That evening, Heinrich greeted the cousins at his front door with an expression Melba thought looked rather embarrassed. She couldn't be sure because she had never seen him embarrassed before. There was something charming in how he looked away and hunched his shoulders. Was he blushing a little?

Did she dare hope he would announce he had changed his mind, he was ashamed of blackmailing them into having dinner with him, and they could go home?

"Come on in. At least, for a little—I mean—well, it'd be rude to make you go around the house, wouldn't it?" He shrugged again and stepped back from the door and gestured for them to step inside.

Cilla went in first, but only because Melba took a step back. They had come near to arguing over Melba's teasing about Heinrich having a crush on her since kindergarten. Heinrich had asked them both over, and he was just in another of his "us against the world" phases. Meaning the three of them, as the oldest residents of the short street, had to stand against the newcomers and young families. Melba would have agreed with Cilla's reasoning, because yes, Heinrich did do that from time to time. But where did that leave Helen, who was certainly older than them? Then again, Helen certainly acted several decades younger than them, so maybe Heinrich had written her off as a lost cause.

"Oh, my," Cilla said, pausing just long enough Melba nearly stepped on her heels. "What is that incredible smell?"

Melba caught herself holding her breath, but Cilla was smiling and taking deeper breaths, and Heinrich was smiling. No, that wasn't a smile, that was a big, proud, face-splitting grin. She sniffed. Her mouth immediately started to water.

Heinrich led them through the house, which wasn't anything like Melba had expected. She had always seen Heinrich as one of those hoarders who were getting far too much coverage on TV. Why encourage people's emotional problems by giving them attention and temporary celebrity status? Heinrich's house was a throw-back to the sixties in colors and styles of furniture, but everything was clean and neat, very little clutter. She had to laugh, glimpsing the TV room as they went from foyer to dining room to kitchen. Complete with an enormous, red leather recliner with cupholders built into the arms, seated square in front of a flat-screen TV that had to be five feet wide, sitting in an entertainment center that took up the entire wall. And if she wasn't mistaken, there were three video carts holding gaming systems.

They followed that incredible, spicy, sweet, fruity, meaty aroma out the kitchen and onto the deck. This, just like the TV room, was a total break from the décor of the rest of the house. Starting with the gleaming silver gas grill with an attached cooler and several gas burners, and a stand holding multiple barbecuing tools. A tall, thick hedge surrounded the entire yard like an impenetrable wall. That was standard Heinrich. How many of his neighbors knew this incredible setup existed? Probably none of them, Melba suspected. Just how many people had Heinrich invited over to barbecue? He proudly lifted the grill lid, releasing a thick cloud of spicy smoke, and two racks of ribs dripping juice and sauce onto the briquets.

"I'm guessing that barbecue sauce has applesauce in it?" Melba said.

"Yeah, kind of predictable, huh?" he said, shrugging again.

What had happened to Heinrich the surly curmudgeon who snarled at everyone? Were they twins? Or was this a Jekyll-and-Hyde situation, and he took some kind of potion when he left his home every morning to go to his shop? Or maybe, more likely, he took a potion at the end of the day when he went home, to make him this charmingly awkward fellow?

"You're the king of applesauce," Cilla hurried to say, and patted his arm. "I'd be disappointed if you didn't use it. And that smells incredible.

Thank you."

That got a wide-eyed stare from Heinrich. And then ... was it possible he was blushing? He was red-faced most of the time, so the change in coloring was hard to detect. He certainly seemed to like being touched by Cilla, even if startled.

"Can we help you with anything?" Melba asked, mostly to stop herself from staring. If she wasn't careful, the real Heinrich might return. She much preferred this one, thanks very much.

"Oh, no, no, just sit down and make yourselves comfortable. It's all ready. Just gotta ..." He made a swinging gesture. "Serve it up."

The table on a lower level of the deck certainly seemed fully prepared, with bread and butter, pickles, cheeses, bowls of potato salad and baked beans and three-bean salad. Heinrich hurried into the house and came out with an enormous copper platter that Melba wouldn't have been surprised was a mate to the cauldron he brought out every year for applesauce day. He expertly sliced the ribs into separate bones, filling the platter, set it on the table, and stepped over to the cooler to fetch their drinks. Melba silently apologized when the selections turned out to be multiple flavors of iced tea. No beer to be seen. She had the awful feeling she had been making off-target assumptions about Heinrich. As Cilla and Heinrich chatted about applesauce day and his experiments with using it in cooking, she wondered what exactly had changed him from this charming, eager-to-please host into the curmudgeon that he showed the world every day.

"You really should consider setting up a booth at the fall street festival and selling your applesauce," Melba said. "Have you considered making a cookbook with all the recipes you've come up with?"

Heinrich got that stunned look that made her think of robots that had been forced to reboot in a really cheesy science fiction movie. Then he grinned and shook his head.

"Don't go teasing me now, Melba. I know you're trying to be funny, but ... well, I know you don't mean to hurt—"

"She's serious," Cilla broke in. "You are, aren't you?"

"Would I have this many bones on my plate if I wasn't serious?" Melba gestured at her plate. Her face warmed. True, she had been eating while they talked, but she did feel something like a glutton, with as many bones as the two of them combined. "This is incredible. You ought to sell your barbecue sauce to Frenchy's. Or at least enter it in the rib burn-off in Strongsville next summer. And everyone loves your applesauce. The historic village sells out every year the same day it's made."

"Well ... yeah ... that's true." He shrugged. "Never thought about it being something serious. It's just something I do for fun. My granddad and me, that was something we did together. Miss that old man something awful, even now."

That turned the conversation to memories, and Melba was surprised to realize that yes, they did have quite a few shared memories, growing up in Cadburn Township. She had more memories of Heinrich's grandfather than she realized, mostly because she hadn't connected the quiet, shuffling, threadbare old man to Heinrich's three-piece-suit banker father. His grandfather would sit in the park and teach children to play chess and checkers. He made animals with knotted handkerchiefs and then told stories about the animals, somehow making them move without seeming to touch them, just sitting there on the table.

The three talked and laughed and sighed and reminisced over old friends, long gone, until the sun set and the air got chilly. It was October, after all. Heinrich excused himself to get up and light citronella torches. He shuffled a little more as he returned to the table.

"Guess I should have thought ahead and have you bring something to wrap up. Getting too cold to sit out here this late." He looked around the shadow-filled yard. "Been thinking about getting one of those Mexican clay pot stove thingamajigs. Or maybe one of those fire tables you see in the commercials. Could never see the sense in them, though." He shrugged and settled down at the table.

"It strikes me as something you'd want to share with friends," Melba said. "Although, I can see myself enjoying some quiet time, sitting in the dark, staring into the flames, just thinking. Or drifting."

"Yeah. Sounds kind of nice." The smile he gave her was a little sleepy, a little sad. Melba wondered if some of his usual crankiness came from being lonely. Funny, how she had never imagined a curmudgeon could feel lonely. She thought his solitude would be something he chose, deliberately driving people away.

Chapter Eighteen

The change in pace seemed to signal the end of the evening. Cilla got up first and scooped up several bowls of leftovers and asked where she should put them in his kitchen. Heinrich protested, but not very hard, that they were guests, and he'd do the cleanup. The three of them cleared the table in short order. Melba snagged a wet, soapy rag to wipe down the table, and returned to the kitchen to pause and watch the two of them work in silence, packing up leftovers, rinsing dishes, and putting them in the dishwasher. Somehow, she had never imagined Heinrich having a dishwasher. She would have seen him as someone who handwashed everything. If she had ever wondered about that part of his life.

"Gotta tell you ... you were right," Heinrich said, when the counters were cleared. He paused with the box of dishwasher detergent in his hand. Another shrug.

By this time, it had gone from awkwardly endearing to a little irritating. Melba tried to resist seeing it as an affectation, maybe even an act put on for them, and the real Heinrich was waiting to emerge as soon as they walked out the door.

"Right about what?" Cilla asked.

"You warned me not to talk about the murder. Thought I didn't, but ... well, maybe I let things drop. Everybody's talking about it. Lots of folks ask me, because they know we live on the same street. Kind of burns me, the folks who hope you did it. Maybe I got mad and let slip I had proof you didn't and ..." Another shrug. "Well, got a subpoena or summons or whatever from the Worters, asking me to turn in whatever evidence I had. How they knew it was video from my new security cameras, or I even had new security cameras ..."

Melba flinched. She glanced at Cilla. Fortunately, Heinrich was staring at the box in his hand and not at either of them.

A gusty sigh followed. "Anyway, I wanted you to see it first, seeing as you're being accused, and it just ain't right. Then I'll turn it over to the cops or whoever."

"That's very wise, Heinrich," Cilla said, and patted his arm. "I wish you hadn't ... Oh, this isn't going to come out right. I wish you hadn't felt the need to try to ... well, bribe us to come over. We had a lovely time, and I hope we can do this again. Regularly."

"Yeah?" His face lit up with wonder like some of the children Cilla read to at the library.

He insisted on giving them all the leftovers, and a jar of the barbecue sauce, and walked them home, even though it was only three doors down the street. Both cousins were quiet after the final farewells, and they stood on their front porch, watching Heinrich walk back to his little house.

"Just think of all the time we've wasted, when we could have been friends," Cilla murmured.

"Just think how different the world would be if he had asked you to the prom first. You broke his heart, Cilla."

"I did not!" She gasped and made to elbow Melba, because her hands were too full to allow her to slap her arm.

Grinning at each other, the cousins struggled to open their front doors without dropping their containers of leftovers. They said goodnight and went inside. Melba stowed the food and turned off the lights downstairs and climbed to the second floor in the dark. She changed for bed and curled up to read and smiled when Cilla thumped on the wall with the rhythm that meant, "good night, sleep tight." She rapped out the final sequence, "don't let the bedbugs bite," and finished her chapter before turning out the light.

Wednesday, October 12

Eden joined Allen Kenward at the video lab recommended by Carson Fletcher to view Heinrich's security videos. He had stopped by the police station at nearly midnight with a letter for Allen, containing the website and account screen name and password, where the security videos were automatically uploaded.

For once, Eden was grateful that Heinrich was a paranoid old cuss. He had three cameras focused on the creek, every possible angle to catch someone climbing up the creek to the back deck of Windows on the River, where a thief could try to break into the shops. Not just Heinrich's rare coins and gems shop, but everyone's. The cameras regularly panned, and the lenses adjusted for night vision and infrared, and the programming was sophisticated enough that tree branches moving in the wind didn't trigger the motion-activated tracking.

The video files had blank patches, from midnight until an hour after their group of seven had discovered the body in the shop.

Just like with the frame job, creating fake texts and emails between Ernie and the Tweeds, the erasure was a sloppy job. With permission from Chief Sunderson, Rufus and Eden got to work analyzing the files, and had to conclude that whoever had done the erasing knew how to do it, but either had never done it before, or was in a hurry. There were layers of digital information that with enough time and effort could be finessed to restore what at first glance appeared to be totally erased.

The problem was finding the time and someone with the skill to do it.

Eden considered her options. She discussed them with Chief Sunderson. Then with Rance Harcourt, retired FBI. Proving the innocence of the Tweeds wasn't that high a priority. However, identifying who had killed Ernie Benders, on the chance they might still be trying to retrieve something from the shop, raised the seriousness of the situation. Rance promised to make calls and pull strings, then warned Eden that if he couldn't get someone to get to work on the files in a few days, maybe she should ask Nick West to pull his own strings. Eden agreed, and then offered up some rare prayers that she wouldn't have to come to that.

Thursday, October 13

Eden's cell phone rang early enough that morning to make her curious, rather than irritated enough to ignore it.

"So, any idea who this tech semi-genius is who's giving you fits?"

For two seconds, she didn't know that warm baritone voice, but her gut instinct told her not to hang up even though her knee-jerk reaction was to do just that. Then she recognized Nick West's voice. She bit back a demand to know if he was outside on the street, watching for the first glimmer of light in the glass block windows of her office, so he knew it was safe to call her at the ungodly early hour of 5:53 am.

"In regard to what, exactly?" she said instead, and congratulated herself on responding quickly enough, smoothly enough, not to sound like he had stumped her.

"You know, Heinrich isn't as bad as his first impression might make you think. He's kind of sweet on Miss Cilla. That's why I was keeping an eye on him. That and realizing he added a couple cameras to his security system, both pointed across the creek."

"By any chance ... did you ... access the video of the murderer ... before the hacker got in there and erased it?" She kept her voice quiet, while her heart skittered, waking her up better than the glass of Mountain Dew hissing just a little too loudly next to her keyboard.

"Not the murderer, but somebody was trying to get into the shop, and he came close to running into the real murderer." Nick chuckled. "Thanks for not accusing me of doing the erasing."

"Any clue to who got into those files? And if whoever Heinrich caught on camera isn't the murderer, why did he need to cover it up?"

"My gut says there's more in the shop that hasn't been uncovered yet. Rumors say the late, unlamented Ernie was working with quite a few people. Chances are good some of them didn't know about the others. Someone was desperate to get his contraband out of there, trying to get in through the back door while Ernie was being set up by whoever came in the front door and shot him. Or, I could be wrong, and whoever came in the back door did the shooting. Front door man came out the back door, maybe ten minutes after back door man fled."

"Are you telling me this because you aren't going to turn over the pirated videos to the authorities?"

"Miss Cole, I am hurt by your lack of faith in my integrity," he drawled.

"Why are you helping at all?"

"Saundra likes the Tweed ladies. Anybody she cares about, I look out for too."

Eden took a deep breath, fighting back several sarcastic retorts. The funny thing was that she believed Nick.

"I'm giving you a heads up before I push the button and send the video over to Chief Sunderson. And I'm letting you know I've got friends with equipment three times more sensitive than what you used before to look inside the walls and floor. The last thing either of us wants is for someone to show up, looking for whatever is still hidden in that shop, and end up frightening or hurting the ladies."

"Thanks. It's appreciated."

"There. Was that so hard?" He let out a gusting sigh that made her think he had tried to laugh, but instead just sounded tired. "One of these days, you're going to like me."

"That's not as important as being able to trust you."

"True. But have I done anything to make you not trust me?"

"No." She could almost laugh as she made that admission. The word actually seemed to stick in her throat for a moment.

"Someday, we're going to look back on this rough patch in our friendship, and we're both going to laugh."

Eden thought of eight sarcastic responses to that, in the time it took to wash and dress and hurry down the street, in the hopes of meeting up with Captain Sunderson when she arrived for work.

Half an hour later, Eden, Allen and Captain Sunderson huddled in front of a computer screen. They watched from two different angles as a shadowy figure climbed up from the creek, using the stairs by the Apple Street bridge. He walked along the steep slope behind the shops, then climbed up over the side of the parking deck. The figure had a backpack and dropped it down out of sight behind the deck wall. It most likely contained tools, which the figure used on the lock on the back door.

Light flashed, through the window panels near the roof. The figure by the door staggered backward.

"Gunshot," Allen said.

"Pretty close to the estimate of time of death," Chief Sunderson said, pointing at the time stamp in the lower right corner of both video screens.

A second flash followed. The figure at the door gathered up his backpack and half-fell, half-vaulted over the parking deck wall. Eden muffled a chuckle of satisfaction as he tripped and fell, nearly doing a somersault as he skidded down the slope to the bed of the creek.

"I'm going back to the creek, see if we got lucky and he dropped anything when he fell." Allen closed his eyes and let out a long sigh.

Eden was about to ask him what was wrong, then she heard it. A rumble of thunder. No sound of rain yet, but her weather app had predicted a day full of rain.

"Need help?" she asked. She would prefer to spend the morning snug in her office, listening to the rain drumming on the glass block windows, and making regular trips down to Book & Mug for deluxe peppermint hot chocolate.

"Appreciate it." He looked to Sunderson.

"Better get to it," the police chief said. "I've got to think of how to thank West for his help and impress on him that the ends don't always justify the means."

Eden thought about that as she and Allen headed out. Maybe Captain Sunderson had the messier job.

They didn't find anything. There had been rain in the last week, and some boys had been playing in the creek and on the slopes, getting muddy and shouting, with some kind of game that sounded like a combination of army maneuvers and acting out a fantasy adventure show. If the man in the video had dropped anything, it had either been smashed down into the mud and leaves and other forest debris, or the boys had picked it up and didn't know what they had found.

Friday, October 14

Melba and Cilla made sure they were busy all day Friday, and far away from their shop and the men who responded to Nick's call to action. The shades had been pulled down and a tarp hung against the door so no one could look in. The owners of the shops on either side of them reported sounds like wood being pulled up and drills or saws, and heavy objects being dropped. Everything had been cleared with Tracy. She related later that Nick promised her the floor would be filled in to ensure no one could access the spaces Ernie had created for what was essentially a mail drop arrangement for all sorts of illegal activities and items. In hindsight, losing his lease and Tracy's prompt action in changing the locks had sealed his doom. If the criminal element he was working with couldn't get into the shop in the middle of the night and retrieve their property, then someone was going to pay for that loss.

An unfamiliar number appeared on Cilla's phone as they were getting in Melba's car to head to the library for after-school storytime. Cilla glanced at her phone and showed the screen to Melba. She shook her head, that she didn't recognize the number. Cilla silenced the ringtone. They were halfway down Overlook before her phone pinged to alert her to a voicemail message.

"That's one determined telemarketer," Melba said.

"One of these days, I'd like to get one of them to admit there is no such person as Rachel, or maybe I should join those class action lawsuits they keep talking about to stop those people from calling." Cilla tapped through her phone to call up the message.

"Oh, don't listen. Just delete it." Melba chuckled and flipped the windshield wipers from intermittent to low, as the spatters of drops turned into actual rain.

Charlotte's voice came through loud and shrill, just Cilla's name, the first syllable elongated, before she stopped the message.

"Well, it's a local number, so she's probably calling from her hotel," Melba said.

"Don't know, don't care." Cilla put her phone back in her purse.

The gray skies churned three shades darker by the time they reached the library parking lot. Rain slammed down. Melba looked with longing at the handicapped parking spaces right in front of the door. Yes, other elderly women, and men for that matter, cheated and got handicapped parking tags when they were perfectly capable of walking to the door from at least three rows away, but she wasn't ready to take that step. Being old wasn't an excuse for depriving people who truly, legally needed those spots. Even if it was pouring rain. And her umbrella was in the trunk, not the back seat.

Melba sighted an empty spot directly in front of the doors, just one row back. With some satisfaction, she pulled in, parked, and turned off the engine. Cilla pulled her umbrella out of her suitcase-sized purse.

"You were never a Girl Scout," she said, guessing what smart remark put that twinkle in her cousin's eyes. Cilla pouted for about two seconds, then chuckled as she hit the latch for the door and prepared to push the release button on the umbrella, pointing it into the opening.

Melba gathered up Cilla's purse and her own and waited for her cousin to hurry around the car to her door. They huddled together under the umbrella and took small, careful, slow steps, to avoid splashing the rising water. She shuddered, thinking of that poor Fontaine boy who had been dropped off the Apple Street bridge. If Becca hadn't seen him, he might have been washed away by the downpour that hit that day.

"Are you going to delete that message, or just save it for evidence for the police when they find her dead and we're the first suspects?" she asked, to point her thoughts elsewhere.

"Don't tempt me." Cilla sighed as they reached the covered entryway, and they paused so she could take down her umbrella. "Please don't lecture me like Granny and my parents used to, that I need to feel sorry for Charlotte and God wants me to be nicer to her. Being nice hasn't done any good. I should have royally hacked her off years ago, so she'd leave me alone." She punctuated her words by shaking the rain out of the umbrella.

As if in response, Cilla's phone chattered, signaling a text. She checked it once they were inside the library. Charlotte again.

Saundra hurried over to meet them and guide them to the break room to offer them hot chocolate and paper towels to dry off their shoes. They laughed together over the sudden downpour, and the fear that no children would show up at all. Melba's phone chattered at her with an incoming text. By mistake, she didn't check the number before she looked at the message. She fully expected it to be one of those obnoxious realtors asking if she was ready to sell her parents' home. It had been sold twenty-four years ago, but the database the vultures used was out of date and they thought Melba still had it in her name. No matter how many numbers she blocked or how many times she responded with "Wrong number, leave me alone," or "Stop harassing me," they kept calling. She had given up responding politely with, "I don't own that property," years ago.

> *What's wrong with Cilla? Have her come get me. I'm down at the park without a car and it's raining.*

"Yes, that's Charlotte's number," Cilla said, when she showed it to her.

"How did she get my number? You wouldn't give it to her."

"Of course not."

Melba chuckled, even knowing she was being cruel. "Which park did she go to? One without any shelter?" She tucked her phone in her purse and put it in Mrs. Tinderbeck's office for safekeeping.

"I don't care if I'm being mean. Serves her right for going out in this weather without a car or even an umbrella." Cilla frowned. "Although, come to think of it, that doesn't sound like Charlotte at all. I mean, going walking, period."

Melba sighed when she saw Cilla step back into the office to retrieve her phone. "What are you doing?"

"Telling her she has to wait, we're going to be busy for the next hour-and-a-half. And asking what park she went to." Cilla smiled sweetly and tapped away with her thumbs. She had gotten the knack of that a lot faster than Melba, considering they both refused to text. Sometimes, despite their wishes, it was necessary. The phone blipped, signaling the text had been sent, and she frowned.

"What?"

"I didn't catch it, but I told her half an hour, not hour-and-a-half." She turned her phone so Melba could see the screen.

Busy. Can't leave for ½ hours. Which park?

"Ready, ladies?" Saundra beckoned for them to follow her.

Cilla sighed and tucked her phone back into her purse, then pulled the office door closed behind her. Melba took a deep breath, wiped her hands on her sweater and said a quick prayer that she wouldn't be fumble-tongued today. She could hold her own with grumps, pushy telemarketers, and business supply salesmen who insisted she needed all sorts of supplies for the shop that she most certainly did not need or want or would use in ten years. Facing a gaggle of kindergarteners through third-graders at storytime? That was a little frightening. Children asked the most amazing, amusing, and sometimes embarrassing questions. She adored them. She just lived in dread of looking like an idiot in their eyes. Cilla was the one who had the magic touch when it came to children, and she would be the voice and face of Brighten Your Corner when they offered candle-making classes.

Chapter Nineteen

Only six children showed up for storytime, and they were all children Melba knew from church and Vacation Bible School when she and Cilla had helped with the crafts tent. Two little boys immediately latched onto Melba's hands, wanting to sit with her. This wouldn't be so bad after all.

Saundra introduced the cousins to the children, who immediately laughed and said they knew who they were, and asked if they were going to do crafts.

"Maybe next time," Cilla said. "It depends on the story we'll be reading to you. Or, you know what? Miss Melba and I are opening up a candle shop by the end of the month. We're going to have classes where you can make candles. Would you like to do that?"

The two boys clutching at Melba didn't seem so sure they liked the idea, but the other four let out excited cheers. That earned smiles and some laughter from their mothers or older siblings, who were sitting to the side and observing or working on what looked like homework or crocheting. Saundra brought over a stack of books and Melba settled down in the middle of the children on the floor pillows, while Cilla looked through the stack of books.

"Oh, this is a good one. I remember this from when I was little." She held up *Mike Mulligan and His Steam Shovel*. "Should I start with this one?" Cilla pretended great shock and disappointment when five of the children said they didn't know that book. The little boy on Melba's right bounced up and down on his pillow declaring it was his favorite.

~~~~~

"Bingo bango," Rufus said. His fingers went into overdrive on his keyboard.

"What?" Eden half-raised from her seat and looked around the curve of the workstation to where his wheelchair sat in front of three monitors.

"That same black sedan the spook's people spotted at the shop."

The monitors flashed between the different cameras in the Tweeds' security system, faster than Eden could register the scenes. She grinned. Rufus had picked up Troy's nickname for Nick.

"What's he doing?"

"Besides aiming some interesting little contraption that I can't see clearly but is sending out some signals trying to shut off the alarm system?" Rufus growled out something that was probably Italian, from his father's side of the family. "Jerk's wearing a hoodie, and with the clouds and overcast and ... can't get a good look at his face. It's a rental. Taking a little time getting the company to cough up identification on the guy."

"If he's one of Ernie's old friends, chances are the credit card and ID are fakes, anyway," Eden said. "Especially if he knows there's security to overcome here. What does he want with the Tweeds?"

"Well, all that dirt we've been digging up on that Charlotte chick is pretty interesting and getting kind of nasty. She owes a lot of people a lot of money. She's been running scams for years, trying to get other people to take the fall. Catching up with her, probably. If she's been telling everyone the Tweeds are her partners, someone might figure they're more likely to pay up than she is." He snorted, his fingers never stopping their rapid-fire dance on the keyboard.

"What?"

"The spook sure has some interesting connections. Any chance of getting one of his friends to take Charlotte and drop her in a really deep hole?"

"Won't hurt to ask." Eden turned enough to look at him, just as he was looking over his shoulder at her. They exchanged guilty grins, then both went back to work. She opened up a new screen in her email and sent a message to Nick. She reported what Rufus had detected, linked to the video collected on his monitors, added an update on what was being done to stop that interesting high-tech gizmo from interfering with the security system, and asked if Nick had any friends who could handle a "necessary disposal job."

He responded ten seconds later with several different grimacing smiling emojis. Nothing more.

She sighed but smiled anyway. That was the Nick West she was coming to know, much against her will.

In the next twenty minutes, the driver of the black sedan moved his car to three different positions, trying different angles to aim his scrambling beam at the right place to hijack the security system. Finally, he drove away. Eden was slightly impressed, and a little worried, to discover when she got into the rental company's files that the credit card and identification had been erased. Chances were good, with hacking skills like that, the guy in the hoodie hadn't needed to use fake ID. What were the chances the security system at the rental office caught that information on camera? And what would it take to access those files? Preferably without asking Nick for more help.

On a hunch, she contacted Carson Fletcher, who agreed with her idea and took it on himself to notify local law enforcement to look for the car. Chances were good it would be abandoned, not turned in to the rental company at the end of the day.

~~~~~

Storytime took nearly two hours, by the time the children gave goodbye hugs and a long list of the stories they wanted to read next time. Then their parents and older sisters had to say something, and there were the expected questions about the shop, asking about the rumors of the trouble, what was going on inside today, and when classes could start. Two mothers thought candles would be good Christmas presents for grandparents and teachers.

Melba hadn't thought of that, but Cilla handled those questions with ease and implied that yes, they already had plans in the works for special designs just for the holidays. The moment they got their purses from Mrs. Tinderbeck's office, Melba reached for her phone to Google Christmas candle molds. She stopped short, staring at the notifications for six new texts.

"Charlotte has been pestering me. I don't even want to know what she's been accusing me of. Probably holding you prisoner and keeping you from getting to your phone." Melba looked up to see Cilla frowning at her own phone. "How many times did she call you?"

"Just once more, then everything is texts. That just isn't like Charlotte."

"She does like to talk."

That got an eye roll from Cilla. Sighing in unison, they headed for the break room to get their jackets and umbrella. Leave it to Charlotte to take all the air out of their good spirits after what had been a delightful afternoon.

Twila's nasal tones buzzed across the library. Honestly, didn't that woman know what a library voice was? Melba looked over to the circulation desk, pitying whoever had earned the woman's wrath today, and saw Ted Shrieve. In uniform. Looking very somber as he searched the library. Their gazes met. He grimaced and raised a hand, beckoning for her to stay there. Twila kept talking as Ted walked away. She ended on a shrill "hmph!" and snatched up the ringing phone.

"Oh, Teddy, why do you always get stuck with the bad news for us?" Cilla reached out to pat his arm. "Now what happened?"

"Outside," he said, and glanced over his shoulder at Twila. No more needed to be said.

Saundra retrieved her jacket and followed them. Ted led them to a little picnic shelter tucked behind the library. Melba hadn't even known it was there, and guessed it was for library employees to use on their breaks.

"The short version," Ted said, staying standing when the women settled at the table, "is that Charlotte was attacked in the park just past the skate and scooter rental shack. Jim Russo found her less than an hour ago.

Unconscious. Pretty nasty cuts and bruises. Someone went to town on her with a couple of those baseball bats they keep out back of the shack, for anyone to use."

"Wasn't anyone at the shack to see it?" Melba reached for Cilla's hand, aching at the wide-eyed shock and guilt driving the color from her cousin's face.

"They shut down during the day on weekdays, during the school year. Only open evenings and weekends." He shrugged and took a deep breath. From the way he couldn't meet their eyes, clearly the bad news hadn't been spoken yet.

"What else?" Saundra reached across the table to clasp Melba's other hand, and Cilla's.

"She came to about twenty minutes ago, while the EMTs were getting ready to lift her into the truck. Full-on panic mode." He looked around, everywhere but at them. His mouth pursed like the words waiting there tasted bad. He took a deep breath. "She claims you did it, Melba."

"Never!" Cilla cried. Her hand tightened on Melba's to the point of threatening to crack bones.

"They've been here more than two hours," Saundra hurried to say. "When did the attack take place?"

Ted shrugged. "Have to wait for the doctors to finish with her, but Jim did say he saw her walking around by the shack when he went past on his rounds, and he keeps a pretty regular schedule. I'll call him. Should clear you ladies right away." He stepped away, pulling his phone out of his pocket.

"Oh," Cilla said, straightening. "We have proof. At least, proof when she was still—when she wasn't hurt yet. All those texts, and that phone call. Charlotte called and texted us, wanting a ride. But it still doesn't make any sense she'd go to the park without her car."

"Show me," Saundra said. "No, wait. Let me call Eden. She has a whole lot more experience in this, and we need to be very careful." She gave them an encouraging little smile and got up to hurry back into the library.

"Maybe we should talk to Bill Worter?" Melba said.

"Please, Lord, don't make us need a lawyer," Cilla whispered.

Saundra came back, talking on the phone with Eden, while Ted was making more phone calls. He had gotten through to Jim, who was helping someone who had gotten stuck in the mud and would call as soon as he was free. It was nearly impossible to keep from overhearing him talking to Captain Sunderson, then a nurse in the emergency room, requesting updates.

"Jim pulls into the parking lot by the rental shack around 2:45 every day," Ted announced, coming back to the table. "He confirms he saw

Charlotte pacing back and forth, and asked if she needed help." He grimaced. "She snapped at him, told him to mind his own business, and then chewed him out because the door was closed. She got offended when he asked if she wanted to rent skates or scooters. From there he takes the long loop through the park, so he didn't come back for nearly an hour. When he did, he found her lying out on the edge of the creek, with the baseball bats all in the water."

"Kind of convenient," Eden said, startling them. Melba hadn't seen her approaching, so intent on what Ted was saying. "Hard to get fingerprints from wet wood."

"Why would she lie and say we attacked her?" Cilla said.

"She didn't accuse you. She accused me." Melba shrugged. "Charlotte has always tried to separate us, keep you all to herself."

"Kind of extreme," Saundra said. "Beating up on herself to frame you."

"Yes, well, Charlotte is ..." Cilla looked up at Ted. "You've seen enough of her to know what she's like."

Ted nodded, his face wrinkling with distaste.

Eden and Ted studied the messages on the cousins' phones, noting the times they came in, ending with Charlotte's voicemails to Cilla. Melba shivered at the last one, sensing something odd in the woman's voice. She was too sweet, she decided. Too conciliatory. For one thing, Charlotte never admitted she was wrong, never asked for forgiveness, yet she did both, before asking Cilla to bring Melba and meet her in the park.

After Cilla texted her that they would meet her in half an hour, Charlotte alternated with texting her and Melba. She demanded Melba leave Cilla behind, they needed to settle their problem in private. Then she switched to Cilla, begging her to see reason, begging her to admit that Melba had always "had it in" for her.

At the half hour mark, Charlotte demanded to know why they hadn't come for her. Five minutes later, she devolved to, "Where are you?" and "How can you be so mean to me?"

At the forty-five-minute mark, the texts stopped.

That coincided with the estimated time of the attack. Charlotte couldn't have remained unconscious for very long with the rain in her face. She was moaning and starting to move her arms and legs when the park ranger found her.

"I'd say you two are cleared completely, just on this evidence," Ted said. "But ..."

"But Charlotte is accusing Melba," Eden said, filling in what he was reluctant to say.

~~~~~

By nine that evening, they had a few answers, but those led to more questions.

Charlotte reacted badly to the sedative they gave her for her nerves, combining with the anesthetic when they sewed up several small cuts and the pain killer for her throbbing headache. She settled into a babbling state, alternating between giggles and baby talk and begging the nurses to keep "him" out of the room.

She wouldn't say who "he" was, but he had given her Melba's number and had her send all those texts to bring Melba down to the park. He got angry with her, telling her she was useless and a failure. She protested that it wasn't her fault, he got the wrong one, the key was in the right one. She went into hysterics when someone asked her what "the wrong one" was, and asked what key she was talking about.

After she told the man he got the wrong one, he had hit her with the baseball bats. Again and again. When one broke, he pulled out another. And he told her to blame it all on Melba, or he would come back and make sure she never woke up.

Repeatedly asking her who "he" was, from the doctor, the nurses, and then Allen Kenward, drove Charlotte into hysterics. Further sedation sent her into incoherent babbling. She was clearly too afraid to give them the truth.

Saturday, October 15

Allen Kenward knocked on Melba's door at the headachy hour of 6:30 that morning. She had one eye open and was clutching her robe around herself, and vowing she would never again stay up until nearly 2am, drinking hot chocolate and washing down three different flavors of Oreos while binging the Thin Man DVDs.

The evening started with Saundra inviting the cousins to stay at her apartment, but Cilla had refused. She felt that would be bowing to whoever was apparently targeting them. They asked her to come for the evening instead. Then Eden, Kai, and Troy had come over with provisions for a picnic, full of all sorts of salads and treats, finger food and fancy cheeses, pickles and olives and decadent pastry. Eden claimed she wanted to do some updates to the security system, but Melba knew there was more to it than that. She was perfectly happy to let Eden keep her secrets and trusted her to tell them when the situation got truly serious. Not knowing was a relief lately.

They had declared Friday as girls' night, and Eden had stayed for the first three movies, before calling it quits. Saundra stayed, which was a comfort, and was right that moment sleeping in Cilla's guest room, since the labyrinth chest was in Melba's guest room. She didn't have a bed in there, anyway.

Seeing Allen standing on her porch in the rainy gloom helped Melba get her other eye open. Amazing, what adrenaline could do to clear the sugar fog from her brain.

"Now what's happened?" Her voice cracked. She coughed to clear her throat. "Sorry, Allen. I'm still half asleep."

"Totally understandable." He tipped his head toward the other half of the duplex. "Mind waking Cilla? She needs to hear this, too."

"That bad?" She stepped back and gestured for him to come in. "Coffee?" She led the way to the kitchen, called Cilla's phone, only letting it ring twice, hung up, rang twice again, and then got the coffeemaker going. She gave herself two minutes to get a response to their standard "sorry to bother you" signal. Then she would go in and upstairs and wake her. After pouring water into the reservoir, she gestured for Allen to take a seat at the kitchen table, then dug into the freezer for the box of toaster pastries. Cilla responded with a single ring. Her signal she was on her way. The first batch was ready to pop by the time Saundra and Cilla joined them.

"What happened? Is Charlotte all right?" Cilla sniffed and changed course, heading for the toaster.

Melba cocked an eyebrow at her. Cilla chuckled but didn't say anything. It was a long-standing, teasing argument. Melba had a six-slice toaster, and Cilla regularly asked nobody in particular why she needed more than four slots. They were two old women who couldn't eat more than two slices at a sitting, so why need to toast more?

"Interesting fallout from yesterday. Seems Charlotte wasn't playing fair with her partner. Yeah." Allen nodded. "It was a partnership. She was supposed to get you out to the park, probably to get you away from the house. Helen reported that about ten minutes after she saw you pull out of the driveway, a man parked across the street and just sat there, watching your house. Didn't do anything. Just watched. Considering what happened, I'm thinking he was waiting for you to leave, to go meet Charlotte. But you were already gone." He gave them a grim smile.

"How long did he sit there?" Saundra asked.

"According to Helen, more than half an hour. It fits the tentative schedule we put together from eyewitnesses and the texts you received. He drove to the rental shack and apparently parked to hide and watch and wait for you to show up. We found some deep tire tracks in that low, muddy patch beyond the trees on the far end of the parking lot. When you still didn't show up when your text said you would, he switched to plan B, where he dragged her over to the creek and went at her with the baseball bats."

"He wanted us out of the house," Melba said, thinking aloud. It made sense. She caught her breath. "To get at the labyrinth chest? We've been thinking all this time that someone broke into our shop for whatever Ernie hid, but what if it's been the chest the whole time? What if someone else hid something in it over the years, and they came back for it?"

"No way of knowing until we find him. Charlotte's not talking, because she can't. Hysterics, mostly, but she's been in so much pain, the doctors went back and found some cracks in her jaw." Allen held up his hand to stop Cilla's next question. "This is the part where it gets really interesting. We had an attempted break-in at Charlotte's hotel room."

"I don't suppose the hotel had security cameras?" Melba said.

Allen nodded but didn't seem very happy about that.

"What's wrong? You didn't get a clear image? He was wearing a hat, something that hid his face? He knew where the cameras were, so he kept his back to the cameras?" Saundra guessed.

Allen scrubbed his face with both hands, then sat back in the kitchen chair. "That coffee ready?"

"What's wrong, Allen? Who is it?" Cilla said.

"Oh, no," Melba whispered, as the answer slapped her between the eyes. Who had a good reason to want to get at the labyrinth chest, didn't like Charlotte at all, and had technical know-how when it came to security? "What did he do?"

"Had some handy little gizmo to override the electronic locks. The big-ticket hotels run into people using those things a couple times a week. Especially when there are electronics shows in town. The geeks have to show off, and they end up messing up the entire security system of the hotel, sometimes, going overboard when they just want to get into one room. This hotel has some experimental system that alerts them when someone tries to play games with the key card system, and activates some automatic responses, to stall the would-be burglar until security can get to the room. Plus, they had a double alarm go off. Someone shut down the security cameras. They got the cameras up pretty fast, because again, they've had this trouble before, and got a couple good pictures of the guy before he ran for it."

"Who?" Cilla said.

Chapter Twenty

"David?" Melba whispered. That disappointed look Allen wore made sense now. She wished she had been wrong. Those two had been summer friends since they got dumped into the wading pool by the gazebo when they were toddlers.

Cilla inhaled a sharp little gasp and pressed a hand over her heart.

"Have you caught up with him?" Saundra asked.

"The guy's got alibis. We're working on unraveling them, but until then, he's in the clear."

"Do you think he'll try to get in again?" Cilla said. "What does he want?"

"David brought up the treasure hunt," Melba said, thinking aloud as an idea unraveled in her head. "I don't know what good he thinks it will do him after all these years."

"What good will it do him to get at the chest, if he can't get it open?"

"I want to know what he was doing working with Charlotte," Saundra said. "Something just doesn't add up."

"That's an understatement," Melba said, her voice cracking with a chuckle. "Although ..." She leaned back in her chair, feeling a little dizzy as her brain seemed to spin, trying to put disparate pieces together. "The last time we talked, he was being nice to Charlotte. He asked me to give her the pillow." She caught the confused looks Allen and Saundra gave her. "Every time Charlotte shows up, she tries to steal an embroidered pillow Granny made. That specific one. She claims it has sentimental value. It's really rather annoying, how intent she is on having it. And yes, we're rather childish, taking such joy in frustrating her every time. We hide it whenever she shows up."

"But you're right, it seems odd David would turn around and ask you to give it to her," Cilla said.

"What's so special about the pillow that she wanted it?" Saundra asked.

Both women shrugged. "Other than that she kept taking it without permission, and we always took it back?" Cilla added.

"Did you give him the pillow?" Allen said.

"Of course not," Melba said. "I gave him another dusty old one. I can't even remember who made it. I thought it would be rather funny, Charlotte's reaction when he handed her the pillow and she realized it was the wrong one."

"Wait," Saundra said, holding out a hand. "She was babbling about how he got the wrong one ... the wrong pillow?"

"Why would David pound her senseless arguing over the wrong pillow?" Allen said, speaking slowly, as if he needed to test the idea aloud.

"What's so special about the pillow? Other than Charlotte wanted it so badly," Saundra hurried to add. "Is it some special design?"

"Well, it's ..." Cilla caught her breath. Her eyes got wide as she turned to Melba. "It's a keepsake pillow."

"Keep-safe," Melba corrected her.

"Whatever. Granny had enough for all us girls. She used to hide treats in the pillows, or clues to a new treasure hunt. She'd leave the pillows on our beds when we came for sleepovers."

"Treasure hunt." Melba could barely whisper the words.

"Where's the pillow?" Saundra said.

Melba's legs shook as she led them upstairs to her spare bedroom. Her hands shook just as much when she pulled open the accordion door and shoved aside the hangars full of tablecloths and winter clothes, then went on her knees to reach into the little alcove where she had shoved the milk crate with Cilla's paperwork. And the heart pillow.

The little pocket that used to hold treats and slips of paper had been sewed shut with thread that almost matched the colors of the original embroidery. Melba squeezed the pillow as Cilla rummaged in her desk for scissors. Her heart skipped a few beats when she felt the hard, narrow object that filled the pocket, maybe three inches long and an inch wide.

"The sewing is too neat for Charlotte. She hated sewing. Always got vicious when we invited her to join us in crafts." Melba took a deep breath and met Cilla's gaze when she turned back to her with the scissors. "I'll just bet you anything, Granny put the key in here, after Charlotte got caught messing with the chest the last time. And I'll just bet you she got hold of the list of clues for that last treasure hunt, and decided she'd punish us all for cutting her out, and she's been hunting for the chest all these years."

"And she talked David into helping her?" Cilla shook her head. "That still doesn't make any sense."

"Maybe David knows what the treasure is, and it's still valuable after all these years? Maybe he offered to cut Charlotte in if she helped him?" Saundra offered.

The two cousins locked gazes.

"That makes a lot more sense," Cilla said, nodding.

Melba carefully snipped the stitches and turned the pillow upside down, gently shaking it. A thin, dark object slid out. Allen snatched and caught it just before it hit the floor. He grinned and held out his open hand.

The key looked old, a very simple design. Dark metal, probably tarnished from age, with several tabs poking up from a thin rod.

"Well, it looks like it could be old enough," Saundra said. "It looks more like a decoration for a steam punk costume. A skeleton key."

"Makes you wonder what family skeletons are about to fall out of the closet," Cilla murmured. She glanced at Melba, nodded, pressed her lips flat, then reached to take the key from Allen's hand. "Shall we?"

Half an hour later, they had pulled out every drawer of the labyrinth chest as far as it would go, and even, with Allen's help, tipped the chest back against the wall, to look underneath it. No keyhole. Melba was ready to sit down and cry, or maybe laugh. She wasn't sure what that pressure in her chest and the back of her head threatened to turn into. The doorbell rang, at the same time someone pounded on the back porch door. Melba went to the back, and Saundra went to the front.

Nick was at the back door. He signaled Melba to listen, and she heard Eden's voice coming from the front door.

"Your friend across the street got worried," Nick explained, as Eden and Saundra joined them in the doorway between the kitchen and living room. "She saw some character sneaking around in the bushes just before dawn and was going to call me when the police showed up. She didn't call, until he was here long enough to make her worried again."

"Why would she call you?" Saundra asked.

"I asked her to," he said with a shrug and that glint of mischief in his eyes that reminded Melba so very much of Kai and Troy.

Come to think of it, there was a lot about Nick that reminded her of Kai, Troy, and Eden, when they were having fun, getting creative. Especially when they were standing against the arrogant and nasty element in Cadburn, such as former Trustee Roger Cadburn and his cronies.

"Yeah," Allen said, reaching the bottom of the stairs. "Should have thought of that. I guess we got a little caught up in finally solving the mystery."

"Solve it how?" Eden said.

Allen made his farewells. He was on duty, after all. Melba led the way to the guest bedroom while explaining this new development.

"Maybe it's not a genuine Duchene after all?" Cilla said on a sigh.

"Oh, it is," Eden said. "I did enough research and backtracked the serial numbers burned into the wood on the bottom side." She stepped over to the windowsill where the key sat. "The keyhole is hidden in plain sight, and the key is ... the key," she said with a shrug. She picked it up and held it up, comparing it to the dark metal fittings decorating the front of the chest.

Nick sat on the edge of the steamer trunk Melba used as a table when her desk was too crowded. He crossed his arms and watched through half-hooded eyes. He waited until Eden had studied all the hardware on the front before saying, "Isn't anybody concerned about the guy skulking around in the dark?"

"We know it's David," Cilla said, never taking her gaze off Eden.

"Isn't anyone worried he's going to keep coming back and keep trying, until he gets whatever he thinks is inside?"

"Of course we're worried." Saundra turned to face him and crossed her arms. "What are you suggesting?"

"Nothing yet. Except that this guy needs to be trapped, good and solid, with evidence and witnesses to lock him up tight, like the *a'nogash* he is."

Eden flinched, and her head snapped around to stare at him a moment. Nick's smirk got a little bigger. Saundra frowned, looking back and forth between the two of them several times, then shook her head.

"What kind of trap?" she said, as Eden moved to study the decorative hardware on the right side of the chest, working her way up from the bottom.

"Well, it seems to me this Charlotte was set up to trap you two. Maybe all three of you were supposed to end up on the wrong end of a baseball bat, and land in the creek. Why don't we return the favor?"

"Make Charlotte the bait to catch David?" Melba offered. Mostly because the other option, of taking a baseball bat to David, was just a little too attractive right now. That frightened her. Granted, her headache from all that sugar and fat was taking its own good time to fade away, but doggone it, David had been raised better than that. He was a Tweed. Granted, his father had been a selfish rabble rouser when he was younger, but he had reformed. David had seemed to reform from the conniving ways of his youth. Perhaps in this instance, appearances were deceiving.

He deserved a taste of his own medicine. A strong enough taste to cure him once and for all.

"Yeah, bait." Nick nodded at Eden. "Whatever happens today, we keep it secret that you have the key. You get another key that looks old enough to pass for it but won't open the chest."

"If we get it open at all," Eden muttered, and grunted softly as she got up off her knees, to study the hardware halfway up the chest.

"Oh," Cilla said. "We can give Charlotte the pillow, as a get-well gift. And put the fake key in it. But we have to make sure David knows we gave her the right heart this time."

"If she's as desperate for money as all my research says, she's stupid enough to call him and let him know she has it," Eden said.

"No." Melba could almost laugh. "Charlotte is vindictive enough to try to get at the chest and keep the treasure for herself."

"Don't you think we should find what the treasure is, whatever is hidden in the chest, before we set up a trap and risk either of them getting their hands on it?" Eden frowned and stepped back and tipped her head to the left.

"What?" Melba said. Eden studied the chest with an intensity that could have bored a hole through all that old wood and hardware.

"What do you think?" She held up the key, the scrollwork end on the right and the teeth pointing down on the left.

Saundra stepped up and looked between the key and a design of keys embossed in four parallel lines, two-thirds of the way up the side of the chest. She nodded and reached out to touch one of the keys.

"This one is different." She stepped back, out of the way so everyone could see.

Eden slid her nail under the embossed key Saundra had touched. She frowned and ran her nail all around the edge. A soft crack whispered through the air, and Melba nearly laughed, realizing they were all holding their breaths. The metal rectangle popped out of the space and tumbled to the floor, hitting the carpet with an anti-climactic lack of sound.

In the spot where the piece of metal had been, Melba saw the dark hole. Even from five steps away, it looked the right size to fit the key, which Eden now held out to her and Cilla.

"Who wants to do the honors?"

Melba nudged Cilla, who nudged her at the same time. Their elbows hit at just the right angle to send a tingle-jolt up her arm. They laughed and caught at each other's hand.

"You do it," Cilla said, nodding to the younger woman.

Eden's hand was steady as she reached out to insert the key in the keyhole. She took a deep breath, glanced over her shoulder at Melba and Cilla, nodded, then slowly turned the key.

It didn't want to turn at first. That much was obvious. Well, of course, how many years had it been sitting there, hidden and unused? How bad were the conditions in the various places where it had been stored, so the wood got damp and swelled and dried out and warped, and maybe dust or grime got into the keyhole, into the mechanism?

The dull click as the key turned sounded loud in the quiet room.

A creak. A few snapping noises, like wood unsticking where it was meant to come apart but had fused over the years. Melba knew that sound well, from the dropleaf table she hadn't had to open since she moved into the duplex, until that yard sale she and Cilla held for the youth group at church, six years later.

"Will you look at that?" Cilla murmured, as the top of the chest lifted up like a lid, pivoting back on hinges that squeaked and protested.

Eden went up on her toes to look inside. She grinned over her shoulder at Melba and Cilla. "Shall I? Or do you want to?"

"For heaven's sake, get it over with!" Cilla trilled a nervous giggle.

The accordion envelope crinkled and split along multiple folds as Eden slowly, carefully lifted it out. Nick got up off the trunk, clearing the only flat surface in the room large enough to take it. Dust and shreds of paper trailed behind Eden as she crossed the room and set it down on the trunk lid. More pops and creaks drew everyone's attention back to the chest.

Nothing was visible. Saundra hurried to the other side. She let out a little gasping laugh and bent down out of sight. When she stood up again and rejoined them, she held out a limp, dusty Raggedy Andy.

Melba pressed a hand over her mouth and held out her other hand. She blinked away tears she blamed on the little cloud of dust that rose up as she clutched the doll barely larger than her hand.

"Oh, that Charlotte," Cilla snapped. "I knew she was lying. She couldn't keep her story straight. First she tossed him in the creek, then in the incinerator in the cellar."

Melba raised the old doll to her lips to kiss, then thought better of it and held him out at arm's length, shaking more dust off him.

One leg fell off, and strands of faded red yarn followed. She laughed, because the only other alternative was to burst into tears, and really, crying over a doll she hadn't thought about in decades was ridiculous. Still, she remembered the sniping and teasing for nearly a week before Andy vanished, and Granny Tweed caught Charlotte cutting Anne into little pieces. Charlotte had targeted the dolls from the moment she arrived that fall. She had insisted that Melba should be nice and give her a welcome present. Melba's response that she wasn't allowed to tell lies and Charlotte wasn't welcome had started a long chain of nasty pranks and demands and taunting, until Charlotte was banned from Granny's house and Cilla had to stay home with her, to keep her company. They had been eight and nine years old that fall.

"Somehow, this isn't the treasure hunt I was hoping for." Melba shook her head, wishing she could as easily dislodge the memories as the dust.

Nothing else came out of the other compartments that now opened easily. With some trepidation, they turned to the accordion folder. Saundra suggested they use gloves, to keep skin oils off the old, probably fragile papers. Depending on how old they were, the acid content might make them prone to breaking or staining. They moved to the kitchen, where there was more light. Cilla ran downstairs to get one of the vinyl tablecloths, to protect the table and contain the dust. Since she had some practice handling old books, Saundra was given the task of removing the first thin bundle of papers. Eden let out a "huh" that warned Melba this was going to be interesting.

"Looks like legal documents." Eden grinned and glanced around the group sitting several steps back from the table. "Financial documents."

An hour later, after Eden snapped pictures of the bundles of what looked like stocks and bonds and other documents pertaining to corporations Melba had never heard of, they agreed to bring in legal help. Eden called Lisa Pascal for advice. Lisa passed them on to her boss, Bill Worter. He handled all sorts of investment and legal financial matters for the firm. The speed with which he showed up at the duplex after Eden emailed the photos to him gave Melba a good idea of just how valuable these old documents might be.

"None of these corporations exist any longer," Bill said, after gingerly examining only a few of the cover documents. He wore gloves he had brought with him, and goggles with magnifying lenses that swung down into place. A sign of his experience with such things. "They've all either dissolved through bankruptcy or the owners just shutting down, or they were swallowed up by other, larger, more successful corporations. It's going to take months to do all the backtracking and determine which ones were swallowed up and which ones just vanished. I can tell you that as historical documents, some of these can be quite valuable. The ones that lead to current companies ... well, that's going to take a lot of digging to know if it's worth the time and effort and legal filing fees to determine if they represent equal shares in the company. With splits and divisions and write-offs ..." He shrugged. "Who knows?"

"How do we know what to do with the shares or money or whatever results from this?" Cilla looked a little dazed to Melba, which made quite a bit of sense. The implications made her feel a little dizzy, too.

"Could there have been clues in her will?" Saundra asked. "Something that didn't make sense back then, but in light of this, makes sense now?"

Melba and Cilla looked at each other for several moments, then slowly turned to Bill.

"What a coincidence," he said, giving a very bad impression of innocent surprise. "Dad was your family lawyer and inherited the job from our Uncle Charles." A snort escaped him. "We could probably pay all our overhead expenses, just charging storage fees for all the family documents we've held onto over the years."

That broke the shell Melba felt enclosing her brain and emotions. She sputtered a laugh.

Sunday, October 16

Melba felt as if she had already put in a full day's work by the time she and Cilla headed for church. Neither of them had been able to sleep. She had only been moving around in her kitchen for maybe twenty minutes, trying to calm her churning thoughts by indulging in some baking, before Cilla heard and joined her. She brought over the leftover picnic food from Friday night and her computer. They took turns composing a letter to send to all their relatives, in between baking cranberry orange muffins, setting up a loaf of onion soup bread in the bread machine, and starting in early on their regular Christmas tradition of cookie and muffin mixes in gift jars.

They were both so relieved to have that task done, they agreed to send the email in the time between getting washed up and dressed for church and when Saundra picked them up in her car. They asked all their relatives in the email list to pass the letter on to everyone they were in contact with who wasn't in contact with Melba or Cilla.

They deliberately left Melba's car sitting in the driveway to discourage David from trying to break into the house and get his hands on the labyrinth chest, or perhaps search for the heart pillow, while they were at church.

The last report from Allen Kenward was that Charlotte refused to speak to anyone, except to ask for more pain medication and complain that she wasn't allowed any alcohol. Whenever an officer showed up, she went into hysterics. Melba believed that Charlotte did that so she could be sedated again. When would the obstinate old fool realize that eventually, she was going to be released from the hospital and have to face the consequences of her choices and actions? Did she even know yet that Captain Sunderson had taken all her possessions and put them into protective custody, and sent the rental car back to the leasing company? She had no one to turn to except the authorities, and nowhere to go, until she started cooperating.

Chapter Twenty-One

Melba tried to feel sorry for Charlotte. The best she could manage was to not feel any satisfaction that the irritating woman was finally getting her just desserts.

Definitely, she needed to spend some extra time in prayer and sitting in God's presence and repenting of her nasty thoughts over the last few weeks. Especially her moments of gleeful satisfaction and "She got what she deserved" thoughts.

Nick showed up after the service and reported that the upgrades to the security systems for the house and shop were finished. Someone had tried to follow them when he, Troy, and Kai moved the labyrinth chest from the house. He had taken them on what he simply referred to as "the scenic route," before taking the chest to the shop and tucking it in a corner in the back room where it couldn't be seen from any window.

The modified trap had been set. Now all they needed was for David to try to break into the house or get at Charlotte. Tomorrow, if nothing happened today, Cilla would visit Charlotte in the hospital with the pillow. If nothing happened after that ... they would think of more ways to up the ante and add pressure to David, until he made a stupid mistake.

Melba decided to be amused that she felt much better about Nick sitting at the end of the pew, watching over her and Cilla, than she did about all the "spy gizmos" as Saundra referred to them, keeping watch on their house and shop and Charlotte.

Monday, October 17

By Monday evening, all the pieces and preparations and people were in place. Except for David. He went about his business and daily routine without a glitch. Efforts to track his whereabouts on the day of the attack on Charlotte and the attempt to break into the security system at the duplex hadn't succeeded yet. Nick had quite a few technical connections, but none of them could play the tricks that were falsely portrayed on TV, such as being able to reactivate phones that had been turned off and turning the GPS against the phone's owner. Either David had accomplices who were helping to hide his tracks and play decoy, or Ernie's former associates were guilty of some of the shady actions after all.

All indications were that David was at work when Charlotte apparently roused from her stupor, found her clothes, and slipped out of the hospital without attracting any attention. He stayed at work all day and went home and didn't make any phone calls, other than to order pizza delivery. He stayed home all night. It was the last night of the World Series, after all.

The painting had resumed at Brighten Your Corner. Cilla and Melba spent a peaceful day in Cilla's kitchen, working on their first batch of candles to put on the shelves of their shop. They had to run out to the shop twice to take delivery of supplies and furniture and were delighted with how quickly the painting was coming along.

Melba spent most of the afternoon going through the flood of email from relatives. Far too many of her relatives, apparently, didn't know how to read and follow instructions. She and Cilla made it clear that all the legal paperwork had been turned over to Worter, Worter & McIntosh, and they would report to the Tweed clan once they had some news. Yet more than a third of the Tweeds deluged her with questions about the paperwork and how the wealth would be divided up and asking for estimates of how much all the old stocks and bonds were worth.

On a positive note, Clyde Bancroft reported that he and Uncle Jerome's estranged daughter, Maureen, had been in contact for some time. She had freed herself from her con man husband and Clyde hadn't heard from his mother in decades. He apologized for not letting the family know about the chest when he first found it in Jerome's estate, but he had chosen discretion rather than valor, and followed his stepfather's instructions for handling the troublesome matter, rather than stir up a new family feud. He expressed great interest in the trail the labyrinth chest had taken since it vanished from Granny Tweed's house.

Thursday, October 20

By the Guzzlers meeting that Thursday, Kai had allowed himself to jump wholeheartedly into preparations for the fall street festival. Other concerns had calmed down, so he didn't feel that twinge of guilt every time he focused on the coffee shop, rather than friends. The Tweeds were moving ahead on decorating their shop. Tuesday, they had approached him about creating a special drink to celebrate the grand opening of Brighten Your Corner. They wanted to give coupons for the drink to the first twenty customers, in exchange for having fliers for the shop on the counter when customers came in during the festival.

More important, no more suspicious characters had been spotted sneaking around the back parking deck of Creekside Shops.

The Tweeds were excited about the refurbished counters they had found at a used furniture store in Strongsville, that had been delivered and put in place that afternoon. They wanted Kai and Saundra to come see them, with an idea of setting up an entire array of candles that looked like drinks from Book & Mug. He and Saundra agreed to come over right after the meeting. The Tweeds bustled out of the coffee shop with the rest of the Guzzlers, calling out for him to hurry, they might change their minds on the walk over.

"I don't know how they do it," Saundra said, following Kai back to the counter with the second tray of dirty sample cups. "After all they've had to put up with the past couple weeks, they're as excited as if everything is going perfectly. They've certainly got more energy than I do!"

"Yeah, well, I'm convinced all those little kids you deal with all day are vampires." He grinned when she made a disgusted face at him. "I'm serious! They're just sucking you dry from the second they run into the library. Miss Saundra, Miss Saundra, tell me a story right now!" he squeaked, in a Mickey Mouse voice.

She laughed and gave the tray of dirty cups an extra shove toward the bus tray.

"Where are they?" Nick appeared from around the far side of the counter. He slammed his flat hand on the surface, hard enough to make a couple mugs and some flatware rattle. "Do little old ladies always move that fast?"

"You don't hang with grannies very much, do you?" Kai gestured out the front door. "They're heading up the bridge. You're gonna lose your magic decoder ring for this, Sherlock."

Nick gave him a narrow-eyed look, then grinned. "I was checking with Eden on a couple things and thought I'd see how they're holding up. If that's all right with you?"

"Be my guest." He flinched at the smile Saundra wore, looking back and forth between them. It was the same look Eden used to give him and Troy when they were much younger, working their way out of foster care. The equivalent of, *Boys. Can't live with them, can't shoot them.* "I appreciate you helping out. The ladies are ... family, I guess."

"Yeah, well, I'm not doing it for you. Saundra asked me to help out. Just doing my big brother duty."

Kai wondered if he imagined it, or Nick really did put a little extra emphasis on "big brother." Saundra just sighed and stepped behind the counter to transfer the dirty cups to the bus pan.

"Any progress on figuring out what was up with Ernie?" he asked and moved over to the other side of the tray, to empty it.

"The other agencies aren't talking, other than to acknowledge they aren't talking."

"Other agencies?" Saundra said. "Which one do you work for, again?" She fluttered her eyelashes at him, earning a chuckle from him.

"The Federal Bureau of Don't Hack off Cleo by Being Stupid." He leaned on his elbows on the counter. "Don't suppose you can babysit my place for some furniture deliveries next week?"

"Your place?" Kai hoped he hadn't heard right.

"Sorry." Saundra punctuated that with a handful of spoons thrown into the bus pan. "In all the ruckus, I forgot to mention, Nick's moving to town. In the same unit as my friend Charli's townhouse."

"Moving to town?"

"Don't panic," Nick said, his usual smirk returning. "It's just a place to crash every month or so. I'm on the road most of the year. But ... yeah, this is a pretty nice little town. I could do a—" He frowned and reached into his back pocket, then stepped away from the counter as he pulled out his phone.

Kai was sure Nick was about to say, "a whole lot worse." He scrambled for something to say, but Saundra was watching Nick like she expected bad news.

Considering she knew Nick pretty well, that was probably a bad sign.

"They're going to their shop?" Nick snapped, coming back to the counter. He pointed a finger at Saundra before either of them could answer. "Call the cops. Stay here." He ran out the door.

Kai didn't think. He ran after Nick.

Didn't see him.

Common sense said he was running up to the Apple Street bridge. It'd take longer to find his car, get in, and drive up to Creekview. Kai ran without looking for oncoming traffic.

Did the guy deliberately dress in black so he could go invisible?

Nick was nearly across the creek when Kai reached the bridge. The guy could run. Did the feds recruit track stars or something?

Kai was halfway across when Nick stopped and waited for him to reach the Creekview end of the bridge.

"They're not inside yet," Nick said, his voice low. "You make sure they don't go any further." He gestured down Creekview, where the Tweed sisters were chatting with someone, standing on the sidewalk, illuminated by the lights from Morning Folks Café. Two doors down from their dark shop.

"What's going on?" Kai grabbed his arm when Nick turned to run again.

"I bugged the place. Saundra asked me to look after them. Someone broke in. We don't want the ladies hurt, do we?" He shook off Kai's hand and ran, darting down the driveway to the back parking deck.

No, Kai didn't want the Tweeds hurt. His imagination painted a grim picture of arriving in another ten, fifteen minutes with Saundra, expecting an update from the delighted ladies, and finding them ... what? Tied up? Knocked out? Shot by whoever had broken into their shop once again?

Why would anyone break in? Hadn't the police and ATF and whoever else was involved already found all the hidey holes Ernie and his creepy friends had been using?

Kai picked up his pace as one of the Tweeds gestured to the door of their shop, probably inviting whoever they were talking with to stop in and see what had been done.

Not good.

"Melba, Cilla! Wait up!" He made a mental note to get that gym membership he had been putting off for a couple years now. Running the coffee shop had always felt like more than enough exercise, on his feet all day, hauling bus pans, using the stairs instead of the elevator, and lifting boxes of books. His aching legs, pounding heart, and straining lungs claimed otherwise.

Now he was close enough to see they were talking with Greg and Ginny Wells.

"What happened to Saundra?" Melba took a couple backward steps, gesturing at the front door with keys in her hand.

"She's—" Kai bent forward, bracing his hands on his thighs, and took a couple deep breaths. "Calling the cops. Don't go inside."

Lights came on inside Brighten Your Corner. Everyone turned. Cilla gasped.

She was right to gasp. A man lay face-down on the newly stained floor, a smear of blood leading to his face, which was turned away from the window. Just a few steps away, a new hole gaped in the floor. A pickaxe and a sledgehammer lay between the man and the hole, with broken pieces of board scattered around him.

Nick West and a big man in a black hoodie and black jeans stood on the far side of the hole, leaning down to look inside.

"Now what?" Melba groaned. She took a deep breath, threw her shoulders back, and stomped up to the door of her shop. Her hand didn't shake as she jammed the key into the lock.

"Melba, don't!" Kai shouted and leaped to stop her.

Nick and the stranger looked up. Melba twisted out of Kai's grip, yanking the door open, and stomped into her shop.

"Would anyone care to explain just what is going on now?" she demanded.

"Ma'am, I'm Agent Tony Malcolm, ATF, and this is hopefully the last member of a pretty nasty gang of arms dealers." He gestured at the man lying on the floor, who didn't move a muscle. Probably unconscious.

"The agency's going to pay to repair that floor, aren't they?" Nick said, when Melba just gaped, looking back and forth between the hole and the man.

"Why didn't you take care of that the first time you people were in here?" Cilla cried, pushing her way past Kai to stand with her cousin.

Greg and Ginny watched from the other side of the window, shaking their heads. Their expressions clearly said this was approaching the point of "enough."

~~~~~

"Malcolm and his team weren't involved in the first investigation," Nick explained, once everyone had returned to Book & Mug, and went upstairs to the office to talk in private.

Agent Malcolm and two members of his team were still at the shop, recording every detail. A black agency van had already showed up to haul away the unconscious arms dealer.

"They know how this particular gang works," he continued, "and have experience with the tricks they use to camouflage the presence of their caches. Some are shielded so the standard sensing equipment doesn't work. They came back and found the last cache, and decided to leave it there, bait in the trap."

"They didn't detect the alarms you installed to keep watch?" Saundra said. She caught her breath, visibly fighting a grin. "No, they did detect them, or they even watched you install the system, and they just let you go ahead. That must have been embarrassing."

"Remind me not to tell you where I put the cameras keeping an eye on you," Nick shot back. Saundra just laughed, and his scowl melted into a grin.

Big brother, Kai reminded himself.

"Arms dealers," Eden said. "Everybody knew Ernie was a nasty old cuss, but ... that's pretty hard core. And dangerous. Who'd have ever thought Cadburn would have arms dealers hiding out here?"

"From what Malcolm deigned to share, Ernie was into a lot of stuff. He was basically letting different groups use his shop to store things, as a mail drop, so one group didn't have any face-to-face contact with the other. Some of the traces different agencies have found include some explosives, and what are probably designer drugs." Nick shook his head, gazing down into the mug of his usual black coffee. "Either the guy had no idea what he was involved in, or he was just plain stupid, arrogant, and contrary. Eventually, one group was going to get in a fight with another, and Ernie would have been caught in the middle. Maybe gotten his shop and the rest of the strip blown up."

Everyone was quiet and thoughtful for a little while. Then Cilla sighed and sat forward, resting her arms on the table.

"So ... how quickly are they going to fix that hole in the floor? We'd really like to have our grand opening during the fall festival. Is that too much to ask?"

"No," Eden said. "It isn't. And Nick here is going to pull every string available to him, to make sure nothing else gets in your way. Isn't he?" She fixed Nick with that flat little smile Kai had learned early never to defy.

"Yes," Saundra said. "He is."

Nick's jaw worked back and forth a few times as he glanced back and forth between the Tweeds, Eden, and Saundra. Then he nodded. "Absolutely. I wouldn't settle for anything less."

Mischief glinted in his eyes. Kai muffled a sigh, accepting the fact that Nick was irrepressible. Considering the strings he held, to pull for the benefit of others, maybe that wasn't a bad thing.

"By the way ... Cousin Charlotte got snatched by one of Ernie's old friends, who believed her when she insisted she was the boss. One of Malcolm's people freed her, but not before she got a good, solid scare in her. I think this time, she really means it when she insists she's never coming back to this state, much less this county or town."

Saturday, October 22

Melba found great satisfaction in coming into the shop that morning when the light was still silver and soft, and pulling out all the supplies to make a new batch of candles. Saundra, Troy, and Kai had been her primary helpers yesterday, arranging the display tables and rearranging them, and setting up and adjusting the workshop area. The hole in the floor had been patched overnight, and if she didn't know where to look, she wouldn't have been able to detect the seam.

Her worktable for letting customers see the process was set up horizontal to the biggest display window, with lots of room behind her for all the molds and blocks of paraffin, and a wide workspace on the counter to hold the heating coils and melting pots, and all sorts of bins down the wall next to her to hold the bits and pieces. Wicks and silicone spray, decorative bits to affix to the warm wax, the beaters for whipping wax, all the little tools for peeling and shaping, and the blocks of colors and bottles of scent.

By the time morning traffic started moving down Creekview, she had four candles cooling in their molds and was laying out the decorations to affix on the inside walls of the next four molds, plus three sand pots to create three-wick candles. She hummed along with the radio and chuckled with the morning DJs, and nearly stopped twice to call in answers to the prize quiz they were running. She shook her head a few times at the wrong answers, and chuckled to herself, knowing if she had stopped, she could have won all the prizes being offered that morning. Not that she actually needed tickets to the craft festival at the Cuyahoga County Fairgrounds, or a dozen caramel apples from Sweet Valley Apple Farm, or a shopping spree at Sweet Street Candy Shop. Although right about then, she wouldn't mind four apple fritters from Sugarbush Bakery.

If she kept up this pace, Brighten Your Corner would be ready for the grand opening celebration, in conjunction with the fall street festival. She and Cilla had agreed that most of the candles should be made for holiday themes, to encourage people to think about buying for decorating and as presents. She had ordered a mold for a huge wax jack'o'lantern, to be used as a candy bowl when the children went trick-or-treating through the businesses after school. Melba looked forward to decorating candles with silk leaves, and the scents of cinnamon and pine and apples filling the shop.

A tap on the window startled her. She looked up to see Heinrich grinning sheepishly at her, hands jammed into the pockets of his oversized, bulky sweater. She was about to gesture for him to come in and remembered she hadn't unlocked the door. The shop wasn't officially open for business, of course. She gestured for him to wait, put down the mold for a trio of snowmen, and hurried over to open the door.

Chapter Twenty-Two

"Morning, neighbor," Heinrich said, and shuffled his feet a little. Then he looked over her shoulder. "Cilla around?"

Melba muffled a chuckle. Of course, what else would prompt Heinrich to leave his shop and come all the way across the creek?

"She's working at home this morning, designing labels with Becca. But she'll be here in time for lunch." Melba only hesitated a moment to think. Cilla would scold, laugh, and blush. "Join us? A celebration. Hands across the creek?"

"Yeah?" His eyes lit up and for a few seconds he was the somewhat awkward boy who had been Cilla's shadow in high school. "That'd be ... that'd be nice."

Melba stayed in the doorway, watching him shuffle down the street, certainly moving faster than she would have given him credit for just a few weeks ago. He was almost skipping as he reached the bridge. She stepped back into the shop, shivering a little, and decided to leave the door open just in case anyone was attracted by the lights and activity inside and wanted to get a preview.

Now, what had she been doing? Right, the snowmen candles. She thought about the mold for a cluster of candy canes to wrap around pillar candles. Maybe she could experiment a little, figure out how long to let the wax cool before it was too hard to shape. She would need to practice either layering the wax in colors or get better at painting with colored wax. Nobody liked single-color candy canes.

Where had she put the mold? Melba turned to look around the shop. The door into the back room was closed.

She couldn't remember closing it. In fact, she and Cilla had agreed to leave it open, to hear if anyone came to the back door. The doorbell was broken, and Tracy had given up on the repairman she usually called for fixing the electronics. Melba was expecting a delivery of jars this afternoon, and she wanted to hear the knocking at the back door.

So no, she wouldn't have closed the door into the back room.

Walking softly, fearful the floor would creak at the worst possible time, she went to the door and tried to turn the knob. She held onto it so it wouldn't open. The knob didn't turn.

Her purse with her keys was in the back room. So was her cell phone.

She swallowed hard and hurried to the little podium that would serve as the checkout counter, with the plug for the landline and the credit card machine, and the princess phone painted with candle flames all over it, which Becca had given them as a celebration gift. Her hand shook as she picked up the handset, and her mind went blank, just for a second. What number to call? Eden? Did Nick give her his number? The police station?

"Don't be a ninny," she scolded herself. Any kindergartener would know to call 911 if there was a monster in the basement or coming down the hall.

A muffled creaking sound came from the back room.

The phone was silent. No dial tone. Had whoever was in the back room cut the phone line?

Melba decided right then, she had watched too many murder mysteries on TV.

What would Jessica Fletcher or Aurora Teagarden or Kinsey Milhone do in a situation like this? Or Stephanie Plum, for that matter?

Well, yes, they would probably be stupidly brave or curious enough to go outside and around the shops to the back door and confront whoever was back there — another creak, a louder one, came from the back room. Was that the sound of wood being pried apart?

That meant David was back there.

They were ready for David to break in, weren't they?

Melba knew one thing none of those female sleuths wouldn't do.

"Please, Lord, protect me. Bring help. End this whole ugly mess before anyone else gets hurt?" she whispered.

Then she hurried to the street door and yanked it open and didn't care if David heard the noise. Let him think she was running away. Let him get confident and cocky and make mistakes.

A sob escaped her, making a lie of her short burst of bravado, when she saw the Cadburn township black-and-white sitting across the street in front of Valerie's shop. Melba waved her arms as she hurried across the street and was nearly to the other sidewalk before she thought to look for oncoming traffic.

The car was empty. She looked around. Had the officer on duty gone into Morning Folks for breakfast?

A car came up the street from Apple and skidded to a stop behind her. Melba turned around to see Ted leaping out of his patrol car.

"Are you all right?" He caught hold of her arm and hustled her down the sidewalk to Valerie's shop. For a second, all she could do was point at the empty patrol car. No breath to speak. "He's out back, keeping an eye on things." The door opened with the Westminster chimes as he guided her inside. "Take care of her?" he called to Valerie, who was standing at her desk, with the phone to her ear. Then he raced out the door again and across the street.

Naturally, the take-down occurred behind the strip of shops, and Melba was grateful she didn't have to see that. For the sake of David's parents, if no one else. She sat with Valerie at her long worktable with a good view of the shops across the street, sipping a huge mug of hot coffee, heavy on cinnamon cream and sugar and watched as Ted and Bill Shipman escorted David, handcuffed, to Ted's patrol car. Eden had arrived just minutes before that, and stayed out of sight, watching until the two officers declared the building safe. She went around back, entered through the back door, and unlocked the door to the back room by the time Melba crossed the street again, with Ted on one side, and Valerie on the other.

The top of the chest was dented, showing where David had tried to pry it up, using the crowbar discarded on the floor.

Eden and Ted helped her go through the back room, identifying anything that had been changed, moved, broken or stolen. Melba laughed, and feared the sound was a touch hysterical, when she discovered that David had taken time to take all the cash from her wallet, and her debit card. Probably to punish her for being there when he expected the shop to be empty. According to Ted, he had cussed up a storm, blaming Melba. As if she didn't have a right to be in her own shop? Eden laughed at that and explained that she and Rufus had allowed David to hack into the security system and inserted false video to trick him into thinking the shop was empty. She apologized for leaving Melba in the dark, but they couldn't warn her without alerting David that he had been caught.

Melba stayed in the back room when Ted left to drive David to the police station. She fussed with the arrangement of the drawers and compartments of the chest, trying to decide how best to use it to display candles, and grateful David had only strained the gears for the top compartment. No more damage beyond that. Eden and Valerie stayed with her. Becca and Saundra joined them in time for lunch, which Troy insisted on providing. Cilla and Heinrich arrived while they were setting up around the work counter, and Troy and Valerie were hauling some folding chairs across the street from her office, so they could all sit down. Melba had to go through the story again. She got distracted several times when Heinrich caught hold of Cilla's hand, then put his arm around her, visibly protective of her.

Well, that was one of the few nice things that had come out of the whole ugly mess.

"It's finally over," Cilla whispered.

"No," Melba said, welcoming that shiver that washed over her. The good kind of shiver, like she got on the first day of summer camp or walking up the front steps to Granny's house for Christmas. "We're just getting started."

"I'll drink to that." Kai raised one of the jumbo-sized cups filled with the new iced fall drink, apple cider frappe with thin maple sugar leaves floating on top.

Everyone raised their cups.

"To Brighten Your Corner and our grand opening."

"Long may your candles burn," Troy said. Eden groaned, which got chuckles from the others.

One week until the fall festival and their grand opening.

Lord, thank You for getting us through this. Make us a blessing.

The chorus of the old Sunday school tune wove through her thoughts as they chatted about the festival, past and future, and candle designs and the treasure hunt that had been delayed more than forty years.

> Brighten the corner where you are
> Brighten the corner where you are
> Someone far from harbor you may guide across the bar
> Brighten the corner where you are

Brighten the Corner Where You are
Ina D. Ogden, 1913
In the Public Domain

The End

THANK YOU!

Thank you for reading this book from Mt. Zion Ridge Press.

If you enjoyed the experience, learned something, gained a new perspective, or made new friends through story, could you do us a favor and write a review on Goodreads or wherever you bought the book?

Thanks! We and our authors appreciate it.

We invite you to visit our website, MtZionRidgePress.com, and explore other titles in fiction and non-fiction. We always have something coming up that's new and off the beaten path.

And please check out our podcast, **Books on the Ridge,** where we chat with our authors and give them a chance to share what was in their hearts while they wrote their book, as well as fun anecdotes and glimpses into their lives and experiences and the writing process. And we always discuss a very important topic: *Tea!*

You can listen to the podcast on our website or find it at most of the usual places where podcasts are available online. Please subscribe so you don't miss a single episode!

Thanks for reading. We hope to see you again soon!

About the Author

On the road to publication, Michelle fell into fandom in college and has 40+ stories in various SF and fantasy universes. She has a bunch of useless degrees in theater, English, film/communication, and writing. Even worse, she has over 100 books and novellas with multiple small presses, in science fiction and fantasy, YA, suspense, women's fiction, and sub-genres of romance.

Her official launch into publishing came with winning first place in the Writers of the Future contest in 1990. She was a finalist in the EPIC Awards competition multiple times, winning with *Lorien* in 2006 and *The Meruk Episodes, I-V,* in 2010, and was a finalist in the Realm Awards competition, in conjunction with the Realm Makers convention.

Her training includes the Institute for Children's Literature; proofreading at an advertising agency; and working at a community newspaper. She is a tea snob and freelance edits for a living (MichelleLevigne@gmail.com for info/rates), but only enough to give her time to write. Her newest crime against the literary world is to be co-managing editor at Mt. Zion Ridge Press and launching the publishing co-op, Ye Olde Dragon Books. Be afraid ... be very afraid.

And please check out her newest venture: Ye Olde Dragon's Library, the storytelling podcast. Interspersed between the chapters will be interviews with authors of fantastical fiction. Listen to the podcast on your favorite podcast app or listen on the website: www.YeOldeDragonBooks.com, and click on the Ye Olde Dragon's Library link.

www.Mlevigne.com
www.MichelleLevigne.blogspot.com
www.YeOldeDragonBooks.com
www.MtZionRidgePress.com

NEWSLETTER:

Want to learn about upcoming books, book launch parties, inside information, and cover reveals?
Go to Michelle's website or blog to sign up.

Thanks for reading!
If you enjoyed this book, would you help Michelle by posting a review on Goodreads?

Are you a member of Book Bub? If so, please follow Michelle on Book Bub, and you'll get alerts when new books are coming out.

As a way of saying thanks, Michelle invites you to the Goodies page on her website. It will change regularly, offering you a free short story, a sample audiobook chapter, sneak peeks at new cover art, inside information on discounts and new release dates, etc.

Please go to: Mlevigne.com/good-stuff.html

Also by Michelle L. Levigne

Guardians of the Time Stream: 4-book Steampunk series
The Match Girls: Humorous inspirational romance series starting with **A Match (Not) Made in Heaven**
Sarai's Journey: A 2-book biblical fiction series
Tabor Heights: 18-book inspirational small town romance series.
Quarry Hall: 11-book women's fiction/suspense series
For Sale: Wedding Dress. Never Used: inspirational romance
Crooked Creek: Fun Fables About Critters and Kids: Children's short stories.
Do Yourself a Favor: Tips and Quips on the Writing Life. A book of writing advice.
To Eternity (and beyond): *Writing Spec Fic Good for Your Soul.* A book defending speculative fiction.
Killing His Alter-Ego: contemporary romance/suspense, taking place in fandom.
The Commonwealth Universe: SF series, 25 books and growing
The Hunt: 5-book YA fantasy series
Faxinor: Fantasy series, 4 books and growing
Wildvine: Fantasy series, 14 books when all released
Neighborlee: Humorous fantasy series
Zygradon: 5-book Arthurian fantasy series
AFV Defender: SF adventure series

Young Defenders: Middle Grade SF series, spin-off of *AFV Defender*
Magic to Spare: Fantasy series
Book & Mug Mysteries: cozy mystery series
Quest for the Crescent Moon: fantasy series
Steward's World: fantasy series reboot and expansion
The Enchanted Castle Archives: fantasy series

Printed in the USA
CPSIA information can be obtained
at www.ICGtesting.com
LVHW030809150224
771651LV00010B/245